Hexy Witch

DAISY MAY COOPER

Hexy Witch

Spooky Tales From My Weird Life

RADAR

First published in Great Britain in 2024 by Radar, an imprint of
Octopus Publishing Group Ltd
Carmelite House, 50 Victoria Embankment, London, EC4Y 0DZ
www.octopusbooks.co.uk

An Hachette UK Company
www.hachette.co.uk

The authorized representative in the EEA is Hachette Ireland, 8 Castle Court
Centre, Dublin 15, D15 XTP3, Ireland (email: info@hbgi.ie)

First published in paperback in 2025

Distributed in the US by Hachette Book Group
1290 Avenue of the Americas
4th and 5th Floors, New York, NY 10104

Distributed in Canada by Canadian Manda Group
664 Annette St., Toronto, Ontario, Canada M6S 2C8

ISBN 978-1-80419-260-3
eISBN 978-180419-262-7

A CIP catalogue record for this book is available from the British Library.

Typeset in 12.25/20pt Heldane Text by Six Red Marbles UK, Thetford, Norfolk.

Printed and bound in Great Britain.

13 5 7 9 10 8 6 4 2

I'd like to dedicate this book to the pair of ghost legs that I saw.
Thank you for scaring the absolute shit out of me.

'When you have eliminated the impossible, whatever remains, however improbable, *must be the truth*'

Sherlock Holmes in *The Sign of the Four* (1890),

Arthur Conan Doyle

'I ain't afraid of no ghost'

'Ghostbusters' (1984), Ray Parker Jr

CONTENTS

INTRODUCTION

When I was younger, I had a recurrent vision. That one day I would be visited by someone or something from the paranormal. I think we all had this dream – a hope that our tiny lives would somehow cross paths with the *other side*; that our existence was far more fantastical than the deadening drudge of the mortal world. School, eat, sleep, repeat. Sleepovers weren't proper sleepovers without a glut of terrifying ghost stories doing the rounds or a mate shining a torch in her mouth while she hunkered under a white sheet with the lights out or the banging of a headboard against a wall followed by excited whispers around a darkened room: 'What *was* that? Did you hear something? *That* was definitely a ghost!'

But thirty-something years later when – finally – my life and the other side did collide, it resembled nothing like the ghosts of my childhood imagination. Nor was this spirit the moral arbiter of my life that I had also anticipated – a fact my mum had drummed into me from a very young age. Whenever I was caught nicking sweets from the downstairs cupboard and stashing them behind my bed, Mum warned: 'I can't always see what you're up to, Daisy, but Granny Bertie can.'

It was a horrifying thought. Granny Bertie was my dad's mum, who had passed away some years before. We all loved Granny Bertie. She was fun and cuddly, but she could also be quite stern. You never wanted to mess with her. The idea that my dearly departed grandmother could see and judge everything I did filled me with dread, especially as a teenager – taking my first intoxicating draw on a fag in the park; sneaking out of my window to snog my first goth boyfriend. I was so worried about Granny Bertie watching me from the other side that I refused to wank off Mark Jones at the back of the dodgems at Cirencester Mop Fair circa 2000. He dumped me. But, honestly, it was a relief. No grandmother needs to witness that, regardless of whether she's a spirit or not. Because of Mum's warnings, I'd spent 36 years in a bewildering moral maze, worried that Granny Bertie's eyes would be watching my every move. Talk about killing the mood!

Yet on the day I was finally visited by the paranormal, all of those myths got well and truly busted. Whatever this spirit was, it looked nothing like dear old Granny Bertie . . . it had no face whatsoever. It had no eyes. It didn't even possess a head or a torso, for fuck's sake. Even if it had wanted to, this manifestation couldn't see a goddam thing. It wasn't watching me at all. It didn't even appear to care that I was there. But I saw it with my own eyes. I saw it as clear as day . . .

☆

It was around 5pm. There had been nothing peculiar about the day at all. No storms; no thunder; no freak occurrences. Just a sunny summer afternoon. As I remember it, I'd been to ASDA superstore, packing in a family shop before my kids arrived home. Later that afternoon I lay in bed with my then baby son, Jack, while he watched episode after episode of *PAW Patrol*. And that's when it happened. I sensed we were not alone. My body tensed. Then, I heard the pat, pat, pat of tiny feet on the wooden floor. I jolted myself upright. At first, I assumed it was my daughter hurtling in like a whirlwind and I hadn't noticed. Yet when I turned, a pair of legs – child's legs – were running across the room. I peered closer. *What the fuck?* Unmistakably, these were the legs of a little boy dressed in tight white PE shorts. They swooped around the bottom of the king-sized bed as if it was an athletics track and headed straight towards the door. Those legs were physical and solid – then they simply melted away. After their ghostly 100 metres was complete, a strange feeling of calm washed over me. Jack had been watching too. Like me, his eyes had followed this vision around the room. He sucked on his dummy like a contented Maggie Simpson, glanced up at me, then nonchalantly turned back to the screen in time to see the Pupmobile get summoned to its latest emergency in Adventure Bay.

I brought the duvet around my neck for comfort and racked my brain for an answer. *What the fuck just happened?* Seriously, did I just see a pair of disembodied legs run around my bedroom? A topless fucking ghost, but definitely not the good sort of topless. It all seemed so silly and ridiculous yet completely and utterly real. But whose legs were they? Where were they going? Why were they there? Why hadn't this scared the bejesus out of me? Or frightened Jack? Was I going mad? Had someone spiked my tea?

In truth, considering I'd waited almost four decades for this event, it had been somewhat underwhelming compared to other people's first ghostly sightings that I'd read so much about: stories of encounters with headless horsemen and Casper the Friendly Ghost. Visitors to my home had also claimed to have witnessed far more exciting ghosts, like a highwayman and a Roman in full battle gear (more of this later), even though I'd never set eyes on them. Not like this, anyway – an apparition in roaring 5D technicolour.

At this point, I should fess up to having more than a passing interest in this type of phenomena. Some among you will know I am hardly what you would call a sceptic. From day dot I have been a believer. I have always suspected there is another realm, even though I am often doubtful about the myriad ways people try to tap into that realm. Throughout my entire life, I have known that one day I would have a full-on paranormal experience that wasn't just my pale-faced brother Charlie jumping out from behind a gravestone in St John the Baptist Church in Cirencester. Tosser.

And now that I had seen a proper ghost, I wanted to know exactly what the hell it was. I'd *heard* a ghost before (I'll fill you in on this in a bit), I'd also experienced astral projection (yep, you did read that correctly and for the uninitiated, don't worry, we'll get to it in Chapter 20), but this was a whole different ball game. From now on I knew there was no going back to naively daydreaming about fairies or mermaids or unicorns – finding a place of safety and escapism and fantasy in a fucked-up world. It does leave you with an uneasy feeling in the pit of your stomach knowing that there *are* visitations, parallel worlds, real hauntings. And, as nuts as this might sound, I am convinced that it's only a matter of time before the scientific community wake up to this. It's my firm belief that hard, unequivocal proof will happen. Paranormal existence will embed into our consciousness in the same way that we've come to know the Earth is round, understand we're governed by the laws of gravity and accept the irrefutable truth that double caramel Magnums do taste better if you eat them in bed.

But I also know that talking about this stuff still feels *very* taboo. If you say you are a believer in certain circles it's like announcing to a meeting of the Women's Institute that you masturbate. Or dropping the C-bomb in front of a parish priest. The silence is deafening. Yet, thanks to the Internet, it's amazing to see more and more people sharing stories – a growing community of believers, curious sceptics and people who have experienced things that don't have a rational explanation. Yet they know they heard them, saw them, felt them. They know it was real.

Before I started writing this book, I put a call out on Instagram asking followers to write to me with stories:

> You all know I love a good ghost story . . . well, I'm working on something where I'm looking into mysterious comings and goings, and I'd bloody love to hear yours. Have you had an exorcism over Zoom? A scarily accurate (or not) psychic reading at the village fete? Seen the face of a dearly departed relative on a pork scratching or any other unexplained phenomena? Then I want to hear about it . . .

I wanted to test my theory that we're all a little bit curious about this subject. The response has been nothing less than incredible, even from people who remain unconvinced by the paranormal. I've featured some of these stories throughout this book and I want to give a massive shoutout to everyone who took the time to contact me – even the lovely bellend who simply replied 'France' to my post.

One guy emailed: 'Ghost stories. I have a few . . . the shimmering spectre that followed my girlfriend around the house; the ghostly monk that walked in on me and my cousins; the family cat that didn't move on and the old man in the window . . . and one encounter I don't want to talk about.' Please do talk about it one day . . . I implore you!

Another bloke opened up an entirely new field of enquiry, probably far too ambitious for the remit of this modest book: 'I'm a rational dude. Open minded but I don't believe in ghosts. Weird coincidences aplenty and I've had a fucking weird relationship with peregrine falcons. Another story . . .' For that message alone, thank you. Thank you. Thank you.

As for my own journey into the paranormal, this book is the culmination of years spent wondering and dabbling – trying to sort the real from the unreal, the fake from the legit, the sane from the utterly batshit crazy. And, as you will discover in these pages, I've stumbled across the weird and wonderful. I've pissed myself laughing at the sheer ridiculousness of it all and I've cried my eyes out at the profound. I've also done some fucking mental shit all in the name of discovery. Yet in my mind, there's no smoke without fire. This world cannot only be populated by mad people witnessing mad things. The truth is out there somewhere.

Granted, this is not the most scientific investigation. I very much doubt Einstein will be calling me from heaven any time soon to congratulate me on my painstaking research techniques. But what did you expect? That would just be boring, wouldn't it? And truth be told, sometimes, for privacy (and to avoid awkward conversations), names have been changed. And hey, I might have sprinkled in a few extra laughs here and there.

Whatever this book is, it's been an absolute fucking joy sifting through memories and experiences, conversations, random thoughts, pictures and recordings and writing it all down, discovering a world where the mortal and immortal coexist, where this life meets the next life, where past lives are resurrected, where people die and are brought back from the abyss and where the undead haunt every corner of our universe, seen or unseen. Most of all I've bloody loved trying to figure out what the actual fuck it all means . . .

☆

PART ONE

DAISY GETS GHOSTED

1

THIS HOUSE IS BLOODY HAUNTED

The Bates Motel, where its famous inhabitant Norman Bates took on the terrifying alter ego of his dead mother in Alfred Hitchcock's *Psycho*.

The Overlook Hotel where Jack Nicholson stalked the corridors in *The Shining*, announcing, 'Here's Johnny!' in one blood-curdling moment when the deranged writer peered through a hole in the bathroom door that he'd carved with an axe.

The all-American white picket-fence house where demonic spirits were unleashed to create the spine-chilling movie *The Amityville Horror*.

A new build in South Cerney, 20 minutes' drive from Swindon and a stone's throw from Birdland Park and Gardens near Cotswold Water Park – one of the Cotswolds' finest tourist attractions. This example doesn't quite have the same effect does it? Yet it's what I've come to know as a haunted house – *my* house – *my* haunted house.

I first told the story of my house on the radio series and podcast

Uncanny, presented by Danny Robins for the BBC. Doing so felt *very* surreal. Eventually putting into words all that had happened in that house suddenly transformed a sequence of random, unexplained events into something real, something tangible. Now it wasn't just the figment of mine or anyone else's imagination. I was telling it to the world and it felt good, *really* good. Therapeutic, even.

It had all started with some vague sightings by others. Debs, my short, dumpy, fifty-something, batshit-crazy cleaner at the time, had spent months reporting that a highwayman frequently walked through my wardrobe in the hallway, across the kitchen, through the patio doors and into the garden. 'He's polite. Always doffs his cap, Daisy,' she told me before reminding me that I'd run out of toilet roll. He did sound like the perfect gentleman, but I'd never set eyes on him. I logged on to Amazon straight away, ordered up a 24-roll multipack of quilted bog roll and thought about the highwayman fleetingly before he cantered off into the recess of my mind.

Another time Debs claimed a Roman in full battle gear was hovering near the utility room.

'Wait there, Dais,' she said, pointing a bright pink rubber-gloved finger in my direction.

'What is it, Debs?' I stood frozen on the spot. Was it a wasp, a bee, the terrifying sight of my fake tan gone wrong?

'There's a Roman. On your shoulder, three o'clock, Dais.'

My first instinct was to swat him like a bluebottle, but Debs stopped me.

'No, Dais, he means no harm. He's just passing through.'

I didn't sense a thing. Debs also claimed to be a medium – she said she had special powers. But a lot of people say that, don't they? One read of Sally Morgan's *My Psychic Life* and suddenly they're channelling Queen Victoria.

Once, she reckoned that there had been a hangman's tree directly outside my bedroom window. According to her, hundreds had been executed there. After some thought I dismissed this as a passive-aggressive attempt to tell me off for repeatedly leaving my knickers sunny side up on the bathroom floor. Classic Debs. Or maybe it was because I hadn't put her wages up? Of course, I did want to believe my house was some kind of portal. I *really* did. It would be the proof I'd been waiting for – the evidence that spirits are all around us and we just need to tune into their frequency. But nothing ever appeared for me. Besides, it's really fucking hard to take anyone seriously when they turn up at your house wearing a moth-eaten brown woollen hat pulled down over their ears, a shiny green puffer jacket that made Debs look like the Incredible Hulk and clutching a can of Mr Muscle Platinum kitchen spray. If anything was going to come back and bother the living, would it *seriously* make a beeline for Debs?

Then my friend Sarah came to stay. Sarah is a police officer – she deals in cold, hard evidence every single day. Even on an off day she can look like Detective Inspector Kate Fleming from *Line of Duty* chasing down an armed gang leader. Fear is not in her feelings vocabulary. She's also a massive sceptic. That night we ate a Chinese takeaway and downed a few glasses of wine. Sarah slept on the top floor of my home in the bedroom where I usually put guests (it was a three-storey house and my bedroom was on the middle floor), but when she came downstairs the next morning I noticed she looked pallid, rubbing her eyes like she'd barely slept a wink.

'Hiya!' I shouted over. 'Got a hangover? Fuck me, I feel like shit.'

'No . . . Is everything okay, Daisy?' she asked hesitantly.

'Yeah, want some crumpets?'

'No, Dais, I mean . . . *is everything okay*?'

'Yeah, sure. What do you want on them . . . Butter? Or jam?'

I've never been very good at picking up on foreboding. The conversation really did need some tinkly background music.

'Was the kitchen as we left it last night?'

'Yeah . . .'

Sarah dragged out a stool, climbed on it then cradled her head in her hands on the breakfast bar. Then, I started to feel *very* anxious. The poor woman was trembling.

'What's the matter, Sarah?'

'This house. It was broken into last night. I heard it. There were sounds like saucepans hitting the floor. When I edged out on to the stairwell, I heard voices. Loud voices. Then, wafting up from downstairs was the smell of cigarette smoke.'

'Why didn't you wake me?'

'I was petrified, Dais,' she admitted.

Apparently, Sarah had been on the verge of calling the police, which is strange because she is the police, so in my mind, she must have been bloody terrified! But then, everything went quiet.

'Nothing's happened here,' I said, gazing around the room confusedly.

'So . . . nothing had been moved when you came down this morning?'

'Nothing,' I replied, but when my eyes locked on Sarah's I knew that she wasn't bullshitting. For most of that morning we tried to figure out what she'd heard. My house was detached and overlooking a large lake, so it definitely couldn't have been the neighbours.

'Are you sure you weren't dreaming?' I asked her for the umpteenth time.

'Positive,' Sarah muttered.

Both of us took a deep breath and stared into our mugs of tea. After an hour or so it felt like we'd run out of rational explanations.

'Do you know what I think?' I said wearily. Suddenly, I was faced with the possibility that Debs may not be telling massive porkies after all, although I did still think that she used the paranormal just to be a spiteful cow.

'What's that?' Sarah looked up quizzically.

'This house is bloody haunted.' I grimaced.

★

Nothing happened for a few months after that, not until my friend Selin turned up. We'd just started writing the BBC series *Am I Being Unreasonable?* together but I'd known Selin since we were at RADA more than a decade before. She often took the piss out of my obsession with the paranormal. I seem to recall she'd used the words 'absolute bollocks' in the past. Quite frequently, actually. Yet that night, when Selin stayed with her partner in the same room as Sarah had, she crossed over from being an evangelical non-believer into a what

I would call para-curious. And let me tell you, it was an absolute fucking joy to witness.

Normally, Selin sleeps with earplugs in, to shut out the sound of her partner's loud snoring. But not long after her head hit the pillow, she woke up to a strange hissing noise in her ear.

'Pssssss . . . psssss . . . psssss.'

Then, she felt her partner's hand shake her gently. 'Did you hear that whispering noise?' he asked her.

Both of them had heard it, although neither could work out what the voice said, where it was coming from or what it might be trying to tell them.

On another occasion, when Selin came to my house alone, she swore blind she'd heard dogs barking in my downstairs living room. I do not have dogs. She listened from the very same bedroom and, like Sarah, hovered on the stairwell. The next morning, she burst into my room.

'D'you know what? I think you're right, Daisy,' she cried.

'I am right about most things . . . what's the latest?' I answered, rather smugly.

'This house *is* bloody haunted.'

✦

By then, though, all sorts of peculiar activity had been unleashed. There were nights when I'd been sitting alone downstairs watching a true crime story on Netflix when I swore I heard the faint sound of running water. I turned the sound down and listened more closely. As I got up and slowly climbed the stairs, the sound got louder . . . and louder. When I peered around my bathroom door I found the shower tap on full blast with the water gushing. Could I have forgotten to switch it off? I didn't think so. It was a stiff mock-Victorian handle that I had to squeeze shut.

On the landing, two large canvas paintings that I'd recently bought had also been taken down. First they'd been placed leaning neatly against the wall by the stairs. Another time, they were put near the entrance to my daughter's bedroom. It had taken a stepladder to hang them, so the idea that someone could have reached up overnight and moved them was absurd. Even Debs denied trying to dust them.

'I draw the line at the paintings, Dais. Vertigo gets me every time.'

There were other unsettling audible moments, too. I'd started to hear heavy footsteps on the stairs, casually making their way up to the top floor. Whereas at first I gulped hard with fear, I tried to remain open-minded. And these bumps in the (day and) night began happening so frequently that the noises started to blend into the fabric of my everyday existence.

Whenever I searched, no one was there. I tried to inject some calm into the situation: whoever or whatever this was didn't seem to want to threaten me or hurt me, so why should I give it a hard time? *Could we live peaceably together in some kind of Buddhist fantasy?* I wondered. What would the Dalai Lama say? By harming it, would I ultimately harm myself?

This brought on a massive existential crisis that I had not predicted at all. On balance, though, all these stuck taps meant the water bill was reaching unmanageable levels, especially as I was on a water meter, but perhaps that was a small price to pay. Then, I spotted an opportunity. At last, I could conduct my very own paranormal investigation.

Right there, in my own home. By a process of elimination, I could solve this mystery like a slightly sexier Miss Marple.

The activity kept me on my toes for months. Even my dad Paul – by far the toughest audience when it comes to the paranormal – had experienced something. He had been standing by the French windows looking out on to the lake when he'd seen a man, probably in his early fifties, well-to-do and sporting a moustache. He strolled by the hot tub wearing a tweed coat, seemingly from a bygone era.

'Daisy!' Dad called me outside. 'Was anyone coming to fix the hot tub today?'

'It's not broken . . . why?'

'There was a man standing by it a moment ago . . .'

I thought about this for a nanosecond. No one was due to check anything.

'Are you sure it wasn't a nutbag fan?' I asked.

'Don't think so, Dais. Looked more like aristocracy. I've met the fans, remember . . .'

Dad was right. No one had ever turned up at a Q & A or a book or DVD signing dressed like that. And believe me, I've seen some fucking mental sights . . . like the guy who came to one event dressed as a stuffed Dalek scarecrow. He had a wicker basket on his head and arrived holding two solar-powered garden pathway lights as arms. I couldn't fault him for the effort he'd put in.

And, no offence, most fans are lovely, but since the success of *This Country* I have been confronted with some truly alarming things. One morning I pirouetted downstairs and flung open my curtains with joyful abandon. I felt the warmth of the bright sunlight hit my face and gazed out at the lakeside vista. Fuck me, there was a random bloke squatting on my back lawn. I locked eyes with him. He stared back. He was grinning wildly, giving me the thumbs up while the grass tickled his fat arse cheeks. His cacks were around his ankles. The full horror took seconds to sink in. *Is he . . . ? Is he . . . ? Oh fuck . . . he is . . .* My mouth dropped. There was a fully-grown human curling out a massive turd on my lawn while I stood helpless in my pyjamas. With the lightning speed of an ageing Premiership goalkeeper I leaped to cover my daughter Pip's face with my hands. No four-year-old needs to be met with that head on at 7am on a Tuesday morning. It could scar someone for life.

For that reason, I'd employed a security firm to check around the property every hour. They had the key to the only entrance to the back garden – a gate that remained padlocked. When I called them on the afternoon of Dad's sighting, there was nothing in their logbook to suggest anyone had been spotted sniffing around.

'Did the man by the hot tub seem dangerous?' I asked Dad, just to make sure.

'No, he just sauntered past, like he lived here,' Dad said, with a shrug.

Dad never saw that man again. Neither did anyone else, but I was starting to build a theory. Several, in fact. What if this wasn't evidence of the past undead, exactly? What if these noises – these sightings – were just another family living in a parallel universe? A bit like when I once recorded an episode of *Poirot* on VHS tape but, when I watched it back, scenes from *Blue Peter* that hadn't been properly erased flickered through. The competing storylines were insane, as if two realities were interwoven and Konnie Huq was now trying to solve the brutal murder of a wealthy recluse in the Blue Peter garden with Mabel the dog as the prime suspect.

I'd read articles about this kind of phenomena, too. None of it was simple. There's one school of thought that believes these kinds of experiences could be the result of two time dimensions bleeding into one another: that we live in parallel universes where gazillions of alternate realities rub up against each other like pissed-up teenagers at a foam party.

Many have reported similar time slips. Some of the most well-documented cases come from Liverpool, one hotspot being part of its main shopping area, Bold Street. In 1996, one paranormal expert interviewed an off-duty policeman who described in such precise detail what had happened when he and his wife had gone shopping. At the moment they parted, agreeing to meet up later, he suddenly found himself stepping into the 1950s. Box van vehicles sped past him. Men strolled by wearing trilby hats and long overcoats and the women had on pillbox hats, scarves and gloves. Yet at other moments a girl appeared wearing hipster jeans and a lime green T-shirt and carrying a Miss Selfridge bag, like she'd got hopelessly lost on the set of *Call the Midwife*. Two worlds tuning in and out of each other like an old analogue radio. How fucking bizarre is that?

Another famous account dates back to the 1970s when two English couples set off on a road trip through south-eastern France. At the bed and breakfast they stayed at they ate breakfast alongside two French police officers dressed as if they were from the 1900s. There was also a woman in a silk evening gown carrying a small dog under her arm.

Everything seemed to be from another era, including the price: the equivalent of around £2.50 for four people. Absolute fucking bargain! No wonder they headed straight back when they passed through again a few weeks later. This time, though, when they turned into the cobbled lane to find the building, it had completely vanished. No one they asked knew of it. I mean, what business could keep going on those prices? Especially when the Novotel down the road was charging £250. But even more mysterious were the photographs they took while they were staying there. Those very pictures had disappeared off the roll of film when it came back from being developed. It remains a completely unsolved case. Spooky as fuck.

On the day I lay in bed watching a pair of disembodied legs run around my bedroom – the culmination of months of unnatural goings-on – I thought hard about this time slip theory. The little boy; the man by the hot tub; the dog barking; the noise of pots and pans; the shower turning on. Good grief, was this evidence of others taking up residence in my house? Just going about their business? Bumping up against my life? And if so, why did the fuckers never go to Tesco and fill up the fridge? And I never woke to find a random turd floating in the toilet, either. The sort that happens in every single household, an oversized number two that everyone denies is theirs and needs a tsunami of water to flush down.

But there's another theory, too. A theory that suggests we may not always be haunted by ghosts of the past; instead we can be visited by phantoms of the future. According to the theory of hauntology – which asks whether people can be haunted by ghosts of lost futures – these are ghosts that turn up to remind us of all the things we never did, but always wanted to. They can dig into our deepest, darkest regrets (in my case, never having snogged, shagged or married Ben Shephard) or shine a light on our unfulfilled desires (erm . . . sorry . . . Ben Shephard again!).

So were these more intelligent beings trying to communicate something to me about my life? In my career, I'd achieved *a lot*. After years and years of trying, and failing, to get *This Country* off the ground, Charlie and I had bloody done it. My acting and writing career had finally got lift-off. There were four BAFTAS lined up on my sideboard. *Four fucking BAFTAs!* (Though, the least said about the boring-as-shit ceremony I had to sit through the better.) Now I was writing a prime-time sitcom with my best friend Selin. *Yes! Yes! Yes!* Career-wise, life couldn't get any better.

On the other hand, my two-year marriage to my husband Will had hit the skids. Although we'd been separated for a while I was still filled with all the painful rage of feeling trapped inside a miserable relationship, trying to salvage any shred of confidence I had left in myself. Plus we have two children together. Everything felt like such a complicated mess. And now, potentially, here to tell me what an abysmal human being I'd become was a perfect nuclear family living alongside me, flaunting their 2.4 ordinariness in my face, enjoying themselves in my hot tub and using my bedroom as a sports circuit, cooking up family dinners at fuck knows what hour their time. Was this family punishing me? Or trying to tell me that happier days were just round the corner? Had they even noticed me and my pathetic life? It was time for my investigation to go deeper . . .

☆

2

THE HAUNTING OF SOUTH CERNEY

How the hell could a new build in South Cerney be haunted? Churches are haunted, graveyards and cemeteries too. Hospitals, care homes and former asylums are practically all-night raves for the recently departed. But a suburban house surrounded by mainly holiday homes on the edge of a water park? Doesn't seem likely. Also, I was the first ever inhabitant of that house. As far as I knew no one had shuffled off this mortal coil in my downstairs loo, not even an electrician or a builder. And the top floor bedroom, where most of the paranormal activity had been reported, was covered floor to ceiling in tropical palm wallpaper for fuck's sake. Was the spirit world flocking there in the vague hope it would be hotter in winter? A staycation that was a helluva lot cheaper than a last-minute package holiday to Fuerteventura? I was about to find out . . .

They say that the truth is stranger than fiction and so it has come to pass. I was focusing my investigations on the four walls of my house because it didn't occur to me for a single moment that the land around me or the water park itself were any kind of hangout for the undead. Not long after I agreed to tell my story on *Uncanny*, its research team began digging. Over a period of a few weeks it uncovered facts about the area that I had zero clue about.

I'd only ever known of one tragedy in the area. It was seared into my brain because I was a teen when it happened. A local florist had been found dead in the lake along with her young daughter. It was bloody heartbreaking. The woman had become convinced that her disabled daughter's condition was due to metal poisoning, rather than her having cerebral palsy. In fact, she believed the whole world was being poisoned by metal. To treat her daughter, she gave her healing baths using massage oil. One day, she was giving her a bath in olive oil when her daughter accidentally drowned. From her home, the woman took her lifeless body to the lake. Holding her, she walked in and drowned herself. Both were found dead two days later. This was a such a tragic story that stayed with me and I've never forgotten it.

As a 13-year-old, that story bore a hole in the core of my being. It felt so sad and so fucking creepy, like something you'd see in *The Omen*. But fast-forward to the present day, and it didn't explain the boy running in my bedroom or the man by the hot tub or the random Romans, highwaymen or soldiers that had been drifting in and out of my house. The only mother and daughter in my house were me and my daughter Pip. Thankfully we were alive and kicking.

But nothing is what it seems. As I flicked through the research another world leaped from its pages and thwacked me right in the face. What an idiot! I'd been seeing the lake as a lake, but it was more than that. Originally, it had been part of a series of gravel pits, a place where layers of time are mixed together. In that area – and on surrounding sites – remains dating back more than six thousand years, remnants of the early Stone Age, had been found. The bones of mammoths had been excavated in the early 1950s. Roman artefacts had also been discovered, including traces of an ancient burial site. There was Iron Age, Bronze Age and medieval shizzle like you wouldn't believe. Reading the findings was like binge-watching old episodes of *Time Team*.

Desperate to find out more, I fired up my laptop. I did some googling around of the history of the area before I disappeared down one gargantuan rabbit hole of ghostly goings-on. Hours later it was getting dark and I was still hunched over the screen scrolling. (All the while an H&M dress that I'd clicked on a couple of hours before was still following me around the Internet like a rabid Instagram troll.) Most fascinating were the sites that talked about the relationship ghosts have with bodies of water. Lakes . . . oceans . . . Then I got distracted by an episode of *Octonauts*. The one where Captain Barnacles's team get called out to investigate a spooky shipwreck and are confronted with a long-armed ghost squid that turns out to be . . . well, just a squid with a tangled tentacle. *If only my investigation was so simple, Captain Barnacles.*

Back to the blogs and records and newspaper articles, I carried on with my investigation. With every click, it felt like I was about to crack the Da Vinci code. Ghosts had been seen in lots of swimming pools . . . and . . . wait for it . . . hot tubs! *Yes! Yes! Yes!* It turns out that water amplifies spiritual energy. Spirits travel more easily through liquid than any solid object. The lake, the hot tub: it was all starting to make sense. Even so, I'd never heard of a ghost firing up the maximum bubble setting and laying back with a glass of Tesco Finest Prosecco.

As the days rolled on, more information dripped in from the *Uncanny* team. My house had been built on the site of an old abandoned railway line. It had opened in 1881 and closed in 1961. The line was particularly famous for transporting injured soldiers during the South African War between 1899–1902. On a single day in 1901, ten thousand men were transported on twenty-two special trains. Experts suggested that this could be the reason that Sarah, my police officer friend, had heard voices from the kitchen and smelled cigarette smoke wafting up through the stairwell and why random men in uniform came and vanished.

The line was also used during the First World War and moved troops during peace time to Salisbury Plain. Could this explain the man Dad had seen dressed in what could have been period costume? Maybe. But he could have been from a different time slip altogether. *Fucking hell* . . .

Also in the bundle were some really creepy reports dating back to the 1960s. One man reported that he had regularly cycled around the area to attend bell-ringing practice, but whenever he turned on to one nearby lane a feeling of unease spread through him. 'It felt like something was watching me,' he said. 'I wanted to look around but didn't dare. In the road everything was tense.'

It wasn't until 30 years later when he was talking to his mother and she asked, 'When you were cycling, did you ever experience the ghost of Wick Lane?' that he realised what he may have witnessed. Until that day, he'd never spoken about it. He was terrified of being laughed at and over the years had convinced himself it was just a silly figment of his imagination. Apparently, though, a 19th-century pub landlord and greengrocer called William Allaway had died in the exact spot where the cyclist reported that the atmosphere became cold and icy. Something had freaked out the horse pulling Allaway's cart and when it bolted the cart overturned. It threw him off and he was so badly injured that doctors couldn't save him. He died the next morning, aged 27.

And what about the boy I'd seen in my bedroom? That finding blew my tiny mind. Enclosed was a newspaper article from the *Bristol Evening Post* dating back to 1959. There had been an inquest into the tragic death of a four-year-old. He had been at the lakeside with his dad watching the Bristol Hydroplane Club's race meeting when part of the bank had collapsed and he fell into the water. It took over an hour to recover his body and the coroner ruled that he'd died by drowning. But if that was the boy in my bedroom, why did he have no torso and no head?

To be honest, I had felt a bit short-changed that I hadn't been presented with a full ghost, like I hadn't got my money's worth. But if legs were all I had to work with, so be it. One expert suggested that a floor of the house may have cut right through the boy's spirit body when the house was being built. It would be impossible to prove. On that point, the evidence was inconclusive.

☆

Danny Robins at *Uncanny* was so intrigued by the findings that he wanted to come to my home to see for himself where the supposed paranormal activity had happened. I was happy to oblige but also deeply anxious. This was the first time I'd let in a complete stranger to talk about everything that had been happening. Danny describes himself as someone who 'wants to believe'. He's been exposed to far too many accounts of sightings from ordinary people to dismiss the paranormal as hokum. That said, he's never actually seen a ghost himself. I hoped he wouldn't think I was a complete nutcase, poised to call the men in white coats to cart me off. Whatever was going on, I'd seen what I'd seen, even if I didn't yet know the truth about what it was.

'Can Danny stay the night?' an assistant asked when she rang to confirm the visit.

'Sure,' I agreed.

'Can he sleep in the bedroom that's supposed to be the most haunted?'

'It would be my absolute pleasure.'

Even I hadn't slept in that room. Not because I was petrified but because it doesn't have a wide-screen TV and there's nothing that I like more than lying in bed cracking off episode after episode of *Married At First Sight*.

When Danny arrived he did seem genuine. I knew he'd been a stand-up comic in a previous life and I was half-expecting a lot of really shit jokes about dead ends given that I lived in a cul-de-sac. Plus from a certain angle he did look a lot like a more fanciable Mr Bean. But Danny turned out to be nerdishly forensic, the kind of guy who at school would have his nose stuck in a book like a pig in a trough. *Impressive*, I thought, like having a real-life ghostbuster in your house checking out the ectoplasm. Though I was disappointed he didn't leap from his car with a proton pack strapped to his back.

I took him on a guided tour.

'Yeah, it's pretty stiff isn't it,' he said, turning the shower handle off and on several times. He wanted to see whether it was possible for the shower to turn on by itself. It couldn't. And it was Danny who suggested that we file upstairs and test out whether there was a concentration of paranormal activity in my spare bedroom before he bravely spent the night in there.

That was the perfect chance to bring out my most expensive item of ghost-hunting equipment: my REM pod. Seasoned ghost hunters will know exactly what I'm talking about but I will explain for the uninitiated. Some basic models can look frighteningly like a home-made sex toy, the type you sit on. There's a large antenna sticking out from a round base with nipple-shaped LEDs that light up. It works by picking up radiating electromagnetism. For anyone like me who failed their science GCSE, that means its antenna radiates a magnetic field. (For fuck's sake, please, please don't ask me how.) If any movement breaks that field then its lights glow red, yellow, blue and pink. If the signal is weak then a couple of lights will flicker on, more will light up if it's stronger. Human movement could set it off but also, if no human is near it, any unexplained activity.

I am absolutely sure it's been given way more pizzazz and bells and whistles than it needs, though, just so its makers can charge £200 for the device and mugs like me will fork out for it.

My REM pod hadn't ever worked in the past, but I hoped this time it would produce some results. Inviting the high priest of the paranormal round to your home only to sit there in silence, nothing happening, would have been awkward. Humiliating, even. I'd given it such a massive build-up. I'd even mentioned it in passing to the comedian Adam Buxton, and he'd seemed genuinely intrigued too. How fucking awful it would be if it appeared that I'd fabricated the whole tale. I've told some whoppers in my time – like when I was a kid and blamed my wilful misconduct on The Borrowers, the little people who lived under the floorboards and whispered things in my ear – but I'm an adult now, and I've been practising reality for a while despite how mind-numbingly boring it can be. Plus, I bloody love going on other people's podcasts and that kind of deepfake could ruin my chances of being asked.

Selin was staying with me at the time and my dad was round. Safety in numbers, we figured. After Danny had done a full inspection of my bathroom, hallway and hot tub, we finally made our way upstairs to the spare bedroom. I went first, clutching the REM pod. We set it up on one side of the room. We all huddled in an opposite corner. I could feel my heart fluttering like a trapped bird as we sat and waited. My skin became clammy. In the silence my eyes were also drawn to a large coffee stain on the cream carpet, which was annoying.

'We should ask some questions,' suggested Danny after a while. He was recording the experiment on his phone.

'Sure,' I agreed, although it was hard to know where to start. This felt like speed-dating a spirit. What's a good ice-breaker? The only half-decent question I could think of was: what music are you into?

Thankfully, Danny took control of the situation.

'Are we in your room?' he asked.

Our eyes were fixed on the REM pod. There was nothing. No lights. No beep. Just an eerie, empty nothing.

'Do you feel this room belongs to you?' he continued.

Again, silence engulfed the room.

'Was it you who took the painting down off the wall and turned the tap on?'

The ghost definitely wasn't fessing up to any of those antics.

'Are you in this room with us now?'

Suddenly, all four colours of the REM pod started flashing. It beeped uncontrollably. *Holy mother of fuck.* My heart bungee-jumped from my chest into my gut. When I looked over at Selin, she was cowering in the corner with her fingers half-covering her eyes. Even Danny looked shocked. I crossed myself several times: spectacles, testicles, wallet and watch. Okay, not testicles, but you know what I mean.

Then, an even more disturbing thing happened. When the REM pod stopped flashing, Danny replayed the recording on his phone. As he did so a string of fairy lights hanging by the window began swaying, gently at first then more strongly. The house was newly double-glazed and the windows firmly locked shut.

'Are you in this room with us now?' the recorded message replayed. As it did the first time this question was asked, the REM pod lit up again like a Christmas tree.

'Oh fuck, I'm scared,' shouted Selin.

'I'm here, it's okay,' I reassured her, but in truth my blood had frozen. I was no use to anyone. All the colour seemed to have drained from Dad too. It was extraordinary! Why Danny wanted to remain in that room and sleep the night was beyond any of us. I, for one, did not want to wake up the next morning to find him dismembered . . . disrobed . . .

Or what if he just disappeared? I hoped he had good life insurance cover, although I have no clue whether companies even pay out against death by a malevolent spirit. How the fuck could you prove it?

As soon as we could, we all legged it downstairs and wished him the best of luck. It could be a long, long night . . .

In the early hours of the morning, I found myself awake, tossing and turning and worrying about what horror could be unfolding on the upper floor of my house. When Danny came down for breakfast the next morning I looked at him expectantly.

'You're still alive, then?' I joked.

'Yep, just about!'

'What the hell happened?'

Sadly, Danny had no further activity to report. He did admit to being very spooked, though. He even mistook his own reflection in the full-length bathroom mirror for a ghostly figure as he stumbled in for a 3am piss. What an absolute moron. While I was relieved I didn't have a crime scene on my hands, I also felt very disappointed. Were we any closer to cracking the mystery of my haunted home? No, but the evidence was stacking up. I had witnesses to the fact that I was definitely not living there alone.

☆

3

THE GHOSTS OF HALLOWEEN PAST

I have often wondered why I am a believer; why anyone believes, to be honest. Especially if they've never actually seen or heard a spirit. Yet many people do. A shitload, in fact. In the UK a third of people are fully paid-up subscribers to the supernatural. In America that number is closer to half. Then, if you look at somewhere like Taiwan, a whopping 95 per cent of the population are devotees. Whatever they're on, can I have some? I'd love it if everyone in this country took the supernatural as seriously. In Taiwan, they even hold an annual Ghost Month. It's not organised by some amateur enthusiasts trying to push the paranormal on to the general population, like some shit two-for-one promotional campaign for the underworld. The whole event is government sanctioned! There's even guidance issued about how people should behave. To me it sounds fucking brilliant. During the seventh month of the lunar calendar the gates of hell are flung wide open and hungry ghosts are let loose in search of food and money and entertainment. During this period people avoid doing *anything*, which begs the question: when can I move there? For weeks, institutions close down, law courts stop hearing cases and parts of government stop functioning (if that happened here it is debatable whether anyone would notice).

There are also loads of specific activities that people are strongly advised to abstain from. Here's a few of my favourites:

- *Don't plan anything important.* For lazy fuckers like me this is like feeding bamboo to a giant panda and watching it sleep for 12 hours. Whether you were planning to buy a house or a car, get married, have life-saving surgery, go to the dentist, the warning is: just don't do it. Stay at home. This is because Taiwanese ghosts are mischievous and could sabotage anything at any moment just for a laugh. Imagine waking up from an anaesthetic only to find the word 'knobhead' written on your forehead. Or hearing a mystery voice echo out from the church pews just at the moment when you're about to utter 'I do': 'I'm the spawn of Satan, and he's the father!' Awkward.

- *Don't sit in the front row of a theatre.* No danger there. I know, I'm an actor, but I can barely sit through an episode of *Teletubbies*, let alone three hours of *Hamlet*. Anyhow, during this month the front row is completely out of bounds, left empty for ghosts who fancy a night out.

- *Don't piss on a tree.* An absolute classic that my twenty-something self, correction, my thirty-something self, would fail at miserably. All those times when I've been out clubbing and some overzealous McDonald's security guard wouldn't let me barge upstairs to the toilet without buying a Big Mac and fries, even though I was dancing on the spot and pleading with the cunt that my bladder was bursting at the seams. In my desperate search for the sweet feeling of relief I have pissed on trees, behind gravestones, behind the bins at the back of Tesco. But it's in these shaded areas that ghosts like to gather. I doubt any ghost seeking vengeance would have deterred me. Neither would the CCTV cameras.

- *Don't wear black and white.* It's brilliant to know that ghosts in Taiwan understand what's on trend when it comes to fashion. During Ghost Month black and white is a definite no-no. Instead, bold colours are in season. Shame. Red is not my colour but it is supposed to bring luck to ward off evil spirits.

- *Don't take the last bus or train home.* Ghost Month is a time when Uber drivers can cash in big time. This is because the final transport of the day harnesses the strongest yin, or bad energy. Let's face it, it would put a significant downer on any evening if you stumbled on to the night bus, head spinning with tequila shots, sending pissed-up texts to your ex telling him what a fucking loser he is only to find yourself on a superhighway to the afterlife, driven by a phantom driver. I doubt you'd even get your fare refunded.

- *Don't be untidy.* It turns out that Taiwanese ghosts aren't just the fashion police, but the tidiness police too. Like a delirious Marie Kondo in the house of a hoarder, they hate clutter. Everything must be in its place, especially shoes. These must be positioned with the toes pointing away from the bed before you sleep.

This is because shoes act like road signs for the undead. If you point the toes towards you it's tantamount to switching on the satnav and punching in your own name as the destination. Toes pointed away from the bed means ghosts continually circle the M25 with no fucking clue which junction to come off at.

But I have saved my all-time favourite until last:

- *Don't take part in any water-based activities.* The mind boggles. What does that even mean? No washing? No swimming? No surfing or jet-skiing? Does it mean I can't take my kids to AquaVenture – the largest inflatable waterpark in the Cotswolds? Is this because there's a higher likelihood of drowning or because ghosts just want to hang out there undisturbed without having to queue for the Incredible Mammoth Tower?

This last rule does shine new light on one very mysterious incident that happened when I was around ten years old. Dad had taken Charlie and me to the Oasis Leisure Centre in Swindon. Back in the day, it was *the* place to hang out. It had a wave machine; tiles decorated with dolphins and crabs; a glass dome overhead. Oh, and the *pièce de résistance* – the Domebuster slide. Naturally, Dad hogged it, practically batting small children out of the way to climb up the ladder to take turn after turn. One time Charlie and I were splashing around in the lagoon below waiting to watch him emerge from the mouth of the giant blue plastic tunnel when Dad waved to us from the top.

We waved back. He closed his eyes and jokingly pinched his nose with his fingers, as if he was preparing himself to dive into an abyss of ocean. Then he was gone . . .

'Here he comes!' I squealed with excitement.

'Yeah, any moment now!' Charlie chimed in.

Any. Moment. Now.

But it wasn't Dad's feet or head that made their way down the flume first. Instead, Charlie and I watched, our mouths agape.

'Dad?' I shouted.

Dad had not appeared. Instead a large poo surfed out on the crest of a tsunami wave, followed by a lonely pair of bright yellow children's swimming trunks. I mean, for fuck's sake, of all the times and of all the places: 2pm on a Saturday afternoon when the plunge pool is overflowing with families, is *never* the right time to poop down the pipe of Swindon's most beloved water attraction. And the weird thing is, no child ever appeared. Somewhat delayed, Dad put in an appearance a few seconds later – with his swimming trunks on, I might add. Now, though, I wonder . . . *was that actually a human turd and bright yellow swimming trunks or just a ghost having a laugh?*

✫

Reading about Ghost Month did get me thinking, though. Are ghost stories and celebrations like Halloween (which sadly only lasts one night) our way of making it acceptable to be believers for a short time? Do we experience supernatural occurrences because we *want* to believe? Rational-minded people will insist that seeing spirits of any kind is just our subconscious spewing up random shit, like a waking dream or a form of psychosis. If that is true, then I really need more sessions with a psychotherapist.

Surely the first step to experiencing a ghost in your house is believing that there is one? Or at the very least believing that one is possible? Did I see and hear what I did in my house just because I wanted to? There's loads of apparently scientific studies that say that particular types of people are more prone to experiencing the 'unknown'. Extroverts or people who love new experiences are supposed to be more open to these types of things. Cue a massive arrow pointing at my head. Psychologists also reckon that people who are creative could be more susceptible.

Weirdly, the rate of paranormal belief goes up in times of great uncertainty. And, let's face it, we have been staring down the barrel of an almighty shitstorm for several years: Brexit; Donald Trump; the environmental catastrophe; Covid-19; Boris fucking Johnson; the cost-of-living crisis; Britney Spears's latest marriage to the bloke who clearly missed out on a part in *Zoolander*. It's been a dizzying roller coaster of gut-churning anxiety to ride. But it is still strange to think that more people are finding certainty in something that isn't 100 per cent proven rather than in their own lives.

But I do understand this too. When I look back now, I have been primed to be a believer, although I do think it has made me question all that I do believe. What I saw may not be 100 per cent proven, but it was 100 per cent real to me.

When I was younger, though, believing in the paranormal was all about escape: getting as far away from the humdrum of school and teachers and homework as possible. Admittedly with fewer rules than

Mum's house, on the other hand, was like Willy Wonka's chocolate factory. She put out boiled sweets – like pear drops and sherbet lemons, cola bottles, mini chocolate bars and gobstoppers. Before we went out trick-or-treating we'd invite friends round to bob for apples. In Mum we even had our own Halloween dating guru. She'd hand us an apple and a peeler, and we each had to carefully peel the entire apple in a spiral making sure not to break it. Then, we'd turn around and throw the peel over our shoulder. How it landed was supposed to spell out the initial of the person we were going to marry. At the age of seven my peeling left a lot to be desired. It could have been an O or a P, maybe a D. I did go on to marry a W, but that would have been an ambitious reading of the peel by anyone's standards.

Mum also used to go to town with atmospheric Halloween smoke which wafted through the hallway and under doors like eerie East End Victorian smog. It got pumped out from a smoke machine hidden behind a chair in the living room and needed constant topping up throughout the evening. Children from all over the neighbourhood flocked to see it although sometimes it was hard to see in front of you and kids bumped into each other like dodgems.

While Mum loved tending to the succession of ghouls and ghosts and witches that trooped in and out of our house, Dad expressed very little interest. For him, Halloween was the one night of the year when he hid upstairs in his study playing solitaire on the computer until, finally, Mum shut the door behind the last caller.

'Is it safe to come down now?' Dad would shout.

'Oh for goodness' sake, Paul, it's just children having fun!' Mum snapped back.

Dad was never persuaded.

But one year, on All Hallows' Eve, Mum hadn't been feeling herself and by late afternoon she was complaining of a headache.

'I'm just going upstairs for a lie-down,' she told us. 'Dad will need to welcome in the first trick-or-treaters until I can take over.'

'Jesus fucking Christ . . .' I heard Dad mutter as he heaved into view.

Dad was less than pleased. His face looked like he'd rather be stripped naked and boiled in a vat of tar than lean into this annual celebration. 'Happy Halloween,' I heard him murmur dryly at the first few callers he opened the door to. He was behaving like an absolute twat and not putting his back into it at all.

Charlie and I were just about to step out into the night air and begin our own haunting of the neighbourhood, when the front doorbell rang again. Suddenly, I heard Dad's voice lift a few octaves. Strangely, it sounded like he was almost enjoying himself.

'And what have you come as?' Dad cooed.

'I'm a vampire,' a high-pitched voice piped up.

'And what about you?'

'I'm a werewolf!' the other trilled excitedly.

I recognised the voices immediately as the twins who lived at the other end of our street. Dad was good mates with their dad, Martin. Dad clearly didn't want to be shown up as the neighbour who pissed all over the youthful enthusiasm of the under-tens.

'You'll both be wanting some snacks, then,' he said, as he brought both of them through to the table where mum had laid out that year's spread of goodies. By then, it was running low on gobstoppers and boiled sweets and while Dad had sent the previous children off with a bulging Halloween-themed bag, the twins had what looked more like a nylon popsock filled with a solitary stone.

'Sorry, we've run out of pear drops, cola bottles and tangerines, but would you like some special Halloween brew?' he asked.

'Yes please, Mr Cooper.'

'Daisy, can you please fetch a couple of glasses from the kitchen?' Dad yelled. Halloween drinks seemed to be an ambitious new addition to Mum's spread, but I went with it. She'd left an old plastic Coke bottle on the window ledge with a makeshift label on it on which she'd written the words 'Spooky Juice' with thick black marker pen.

'Now, who would like some spooky juice?' Dad cooed again.

The vampire's hand shot up.

'Good lad, here you go.' Dad smiled while pouring him out some of the cloudy liquid. It looked like Mum's delicious home-made lemonade.

'And you?' He turned to the werewolf.

'Yes please!'

'Here you go, get that down you. Put hairs on your chest, that will.' He patted the werewolf on the head.

'Thanks, Mr Cooper!'

Dad beamed. He didn't want to admit it, but he was starting to throw himself into Halloween and it seemed like he was actually loving it. Chaz and I skipped from our front door delighted that he'd been converted. Full of pride, we stopped on the pavement outside the Jehovah's Witness's front door to lob a few eggs at it before we moved on to chocolate-coin-and-tangerine man.

A couple of hours later we returned home, our Tesco bags heaving with enough sweet stuff to stun a brown bear. By now Dad was back upstairs in his study playing solitaire as the Halloween goodie table was almost empty. Unfortunately, Mum hadn't made it down to enjoy any of the visitors' costumes.

Then, the front doorbell sounded. One last straggler, we figured. We heard Dad stir and leg it downstairs. The door opened.

'Hi, Martin,' we heard him say, sounding puzzled.

'Paul.'

Martin, father of the aforementioned twin vampire and werewolf didn't sound like he'd popped round to chat some matey shit at the end of a weary night.

'What's up, Martin? You look like you've seen a ghost.' Dad sniggered at his own joke. He thought it was very funny but it landed like a bowling ball.

'You've poisoned my twins,' Martin announced.

Charlie and I threw a confused glance at one another.

'I'm sorry . . . I've what?'

'Poisoned them. Both of them are rolling around on the floor at home. We're going to have to take them to A & E.'

'I'm sorry to hear that, Martin, but what has that got to do—'

Martin interrupted, rather curtly, 'It has *everything* to do with you, Paul. Do the words "spooky juice" mean anything to you?'

'Yes . . .'

'The boys say they drank it here. Not long after they started feeling ill. They have temperatures through the roof. Not even bags of frozen peas can bring it down. Janet is out of her mind with worry.'

'Gill left out the spooky juice,' Dad stammered. Poor Dad, he sounded very flustered. 'It's her special lemonade . . . it's just water and sugar and lemons, Martin. I can't see how it would have poisoned them.'

At that moment Mum padded down the stairs in her dressing gown.

'Hi, Martin,' she called out as she turned down the hallway.

'Gill . . .'

Dad stopped Mum in her tracks.

'Gill, the Coke bottle with "spooky juice" written on it. It's lemonade, right?'

'Oh that? It's the top-up liquid for the smoke machine. Did it run out?' Mum giggled breezily.

At the door, there was a deathly hush. The kind you get when snow falls, silent and cold.

'*Fuck. Me,*' Dad said slowly.

'Fuck you, indeed,' said Martin.

★

4

ROUTE ONE PRANKERY

My grandmother, Granny Eddie, used to say that the great advantage of dying was that you would get to visit all the places you never managed to go to in life. Of course, in my head, I'd be swirling above rainforests in an erratic cloud of rainbow-coloured butterflies. Knowing my luck, though, I'll get stuck in a ghostly traffic jam on the M4 just outside Swindon trying to get to the Premier Inn. But the funny thing about Granny is that I don't think she started out as a true believer, but things changed when her daughter, my mum's sister, Alison, died tragically when I was around four.

Up until then, I think Granny may have been para-curious but wasn't a fully paid-up member of the paranormal club. She did have her suspicions, though. One story she told us always terrified me. Her husband, my grandad Eddie, had been a jockey and raced all over the world. Before I was born, she'd been visiting him in Hong Kong, where he was living at the time. She was in the apartment alone when she became distracted by the sound of something unusual.

What appeared right in front of her, almost spitting at her, was a gargoyle-type figure. It lunged forward, then back, before fading into the wall.

'I never believed any of that stuff before that day,' she admitted.

But when Auntie Alison died Granny seemed to cross over into another realm. Mum did too. The circumstances of her death were shocking. One night, Alison was alive, the next moment she'd crashed her car on her drive home. Not long after she was pronounced brain dead and her family had to make the heartbreaking decision to switch off her life-support machine. All I remember was that it was a very weird time in our house. The only death I'd experienced up till this was my hamster Chewy, who failed to respond to CPR after being accidentally vacuumed. It was this (non-hamster-related) family tragedy that set Mum and Granny on a never-ending quest to find Alison.

I suppose sceptics would say that it was their way of processing all the fucked-up things that were happening. In the chaos of losing someone close, their search for the afterlife was just a search for meaning: that someone's existence, however short or tragically curtailed, meant something. Otherwise, what the fuck is life all about?

The downside of this newly found open-mindedness was that our phone bill reached off-the-scale heights. Four-digit numbers off the scale. I recall Mum and Dad arguing about it *a lot*. Mum was forever ringing up crap mediums on psychic hotlines, the kind that advertised in the back of women's magazines. It was like living with someone hooked on the eternal possibility that next time she'd have an answer or next time the message from Alison would be clearer. The angry red letters that dropped through the letter box and got shoved in a pile in the airing cupboard seemed endless.

Mum brought mediums round to the house too. Jesus, they were bad. And Mum knew it. I'd arrive home from school, and a stranger with a poodle perm and semi-rimmed glasses would be sipping tea while the noxious smell of sandalwood incense wafted through the house. Sometimes, they'd wave their arms around or shuffle in their chair if they felt a voice coming through. All I could hear was the life force being sucked from Mum, like she was caught in some never-ending feedback loop.

MEDIUM: Did your sister ever own her own caravan?

MUM: Nope.

MEDIUM: Well, did she know someone who owned a caravan?

MUM: Probably. Is this relevant?

MEDIUM: Well, it could be . . .

MUM: Why, is she drifting around a chemical toilet?

MEDIUM: So, is that a yes or a no to knowing anyone who owned a caravan?

MUM: Yes, most people do . . .

For fuck's sake . . .

There was another classic, a variation of which Mum heard *all the time.*

MEDIUM: She loved budgies, didn't she?

MUM: Hated them.

MEDIUM: No, okay. I'm not seeing a budgie. I'm seeing a . . . parrot . . .

MUM: Or an overweight budgie? She didn't like parrots either.

MEDIUM: Okay, so what about cats?

MUM: Yes, she definitely liked cats.

MEDIUM: Black cats?

MUM: No.

MEDIUM: Ginger cats? Tabby cats?

On and on it went. Talk about clutching at straws. A scarecrow pulling its hair out would have less straws to clutch at.

No matter the vaguery, Mum was always ridiculously polite. She'd smile and hand over her crisp £10 or £20 note. Then, as soon as the front door slammed shut she'd throw her hands up and say:

'Well she was full of shit, wasn't she?'

To be honest, all of them were. But then what do you expect when the woman who works in the local sandwich shop doubles as Cheryl Crystal Tits after the lunchtime rush? Mum really was obsessed, though.

She also used to take me to see awful mediums and clairvoyants in the back of dingy pubs. The kinds of pubs with old, swirly carpet that looked like someone had puked pilau rice on to it. At times, Granny used to come too. We'd go to these events maybe once every couple of months and I'm sure if we'd bothered to read the small print then the flyers would have read: 'For entertainment purposes only'.

This, by the way, is the sure-fire way to know if someone is a fake or not. Looking back, I reckon they were all winging it, cashing in on grief and the false promise of finding a connection on the hotline to heaven.

During this time Mum took me to spiritualist church services, mainly held at the Old Memorial Hospital in Cirencester, which has since been demolished. It also doubled as a cyber cafe, was the gathering place for the local history society and was the location of the Buns of Steel step aerobics class for the over-60s. Don't ask.

Sometimes, there would be as many as three hundred people crammed into a back room all praying for a message. Mum was no different. She always made a special point of going when it was Alison's birthday or the anniversary of her death. And when Granny died a few years later, Mum always turned up wearing her engagement ring: a cherished memento to bring that extra element of good luck, she figured.

'I have a feeling, Daisy, I'm going to get picked tonight.'

Mum never was. Pathetic, really. Most of the time, it was like sitting through a terrible version of the TV game show *1 vs 100* – where The One competes against a panel of The 100. To claim the prize money they'd have to eliminate everybody else by answering a ton of *really* crap questions.

Back in the numerous shitty pubs Mum used to drag us to, the medium would tap his microphone. It was always a 'he' with a Northern accent like a failed Blackpool entertainer and he'd be wearing a black shirt half-buttoned like a poor man's Julio Iglesias, an overabundance of cheap gold jewellery, a terrible toupee and

Roy Orbison sunglasses. They always used their psychic act to crowbar in a tune or two in the break, usually a Frank Sinatra number like 'Fly Me to the Moon'.

'So, I've got a woman. She's very caring. Selfless. Probably worked too much during her life.'

At that, 50 desperate hands would shoot up. Bit vague. And, anyway, who is ever going to show up their departed mum or granny or sister as a lazy, selfish twat?

'And she came from a very large family . . .'

Ten hands would go down.

'She had a squint in her right eye . . .'

Twenty more hands would drop, the sighs of disappointment rippling around the room. Or you'd hear mutterings of the more desperate:

'Was it her right eye, Angela?' One old biddy would tap her mate. 'It could have been left, but I'm sure it was her right . . .'

And the clincher:

'She had a club foot and walked with a limp.'

At the end, one solitary hand would be hovering above the audience. On most occasions Mum didn't even make it to the final ten. Auntie Alison never put in an appearance. Ever. Mum and I never won the raffle that bizarrely rounded off any spiritualist event, either. But you do have to ask: would the dead seriously reveal themselves in the same place that an LA Gear holdall, a Paul Daniels magic set, a Frisbee, a radio alarm clock or a set of glitter gel pens were being raffled off? Unlikely, is my view.

Determined not to be part of any ghostly hoax, Granny was

smart enough to put in some groundwork before she gasped her last breath.

'Gill. If the medium says the codeword "bumfuzzle" then you'll know it's me.' The problem was, by the time Granny had passed, Mum was juggling far too many spirits. And the heart-wrenching thing was that when it came to sitting in front of a medium she forgot the bloody word.

So, a word of warning: communicating effectively with the other side does require you to have a decent memory in this life.

And to date, the only visitation Mum has ever had was quite recently, when she was in hospital. Apparently, she woke up to find a parrot perched at the end of her bed giving her a hard Paddington stare. Being a massive hoarder, she does have a dead parrot called Claude wrapped in gold tissue paper in her freezer.

'Do you think Claude's telling you to bury him?' I enquired.

'I don't know, Daisy. He did seem a bit pissed off.'

Fucking livid would be my guess. He's been there, rock solid and sandwiched between the frozen peas and a packet of pork sausages, for four long years.

Back when I was a kid, though, I was more intrigued by the afterlife than anything else. Plus, whenever Mum or Granny took me to a reading there was always the chance of a bucket of popcorn, a can of Coke, and winning a bottle of shampoo in the raffle. Even better, if the session went on very late, I might get the next day off school.

☆

Regardless of the mediums playing fast and loose with the truth of who they could contact, I'd like to think that these fucking appalling experiences have stood me in good stead to sort out the wheat from the chaff, to know who is shitting me or not. More importantly to a cheeky teen, they elevated me into a different league when it came to convincing people of my own imaginary sightings. I call it *route one prankery*.

When I think about it now, it's unbelievable how anyone could have been taken in by it.

My Catholic school was founded during Victorian times. It was an austere building in the centre of town and had been the site of a school in one form or another for almost three hundred years. A picture of its founder Rebecca Powell hung in the library. She had long brown hair and menacing eyes and she looked like a tight-arsed bitch. I hated her on sight, but I also reckoned she was my best hope of getting out of lessons. Not satisfied with feigning a dizzy spell or an achy stomach, I decided to fuck with everybody psychologically.

It was a hot summer's afternoon and the sun was streaming in through the old sash windows. End of term was almost upon us and I was bored to shit. At the back of class, I suddenly started to convulse. I shook my head violently and rocked backwards and forwards. It caused quite a stir.

'Is there something the matter, Daisy?' Mrs Canes called out.

'It's the ghost of Rebecca Powell. She's possessed me.' I did try to foam at the mouth once but it ended up being one massive globule of spit running down my school jumper. Humiliating.

Amazingly, though, classmates were taken in by it. Even Robert, the class sceptic. In the library, I snatched books from the shelf when no one was looking and sent them flying across the room.

'Oh my God. Look! It's the ghost of Rebecca Powell,' I screamed.

I also claimed to have seen Rebecca Powell run across the courtyard with her long hair and white petticoat billowing behind her. Such a ham-fisted supernatural trope, I know, but I was young. I reported chairs unstacking themselves in assembly. I fucking hated assembly with its endless hymns and prayers that droned on and on. *Kill me. Kill me. Kill me now.*

I played so many mind games that in the end children were being taken to the medical room on a regular basis complaining they were about to pass out from fear. Others were so terrified they refused to come to school. A Rebecca Powell reign of terror swept the building. It got so out of hand that the headmistress sent out letters to parents reassuring them that the school was safe. Of course, I maintained that I needed a priest to exorcise me. I became so good at conjuring the spirit of our school founder that I even convinced myself, even though I did know that the ghost of Rebecca Powell was a complete fabrication, imagined by yours truly.

Then something odd happened. Something that shook me into believing that maybe, just maybe, the paranormal was real. One year, around Halloween, my friend Kaya and I set out on a school project together. As I recall, the project was an attempt by our history teacher to make the subject a tad sexier. It was perfect for me as the task set was to look for ghosts. And we knew of the perfect place: Prestbury, near Cheltenham. It had a reputation of being one of the most haunted villages in the UK. On the surface, it's one of those picture-perfect, chocolate-boxy Cotswold villages but running through it is a dark underbelly. I'd always loved its stories.

One tale, which dates back to the 15th century, is that of the Cavalier of Shaw Green Lane. He is rumoured to have been a messenger shot down by an archer while on his way to Edward IV's camp before the Battle of Tewkesbury during the Wars of the Roses. Legend has it that he returns to the exact spot where he was killed.

Another of Prestbury's most well-known inhabitants is the Black Abbot. He runs a regular course from the village church to the high street to a plot of land near a home called Reform Cottage, reputed to be built on the site of a monk's burial ground. Traditionally he appears at Easter, All Saints' Day at the start of November and Christmas, and he glides through Prestbury in a black hooded robe before fading from view.

One evening, as soon as darkness started to draw in, Dad drove us the half hour to the village and waited for us outside the church.

'Don't be long, girls. I'll be right here waiting.' He paused, then chuckled. 'Unless I've been spirited away, of course.'

'Yeah, Dad. Whatever . . .'

Dad *always* thought his jokes were far funnier than they actually were.

We clutched our notebooks and held hands as we walked around the graveyard, going out of our tiny minds with every little sound, even that of our own feet crunching on the fallen leaves.

We saw absolutely fuck-all.

'Shall we go further?' we asked as we approached an exit to the graveyard.

'Yeah,' we agreed.

It was dark and creepy under the dim street lights. We took out our little map and pinpointed Reform Cottage, a white thatched building set back from the main road. By the time we reached it we were trembling.

'Shall we knock?' I asked Kaya.

'You can,' she said, crouching behind my shoulder.

I'm not sure what we hoped to find there, but our project did require us to interview some people. As the church had been locked and we couldn't find the priest, and the Black Abbot hadn't been arsed to turn up to the graveyard and answer a few simple questions, we were running out of options.

We knocked and waited. A light switched on in the hallway and we watched anxiously as a shadow edged towards the glass-paned door.

'Can I help you?' A middle-aged woman peeked out as it opened.

'Yes.' I took a deep breath. 'I'm Daisy Cooper and this is my friend Kaya and we are doing some research about ghost sightings in the area. It's for our school project.'

'Right . . . well, you've come to a good place.' She smiled.

'We have?'

'Yes, why don't you come in?' she said, ushering us forward with her hand.

She had a pinny on and looked remarkably like the woman in the OXO gravy ads.

By now, Kaya and I had been wandering around Prestbury for some time. I knew Dad would still be waiting for us outside the church, oblivious to the fact that we were about to enter the house of a complete stranger. She could be a total nutbag for all we knew. Suddenly all worries about stranger danger went out of the window.

Fuck it, I thought. When the paranormal taps you on the shoulder, you'd be an absolute fool not to follow.

And this woman turned out to be *a-mazing*. Not only did she offer us Coke and crisps, which we guzzled down like we'd been invited to the Last Supper, but she claimed to have seen several ghosts in the village.

'Do you mind if we record you?' I asked.

'No, dear,' she said. She didn't want to be filmed but she was happy for us to use our Dictaphone. Mum still has those tapes somewhere.

'Who have you seen?' I asked.

The Black Abbot was definitely real, she told us.

'You're kidding, really?'

God's honest truth. She'd seen him with her own eyes. Regularly, in fact. And several spirits up by Prestbury Park racecourse. A spirit having a flutter at the Cheltenham Festival. *What are the odds?* I wondered.

She also claimed to be psychic. If we had time she would give Kaya and me a palm reading. I looked at my watch. I pictured Dad's fingers drumming on the steering wheel and the steam building up in his ears. For the second time that evening I thought, *Fuck it*.

'Yes, please!' we chimed in unison.

That reading still haunts me to this day.

The woman drew her seat closer, clasped my fingers and peered in.

'Are you a Leo?' she asked.

Fucking hell . . . nailed it in one. I was born in August.

'Yes, how did you know?'

The woman looked me straight in the eye, and her face beamed with a kindly smile.

'Young lady, you're going to become a famous actress.' She nodded.

It *was* something I'd always dreamed of – drama was all I was any good at in school. But a real, bona fide actress? A famous actress? No way!

'*Really?*' I couldn't believe it.

'Yes, you are, my dear,' she confirmed.

I felt intoxicated. Drunk on the thought of one day becoming a famous actress. So much so that I didn't listen to a single word of Kaya's reading, although I'm pretty sure her name didn't appear in bright lights in some future life. However, I wasn't quite so popular when she and I finally made it back to Dad's car. He was pacing up and down under the faint street light, frantically looking at his watch, steam now billowing from his ears.

'What time do you call this?' he yelled.

'Sorry, Dad. It's a long story but we ended up getting a palm reading.'

'From a ghost?'

'No! As I said, it's a long story, but check this out. I'm going to be a famous actress!'

'Well that's just brilliant, Daisy,' Dad harrumphed sarcastically before he ordered us into the car and we sat in silence for the entire journey home while Dad quietly raged.

It didn't bother me, though. I was going to be famous. Fucking typical, though, that our random palm reader didn't bother to tell me about the scores of failed auditions I would have to endure and the reams of scripts I'd have to learn to get me there . . .

★

5

WHERE DID ALL THE GOOD GUYS GO?

It's July 2019 and I'm messaging Michael Sleggs, our friend and former co-star on *This Country*. There are so many things I want to tell him.

'I really miss you today Slugs', I write. I mean every word of that. I *really* do. My body and heart feels so heavy, and I can't stop the tears from falling down my cheeks.

I'm desperate to tell him all about Limestone Man too. He's a guy who we always used to see around Cirencester who is freakishly tall. The other day when I was in town I stumbled across the opening of a new gym. There were multicoloured balloons in an arch outside its door and 'Eye of the Tiger' was blaring through some tinny speakers. Outside there was a small crowd gathered who'd turned up wearing tracksuits and trainers. Limestone Man was there too. He was dressed in his trademark dungarees, a check shirt and oversized boots with steel toecaps. He towered above the crowd, dancing in the breeze like one of those inflatable tube men you see outside gas stations across America. Desperate Dan on stilts.

'Saw Limestone Man today', I start to write. *Don't send it, Daisy*, I think. I delete the sentence. Then I start typing it again. I want to tell Slugs. I need to tell him. Only Slugs would have understood. Limestone Man was an in-joke. Our in-joke. 'Why aren't you here Slugs?' I say frustratedly. You should be here! I change my mind and start to delete the text for the second time. *He can't hear you, or see you, Dais. Slugs has gone, you fucking moron. How the hell can he even read it?*

Slugs died a few weeks ago. I went to his funeral, so I saw his coffin and all the bouquets of flowers and messages of condolence lined up outside. I still haven't forgiven him for making me sit through every single one of those turgid hymns. Plus, I've had to explain to his family why we can't carry out his dying wish.

'I want my body in a coffin on the show. First episode,' he told me a few weeks before he died. I was sitting by his bedside at his home where he saw out his final days.

By that time, Slugs was so off-his-face on morphine he was saying all sorts of mad shit. But, even by his standards, that was absolutely fucking mental.

'Right . . . I think health and safety might . . .'

'Can you arrange it, Daisy? It's what I want.'

'I'll do my best . . .'

I didn't want to let him down. How could I? He only had weeks to live.

He also wanted the actor Paul Chahidi, who played the vicar Francis Seaton in the mockumentary, to officiate his funeral. That was pretty funny, actually.

So far the bastard has replied to zero of the texts I've sent him.

And, over the past few weeks I have sent him *a lot*. 'Hope you're enjoying it up there'; 'What's the grub like?'; 'Chaz misses you too, we all miss you. Every. Single. Day. It's been so tough filming without you . . . a gaping hole on set.'

And if he'd got those texts he definitely would have texted me back: *'I can't use my phone. I'm a ghost LOL. My credit has run out . . .'*

Funny, Slugs. Very fucking funny.

Why is it that it's only the people you ache to see who never come back to visit you? Auntie Alison still hasn't turned up and that's been years now. And a guy I knew called Lee, who died in a motorcycle accident while we were making the pilot for *This Country*, hasn't put in an appearance either. I don't even know if he's aware that it finally got commissioned; that the massive, crazy journey we started on had a happy ending. He followed every twist and turn like an endless game of snakes and ladders. One week we were up, the next at rock bottom. But we got to the top, Lee! We finally made it! *This Country* was made! And people bloody loved it!

And now Slugs, who was right at the centre of that happy ending, hasn't even bothered to tell us if he likes the third series. It's probably because he's not in it. Narcissist. There was a mention of his death in the first episode, but I bet he has no idea how difficult that was to write in. We *had* to write his death in, though. We had to explain why Slugs wasn't there any more, but more than that we *wanted* him to be there. In spirit if nothing else. He was our guiding force throughout.

Yet maybe contact from the other side is like buses? You wait and wait and wait for one to come and then three spirits turn up at once? Fucking typical . . .

I put my mobile phone away. For a moment I wanted to sit with my eyes closed and remember Slugs's voice. And his blistering sense of humour. I'd never met anyone like him before. Slugs was one of the kindest, caring, most genuine friends we could have wished for. He was unique and so fucking astute, yet at the same time completely tone deaf.

I'll never forget the time he walked up to me on set one day.

'I know exactly who my character is based on,' he told me.

'Yeah, sorry, mate,' I said, cringing. 'Hope you're okay with it.'

'Yeah, fine.'

'It's Paul Fisher isn't it?'

Paul Fisher was another guy we knew from the area. Slugs had no clue whatsoever that his character in the series was actually based on Slugs himself. Extraordinary!

We'd known Slugs since we'd been at school together. He had cancer back then, and he was always in and out of hospital. But when he was cured of cancer we all thought he'd be okay. Over the years, though, he suffered heart problems which was what killed him in the end. How he kept going was anyone's guess. And that's exactly the way we wrote about Slugs when we wrote his death into the script of *This Country* – we talked about the second, third and fourth winds he had. We counted 26 in the end. Twenty-six! Who does that? Unbelievable how he kept going like he did. Every time he was at death's door he'd rally round like a boxer laid out in the ring, seconds ticking. He'd just haul himself up and keep fighting. I fucking loved that about him.

And when I sat with him a few weeks before he died, I was in bits. Yet he was surprisingly blasé.

'I'm gutted,' he told me.

Yeah, I'd be pretty pissed off if the Grim Reaper turned up at my door when I was aged just 33, I thought.

'I'm really sorry,' I said, hanging my head. What else could I say? What could possibly make things better for Slugs?

'No, Daisy, you don't understand. I'm going to miss the Cirencester Phoenix Festival in August.'

'Oh right . . . yeah.'

I'd forgotten that Slugs bloody loved that festival. One: he loved it because it was in the abbey grounds and within walking distance of his house. Two: it was free entry – both days. And three: on that year's line-up was a Michael Jackson tribute act, plus the Rolling Clones, an apparently hilarious take on the Rolling Stones.

'I can't believe it. It's the best year yet,' he said.

'Yeah, shame. It's a corker,' I replied, bemused.

In his final weeks all he wanted to do was watch the film *While You Were Sleeping* on repeat: that bizarre 1990s romcom starring Sandra Bullock. The one where she's the lonely fare token collector who saves a man's life and her family mistakes her for his fiancée. Except the tragic thing about it is that she ends up falling in love with his brother. Weird.

Slugs was scared, though. He did tell me that, and I could see it in his eyes. He'd grown up in a very religious family and towards the end of his life he surrounded himself with the Bible and Christian songs and sermons. He wanted to focus on all the positives, he said. He reckoned he'd had a good life even though he was facing death. And as we talked at that time he said something that burned into my brain like hot coal.

'An angel came,' he said.

'Are you kidding? Which one?'

'No idea, didn't catch its name. But it sat on the end of my bed. It was bathed in bright light and it was smiling down at me.'

'Did it say anything? What did it say?'

'It told me that in seven days' time, I'll have a new body by midnight.'

'What the fuck does that mean?'

'I'm either going to get better or in seven days' time I'll be gone.'

Slugs died seven days later at 11.59pm.

Since his funeral, that's never left me. As soon as he said it, I saw the shift in him. He went from being terrified to being at peace.

I couldn't help but feel disheartened, though. Particularly as Slugs knew of my interest in the supernatural.

'Please promise me that you'll come back as something and show me that you're okay,' I urged.

'I promise,' he said.

Of all the people who would have kept their promise, it would have been Slugs. And he bloody loved pranks. If anyone would have wanted to have returned to scare the shit out of me it would have been him. A tap on the shoulder, a note warning me of a zombie apocalypse. *Something. Anything.* Now, his lack of apparition has made me doubt at times that anything exists in the afterlife, but I know that can't be true.

So now I'm thinking, maybe the people you love the most, the people who were just really good fucking people, never come back to visit you. Maybe their work here is done? Maybe, just maybe, they had a higher purpose? Maybe Auntie Alison died so that Mum and

Granny could become closer than they'd ever been? Maybe she died so that Grandad Eddie, who spent all his life being a miserable cunt, could soften round the edges and become the grandad we really loved and who loved us? Maybe she died so that me and my cousins (who spent many weekends at our house afterwards) could enjoy the most amazing relationship that's lasted so many years? Maybe my friend Lee died so that a similar sequence of ties and bonds could happen in the living world? And maybe, just maybe, Slugs died because he was at peace with everything that he'd gone through. The alternative is that maybe he did get a new body as his guardian angel had predicted, and he's in heaven right now stripped down to his undies and showing off his rippling six-pack in the new Calvin Klein advert.

Come back? Why on God's earth would I do that, Daisy? I'm living the life of Riley up here. That's what he'll be saying.

I guess what I'm trying to say is that maybe for everyone we lose, everyone we grieve for and everyone who we miss every single day there is a higher purpose all along. Maybe their spirit never really dies? Maybe everything that's fucking blinding about them lives on in other ways?

I put my phone away, but I can't ever delete Slugs's number. It would be a tragic twist if he did ever try to get in touch and I'd deleted it, mistaking his text as a message from a random nutbag.

★

PART TWO

IS ANYBODY OUT THERE?

6

SUMMONING THE DEAD

I do believe that I have grown up in the wrong era. These days people can be far too quick to dismiss the afterlife, but in ancient cultures it was widely accepted that there was an afterlife and that the dead regularly came back to visit the living. As normal as breathing. In fact, it was considered bloody rude if spirits didn't put in a regular appearance.

Take ancient Mesopotamia, for example. There the dead mainly hung out in 'the land of no return'. This was a place where souls dwelled in dreary darkness, fed off dirt and sipped from mud puddles. (Weird that from the beginning of recorded history, there was already evidence of an ancient chain of Wetherspoons.) Mostly, these spirits weren't allowed entry back into Earth, but some were given a free pass if they had a special mission to fulfil. This might be righting some kind of a wrong, like if they'd been brutally murdered, or buried without proper funeral rites, or if Mrs Pasternak confiscated their Care Bear after it was found attached to gallows fashioned from two rulers taped together and hung by a school tie. If there are any Care Bear lovers out there, I am sorry. I was six.

Other, more mischievous ghosts also managed to slip out to harass the living just for shits and giggles before slipping back through their portal before anyone noticed.

In the Egyptian era, people believed that a person's soul travelled to the Hall of Truth where it was judged. Cross-examination techniques did seem a bit basic back then, though. Nothing like the tough questioning on *Judge Rinder*. Instead, the soul's heart got weighed on a set of scales against the white feather of truth. If the heart turned out to be lighter than the feather it got greenlit to the afterlife. If it was heavier, it was thrown to the floor and eaten by a monster. Harsh. And no one ever seemed to notice that those scales were clearly very dodgy, which was odd.

But it is fascinating that some of these ideas persist. When I was growing up, whenever Mum saw a feather on the ground she swore it was Auntie Alison trying to communicate with her. And it was kind of beautiful to think that this delicate white feather drifting down from the sky and resting gently on the pavement was someone's spirit trying to make contact. For all we knew, it could be.

I do reckon Mum was pushing it, though, when she said that whenever she heard the song 'Take My Breath Away' by the band Berlin that it was Auntie Alison also trying to say hello. Granny Eddie thought this too. Talk about putting two and two together and making a hundred. It had been Alison's favourite song so they took this to be conclusive proof of her closeness. I often found them nursing a bottle of Chardonnay and rocking to it in unison in the living room. As for it being a message from the other side, I wasn't so convinced. It was written for the film *Top Gun* and had spent a whole month at number one in the charts in 1986. It continued to be a massive hit and got played on the radio for a *fucking eternity*. As if that wasn't bad enough it then became the theme tune to an advert for the Peugeot 405. Besides, Mum also said this about the song and Auntie Alison whenever she chose to play it on our shitty Amstrad cassette player at home. On reflection, this was completely mental.

But it is intriguing how the departed appear to people in a variety ways. In some Chinese cultures it is believed that people who have drowned, or who have died in battle, or remained unburied, refuse to haunt the living unless illuminated by torchlight, like it's going to capture their best angle. Vain bastards. But some Chinese ghostlore also says that if a spirit's special mission is to return to Earth to tell the living something important, then it will only appear in a dream. This might explain why I often wake up with a lingering recollection of being chased naked by a giant Dorito. In the dream I am always running like the clappers, yelling over my shoulder: 'Fuck off, you weird triangular cunt.' If that is the calorie-conscious spirit of body positivity having a word, then sincerely, thanks.

But it also makes another dream I had a few years ago absolutely baffling. In it I was having a torrid affair with Boris Johnson.

'Why do you behave like you do?' I asked him, quite irritated.

Boris's only answer was that, at the time, he was the front man leading the country through a pandemic and that he shouldn't be blamed for anything. Then he took me out for a Pizza Express and we shared dough balls for starters and a Romana for main. Fuck me, it was tasty. If anyone reading this can shed light on the true meaning of that mesmeric gem, please drop me a line.

Mirrors are also supposed to be another way of communicating with the dead. In particular, black mirrors were used a lot in Victorian times. During the ritual, called scrying, the back of the mirror was covered in black paint. During one scenario, the colour might shift into a dark mist. Shapes might appear, or symbols or pictures. In another ritual, a candle got placed behind the glass. If a person stared into it for long enough then their own face might morph into the features of someone else. Apparently, this was the face of a spirit revealing itself. Another hunch was that your reflection could transform into the reflection of your own face as it would appear in a past or a parallel life.

A few years ago I became so obsessed by this that to distract me from my everyday existence, I went in search of a black mirror. Amazingly, I ended up stumbling across one in a second-hand junk shop. The owner told me it had been handed in by a woman whose grandmother had sworn by it. But the granddaughter didn't want to keep the mirror as she believed it would bring her bad luck. I kept it in my bedroom and hoped that every time I sat in front of it, turned off the lights and lit a candle then some kind of apparition would materialise. Sometimes, I sat for hours.

'Is anybody there?' I asked.

Nothing.

'If you are in this room, could you reveal yourself?'

Of course, in my head, I wanted the reflection to be a glamorous actress: a Katharine Hepburn lookalike wearing a sweetheart neckline and long black gloves and with a cigarette holder, stylishly inhaling on a Gitanes cigarette. It never happened.

I did think I caught a glimpse of a flamingo once, but when I looked again I realised it was just my massive nose glinting in the evening sun. Despite many, many tries it was only ever my own face that glumly stared back at me. Terrifying. And the whole black mirror method of summoning the spirits did make me wonder: what if you were an identical twin who'd lost your brother or sister? If that sibling did ever try to reconnect with you, how would you even know?

That said, I don't want to dismiss the mirror technique outright. Just because it has never happened for me, it doesn't mean it can't happen. And several people did get in touch over email to tell me they had seen very clear apparitions in mirrors. One sounded dreadful: reflected in the glass was a grinning man in his early twenties dressed in a lace ruff collar like something from Shakespearean times. Probably there to remind him to actually read *Macbeth* before attempting to write about it in GCSE English. (Confession: I never did.)

Another also swore that he'd seen Count Duckula reflected back– the children's TV character whose series went by the same name. I have no fucking clue what that is supposed to mean. But that would scare the living crap out of anyone.

✱

Probably the most used technique of bygone days is the Ouija board. It's still out there, doing the rounds. I'm not knocking it at all but, personally, I think in the 21st century ghosts have moved on. Why do people assume they always want to make contact using old methods? It feels like going to all the effort of using yogurt pots on string to talk to your mate who lives across the street when you can just use Facebook Messenger. That archaic method of communication should only be resurrected if your battery's dead or you've forgotten your charger.

As for the practice of Ouija, for those who have never tempted fate, let me explain. The Ouija board is a simple flat board typically marked with the letters of the Latin alphabet, the numbers 0–9 and the words 'Yes' or 'No' written on it. It also comes with a counter called a planchette that moves of its own accord to spell out the answer to any questions asked of a spirit during a seance. In effect, it's a line to the spirit world.

The history of Ouija is fascinating, in particular how it got its name. The board was developed in the States around 1890 in response to a growing interest in spiritualism. However, the manufacturer of the first commercial board couldn't think of a name. To help, the head of the company called his sister. She reckoned she was a shit-hot medium. So, while holding her own seance, she asked the board what name it wanted to be known as. Bizarrely, the word Ouija came through. When she asked it what the hell that meant, the board apparently replied, 'Good luck'. God knows in what language.

Whether the board is good luck or not is debatable. Some spirits just want to spell out their name to let the living know they are there. Others want to reek almighty havoc. Proceed with caution, is my advice. Be aware of what you could unleash. I've read some harrowing tales, not least Sam's, who contacted me via email – the title of which was 'Shit Ya Pants Ouija Board'. With a subject line like that I felt compelled to read on, and Sam didn't disappoint. She described how she opened a portal to hell in the bedroom of her student house in Brighton. I'll let her pick up the story:

Me and my then boyfriend decided to do a Ouija board after a couple of glasses of red wine. We didn't have a board so we drew one on some paper and used an upturned shot glass as a planchette. We closed the curtains and lit some candles. We weren't exactly expecting anything to happen. But shit did kick off . . .

We had the spirit of a little boy come through. He claimed to have been kidnapped from a brand new cinema called the 'Duke of York's' (which happened to be at the bottom of my road). He'd been drowned in a butt of water in the back of our property by a man called Jo. All he kept repeating was: 'tell my story, tell my story, tell my story'.

Next, we had an 18-year-old lad come through. He said he had come to Brighton to work as a hangman but all he wanted was to go back to his wife and child who lived in the countryside. Jo was holding him hostage in the house, he claimed.

Twin brothers also came through telling us that they had been students in the house in the 1980s but that they had both died of a drug overdose. Then we had a man come through saying he was 'starving my darling' and wanted 'eels and ale'.

Whooooaaaahhhh! I'll just stop Sam there. I need a breather. And a large puff of an e-cig. This sounds fucking terrifying. Also very intriguing . . . 'eels and ale'? Wild. Right, I'm back in the room. What happened next?

> We had the wife of this man Jo come through and she kept repeating passages from the Bible and asking for forgiveness. We had the daughter of this guy Jo come through, though she was a mouthy little bitch. But if this wasn't all scary enough I then noticed letters being scratched into the wall above the door. A girl called Heloise had scratched 'H 4 L' and my partner's name was Lion. At this point, Lion started crying with fear and I began laughing hysterically.

Is that it? Can I come out from behind the sofa now? (Also, seriously, was his name Lion? Did he ever roar?)

> No, that's not all . . . In the days after we did the Ouija board, the contents of people's mugs and bottles in the house would disappear into thin air. Once when I was drinking coffee, I looked down and my mug was suddenly empty. Then I looked up and tiny handprints in coffee started appearing up the walls with bent little fingers in the middle. I don't think I slept for about a month and I would never turn my light off. When I did it always felt as though a small child was climbing on to my back and stroking my face. Basically, I had a small nervous breakdown and I had to move out. Never to return.

Well, all I can say, Sam, is thank God you exited this black hole of eternal punishment. And I sincerely hope that you now live in a less troubled household and have never touched a Ouija board again.

✫

I have also dabbled in the dark arts of Ouija. We all did when we were younger, but thankfully I've never been visited by multiple spectres taking part in what can only be described as a marathon of epic suffering.

At school, around the same time that I was attempting to scare the shit out of everyone with the ghost of Rebecca Powell, I did initiate a Ouija session. Now, I confess that it was just me moving the planchette. I doubt anyone was fooled.

We did table turning, too – the seance where everyone sits around a table, places their fingers on it before asking the undead to rattle it, tip it or turn it to communicate with the living.

Me and a few mates shut the curtains and dimmed the lights.

'If the ghost of Rebecca Powell is here please reveal yourself,' I said, my voice reaching operatic levels, like I was auditioning for Lady Macbeth.

There was silence. I called again. Then, we heard the ghostly tinkle of my water glass on the wood. *Fuck* . . . There was a collective intake of breath.

'Did you hear it? Oh. My. God!'

Again, the table began vibrating. We could feel it in the tips of our fingers like tiny jolts of electricity running through us.

My mate Kaya started rocking gently. 'I'm not afraid. I'm not afraid,' she kept repeating over and over.

Then the table tipped ever so slightly sending my water glass tumbling.

A scream tore from my throat. Kaya started crying. A couple of the other girls burst into tears too.

As I write, my guilt-o-meter is banging through the roof. That was also me, rattling the table from underneath with my knee. I really am very sorry. May the forces of darkness strike me down.

Charlie and I did have better luck with a later attempt at Ouija, though. Mum had her own board which she brought out now and again in her hunt for Auntie Alison. We weren't allowed at the seances she held, so one night Chaz and I took the board into our bedroom and shut the curtains.

To this day, I do not know what the fuck happened. All I know is that it was not me who touched the planchette. Chaz swears he didn't move it either. But that planchette definitely moved.

'If you are here, can you reveal yourself,' I thundered.

I can only assume that this spirit must have been desperate. My guess is he'd been knocking on the door of the living for an absolute age. I didn't even have to ask twice. The planchette moved slowly.

Fucking hell... Charlie and I sat with our mouths agape.

First, it spelled out K... then an A... then a J... then... a what? An I? Okay, that's weird. And... another K? A ghost named Kajik. Who the actual fuck is called Kajik round these parts? At first I figured that maybe it was a spelling mistake. Maybe it was Kojak, the bald, lollipop-sucking New York detective from the 1970s TV series. Maybe he'd been en route to Bristol but got hideously lost on the M4 interchange at Badbury Wick and ended up in Cirencester?

As it turned out, Kajik did seem to know the area pretty well. Our interrogation of him – and we reckoned Kajik definitely was a he – took for ever. My heart did go out to him because while words are simple to spell out on a Ouija board, sentences are far harder. But we sensed he wasn't there to do us any harm, so Chaz and I held his hand throughout the entire seance.

'What would you like to be free from?' I asked tentatively.

P-A-I-N. He was quite matter-of-fact in his replies.

'Can we help you?' Chaz asked.

The planchette moved to the word 'Yes' on the board.

Our questions went on and on. Finally, we narrowed it down to exactly what Kajik wanted. The request *was* strange. There was a shop in town – a kind of hippy Aladdin's cave filled with tie-dye kaftans and Tarot cards and spell candles. Me and my mate Kaya would always go there after school to take a sneak peak at a book called *Teen Witch* just so we could cast spells on boys in our year and get them to fancy us. Lots of spells required a lock of someone's hair so scissors were always going missing from the technical drawing department. Kajik was familiar with the shop too. He asked me and Chaz to take the bus and visit at the weekend. While we were there we needed to buy a yinyang – a stone featuring the yin and yang symbols that together represent balance and harmony – then toss it into the lake in the grounds of the abbey. If we did he would finally be at peace. We never did get to the bottom of why he chose that location. Chaz and I thought he may have drowned there. Or maybe he drowned someone and was pleading for forgiveness.

Dutifully, we did exactly as Kajik had requested. Having purchased our yinyang, Chaz and I stood on the bank of the lake that Saturday. We said a short prayer. I can't remember the exact words but it went something like:

> Kajik, we know this is daunting,
> But now, stop your haunting.
> Be at peace in this lake,
> We all . . . make . . . mistakes.

'That'll probably do,' I murmured to Chaz with a shrug. Then, we watched as the small black and white painted stone somersaulted in the air and plummeted into the depths of the inky-black water.

A few weeks later, we did try to contact Kajik again, this time with my mate Tiffany Stubbs. Disappointingly, he didn't come through on the Ouija board. Halfway through the seance Tiffany's clock did clatter off her bedroom wall, though.

'Aaaaaaaaaahhhhhhhhhhhh,' we all screamed together.

Tiffany reckoned it was a thousand per cent Kajik, but I suspect the clock hadn't been put up properly by her dad in the first place. We'll never know.

I can only hope that we did set Kajik free in the abbey grounds and that he did find the everlasting peace he was searching for. And if the clock was Kajik, it was the last we ever heard of him.

✦

7

BEAM ME UP, HOTLINE

Call #1: Daisy wants advice on love

'Hello . . .'

'Hi, my name is Pamela.'

'Hi, Pamela, I'm Daisy.'

Wow, I was actually talking to Pamela. *The* Pamela from Pamela Predicts. I assumed that it would be an assistant or someone else. But no, it was Pamela. She sounded friendly. A tad Northern, and I couldn't quite place her accent exactly. But it was gentle, like a babbling brook meandering through Emmerdale.

'Hi, Daisy, thanks for calling Pamela Predicts today. How can I help?'

'Yes, I'm after some advice on love . . . erm . . . I'd like to know whether I should get serious with a guy I've met.'

'Righto, love,' Pamela chirped. 'I can definitely assist you with that.'

Brilliant. I sighed with relief. It's summer 2022 and I'd been blowing hot and cold about this guy for a while, so I figured I needed some spiritual guidance. I found Pamela on the Internet. It was £1 per minute for the call, but it would be worth it. And I get the first four minutes free, which is a nice touch. Terms and conditions may apply, it said, but there's far too many of those to read. Anyhow, it's one more minute than any of the others were offering for the same service.

'Daisy, can I say, it sounds like you have a most beautiful aura around you. You sound very special. I feel we have a bond already. I'm the right person you need to talk to to get the answers you need in your life at this critical time.'

Absolutely! You can say that, Pamela. *Wow*. A beautiful aura? Special – me? Amazing! This sounds promising. I noticed Pamela did speak *very* slowly, though. Soporifically, even. A strange blend of calming and mind-numbingly boring.

'Oh, thanks,' I giggled. 'Really kind of you to say.'

Honestly, I don't know much about auras or what makes a good one but I do remember that Mum accompanied her friend Diane once to have hers photographed at a psychic fair. Diane fancied herself as a bit of a medium and she'd seen an article about it in *Woman's Weekly*.

During the process, Diane's torso would be photographed with a special camera. The energy captured around it would tell her how spiritually, emotionally and physically complex she was. In the magazine pictures she showed Mum there were hazy psychedelic swirls of rainbow-coloured clouds. Diane reckoned hers was going to be bright crystalline white, beaming out like the Angel Gabriel. When it got developed she was disappointed – quite angry, actually. It was pissy green, the colour of algae floating on the surface of a stagnant duck pond. The psychic said it showed she was nurturing, kind and a freethinker, but that was total bullshit. Diane was a complete arsehole.

I didn't know how Pamela had a clue about how beautiful my aura was. She couldn't see me. But I let it pass. *Ignore it, Daisy. Take the compliment!*

'So, I use Tarot to answer all your relationship questions,' Pamela continued.

'Yes, thanks. I saw that . . . in the advert.'

'Ah yes . . . the advert. Where exactly did you see that advert?'

'Erm . . . online. I think it flashed up when I was searching for "Love hotline".'

'Good, good,' Pamela purred softly. 'Now, I hope you don't mind, Daisy, there will be silence on the line while I spread the cards. Are you okay waiting?'

'Yes, absolutely fine. Spread away.'

Seconds ticked by. Then minutes. Pamela took ages. How many packs of cards was she shuffling?

'Okay, Daisy. Are you ready?' she eventually said.

'Absolutely.'

'Well this is a good day. It's looking good. The cards are telling me you need to take a leap of faith on this one. To go for it.'

It was strange that Pamela hadn't asked me anything about the object of my romantic conundrum, Shaun, at all. Or our relationship.

It had all been a bit of a whirlwind. He swiped right on Tinder. I liked the look of him too. Chisel-jawed and with deep-set eyes, but with a slightly wonky mouth. Granted, he was a bit of a love bomber – pinging messages in my inbox like a quick-firing machine gun.

They all start like that, don't they? But I agreed to meet and we'd seen each other a few times. We'd had phenomenal sex. I mean, *fucking* phenomenal. And he always messaged me afterwards to say he'd love to see me again.

'What cards came up?' I enquire.

'Well, let me explain. First is the Lovers. This is the card of unity and duality.'

'Right, what does that mean?'

'Erm . . . that you're a good match. Symbiotic. Together. That kind of thing.'

'Right, well, that's brilliant, isn't it?'

'Yes, it's very good, Daisy. The next card complements it too.'

'Oh wow. Amazing.'

'Yes, it's the Sun. Your luck really is in today, Daisy. It's the sign of positivity and success.'

'And the third?'

'Well, that's—'

Suddenly, Pamela cut off mid-sentence, and I could hear a voice in the background getting closer and closer. It was quite gruff, like Paddy McGuinness might sound like the morning after an almighty bender.

'Jean, d'ya want a cuppa?'

'Shhhhhh.'

'Sorry, Jean, didn't realise you were on a call.'

The voice faded to a whisper.

'Excuse me for a second, Daisy.' Pamela elevated her sing-song voice but she did seem to be quite flustered. I could just about make out some shuffling. I pressed my car closer to the phone to listen more intently. 'Shhhhhhh,' I heard again, but I couldn't make out the rest because it sounded like Pamela, or someone, now had their hand over the mouthpiece.

I waited a few moments.

'Hi, Daisy, sorry about that,' Pamela trilled as soon as she was back on the line.

'This *is* Pamela, right?' I asked.

I did want to double-check. She did say her name was Pamela. *The* Pamela of Pamela Predicts. But now I was confused. Was it Pamela, or Jean? Was any of this for real? I had a vision of Pamela. Coiffured hair, neat lippy, hot-pink shellac nails. But maybe this was Jean, sat in her dressing gown and undies with a face pack on, chatting to me from her kitchen table. Or maybe she was in a call centre in fucking Wigan?

'Yes! *Pamela* of Pamela Predicts,' she said, now quite shrilly. She sounded pissed off, like I may have upset her.

I looked at the clock. Beep . . . beep . . . beep. Shit. I hadn't noticed the time running down. That second, Pamela cut off and an automated voice clicked in.

'You have two minutes left on your call. If you would like to add more time, press the hash key now and follow the instructions.'

Did I want to add more time? Of course I fucking did. We hadn't even got to the bit that I'd been so confused about. The reason I was on the call in the first place.

The dates with Shaun had kept coming. He was perfect. The moon to my sun. Straw to my berry, or whatever. Then last week he told me that he wanted to surprise me.

'Okay . . . that would be lovely,' I replied.

A gorgeous bouquet of flowers, maybe? A meal out? I mean, it would be nice to actually date the guy rather than just shag his brains out.

'Can you give me a clue?'

'Nah, wouldn't be a surprise then would it?' he laughed. 'Just download the Snapchat app, that's all I'm saying . . .'

Okay. Snapchat. That's novel. But, I guess we did meet online, so it's in keeping. Maybe it's a message? A poem? A romantic monologue from *Romeo and Juliet*?

Later that afternoon my phone pinged. Gotta be Shaun. I excitedly opened up the message. Hmmmm. It was a bit hard to make out at first. I could vaguely see Shaun's face . . . then . . . okay . . . What the *fuck* is that? Right . . . okay. No . . . is that a penis? . . . Yup . . . holy shit . . . that is a penis. Is it his? Yes, I believe it is. I stared in closely and saw that it did bend slightly to the right. Okay . . . and that's definitely his hand . . . *Fucking hell . . . No! No! No!* Was he getting trigger happy? *Fuck* . . . yup, he's doing it . . . he's holding the sausage hostage . . . bashing the candle . . . cranking the love pump. *Oh Christ* and that weird groaning sound. And the face! Like he's about to do an angry sneeze. Euuurrggggh! *Fuck. Fuck. Fuck.*

I could barely watch. I tried to avert my gaze but as my eyes moved up past his left shoulder, that's when the full horror hit me. Behind him was a cabinet. A cabinet filled with ornamental pigs: ceramic pigs, plastic Peppa Pigs, pigs that looked like the pig in *Babe* sat in a fucking wine barrel with its trotters hanging over the rim. Two carved wooden pigs mounting each other with a small plaque underneath that read: 'Pig in a poke'. This must have been his mum's or his granny's front room. Shaun was wanking off on a floral sofa with a prize collection of ornamental pigs on full display.

I was so bewildered that later that afternoon I showed the video to my cleaner. And that's when my world turned upside down.

'That's Shaun, who I've been seeing. Do you think I should dump him?' I asked.

I pressed play. Debs looked, then looked again . . . then peered in closer.

'Daisy, his name is not Shaun. That's Neil. He's a teaching assistant at my kid's school. Brilliant with the children,' she said.

Oh. My. God. My head was spinning. Shaun, or Neil, clearly had a caring side. But would I ever be able to forget the ornamental pigs?

So, now you can see why Pamela's Lovers and Sun cards were all a bit unexpected.

Seconds later, I heard Pamela's voice on the line again.

'Great to have you back, Daisy, and thank you for choosing Pamela Predicts. Now, where were we?'

'Erm . . . on the third card . . .'

'Ah yes. This is also looking beautiful, Daisy. The Hierophant.'

'The Hiero-what?'

'The Hierophant. It's a great card if it's a committed long-term relationship that you're after.'

'Sorry, it's just that things have been a bit weird recently. I was edging towards commitment. Then I wasn't, then I *really* wasn't, but now I'm not sure again . . .'

'That happens to a lot of people, Daisy. Maybe you need something extra – to shine a light. It makes sense to be crystal clear, right?'

'Absolutely.'

'So, I do offer chakra cleansing.'

I had no fucking clue what that was.

'Chakra what?'

'It cleanses the body and helps you make better decisions.'

'By phone?'

'Yes, I do mantras by phone. And I have a special offer on at the moment. Five mantras free if you book at the end of this session.'

Wtf? Was Pamela or Jean or whoever trying to upsell me a verbal douche of my chakras? I couldn't fucking believe it.

'Thanks, Pamela. And thanks for your help today. I'll think about it.'

Pamela cut off. I heard another automated voice message kick in but I hung up. *Fuck*, I'd forgotten about the time. I reckoned it had been around 20 minutes. £20 minus four free minutes. I did the calculation in my head: 80p per minute, and I was still none the wiser.

I texted Shaun, or Neil, or whoever the fuck he was. 'Fancy coming over and sharing a bacon sandwich?'

Call #2: Daisy tries to summon Grandad Eddie

'Hello . . .'

'Hi, you're through to Arthur. How can I help?'

'Hi, Arthur, I wanted to try to connect with someone. I saw your advert in the *Wilts and Glos. Standard.*'

'Great, yes. Happy to help. And your name is?'

'Daisy.'

I liked to think I'd become wise to phone mediums, especially after Mum called so many. But I don't want to rule it out entirely. There are good psychics and good mediums out there, I know there are. There are also good psychic mediums and probably medium psychics, even though that's hard to gauge over the phone. At times, it's an incomprehensible array. I just wonder whether anyone decent operates by phone. Maybe face to face is better, but I'm prepared to give it another go.

'So, Daisy, I can do a cold reading for you? On the spot. Are you happy to proceed?'

'Sure.'

Arthur did sound a bit amateur – which could explain the cut-price cost. He had a West Country accent as thick as farm slurry. *Be kind, Dais,* I thought. Mediums do come in all shapes and sizes.

'Okay, well just tell me what to do.'

'Right, yeah. Let's get started.'

Hmmmm. He didn't do half the build-up that Pamela did. I was a bit disappointed that he didn't mention my aura once. And it sounded like he might be on his lunch hour.

'Sure,' I muttered, hesitantly.

'So, I've got a G coming through. Now, can you tell me if there's anyone alive or deceased whose name starts with that letter.'

Oh wow, maybe I underestimated this guy. First shot and he was bang on the money! My mum's name is Gillian, though I hadn't come to connect with her. She's around my house most days. Too much connection, if I'm honest! The person I really want to talk to is my grandad Eddie.

I've always wondered about him. A lot of my childhood was spent trying to find Auntie Alison, or helping Mum find Auntie Alison, and after that Granny Eddie. Grandad Eddie seemed to get forgotten. Yet, when his end came it was pretty fucking spectacular. A triple whammy of death, you might say. One Easter Sunday he got quite pissed in the local pub. Hours later, while he was walking home he had a heart attack. Seconds after that a car ran over him while he was laid out prostrate on the tarmac. Smack, wallop, crunch. It was hard to know when the final blow started or finished. I remember the grim task of having to go with Mum to identify his body. Weird I had to do that as a kid, but it did happen.

Grandad Eddie fascinated me. As well as being a jockey and travelling the world, he had some funny habits. Chaz and I would have to bring him whisky in an egg cup – God knows why an egg cup – plus fetch him his cigarettes.

'Right, you can fuck off now,' he'd say, ordering us out of the room so he could drink and smoke his fag in peace.

One time he made us toast on Mum's old-style cooker – the kind with the grill pan at the top. He left the gas running too long because he couldn't find the ignition. When he finally lit it with a match the flame billowed out so fast it singed off his eyebrows. It was fucking funny, though Grandad Eddie didn't laugh at the time. Or ever, in fact. We did love him, though.

Could Arthur's G be for Grandad? It's not a name as such . . . probably my mum, I reckoned.

'Yes a G. That would be Gil—'

Arthur stopped me mid-word.

'Don't give me a name, Daisy.'

'Okay . . .'

'So is that a George?'

'No.'

'No, not George . . . a Grant perhaps? Or a Gideon?'

'Nope.'

Gideon? *Jesus Christ.* Gideon? In our family? Not likely! Who does this guy think we are – bloody royalty?

'Okay, it's clearer now. Sorry, it's not a G. It's an E coming through.'

'Oh wow!'

Arthur was on fire! Maybe Eddie was there, trying to bell me up. My heart leaped with excitement.

'Yes, well there's an E—'

'Don't say a name, Daisy.'

'Sure, sorry.'

'It's an Evan?'

'Nope.'

'Eli?'

'Nope.'

'Edwin?'

'Yes. That's it! Well, it's Eddie really, but . . .'

I could only think the connection was a bit dodgy and that Grandad Eddie was having trouble with some static on the line. But he was trying to get through, wasn't he? Fuck me! Grandad Eddie on the line!

'Great. And did you do something with him recently? Like visit him? Or buy him something?'

My shoulders sank a little.

'Erm . . . nope. He's dead.'

'Ah, I see. He's passed already.

'Yes, he was my grandad.'

'Okay, yes. Sorry, the spirits seem to be playing silly buggers at the moment. Speaking with them is like texting. You may not get the right answer for ages but one eventually appears.'

Arthur said this with no hint of irony whatsoever.

'Right...'

'Was he a large man with a massive belly? Around six foot?

'Nope...'

Grandad Eddie had the jockey frame. If you weren't paying attention you could have accidentally stepped on him.

'Knee-high to a grasshopper,' I said.

'Right. I do have an Edwin coming through, though.'

Jesus, it is him! The lines are just a bit crossed.

'Is he okay? What's he saying? Does he have a message for me? Does he still tweeze his nose hairs in heaven? That always made me laugh.'

'Yes, he's saying he remembers you very fondly.'

Yes! Yes! Yes! Fucking hell! Grandad Eddie!!!

'What does he remember?' I asked eagerly.

'He says he loved playing in the garden with you.'

'We didn't have a garden.'

'Well, it could be just be a green space. Maybe a park?'

'Grandad Eddie never took me to the park.'

'Okay, well it can be confusing in the spirit world.'

'Anything else?'

'Yes, he's saying he's sorry it took him so long to die. It must have been distressing for everyone. Cancer was it?'

'Erm . . . He died instantly I think.'

Beep . . . beep . . . beep . . . beep . . .

My time with Arthur was up. And there was no automated voice call option to continue. After a very promising start, Arthur did seem like just another scam merchant. I felt gutted. All that build-up and nothing to show for it. I have never called a hotline since.

★

I wanted to share those conversations with you as a cautionary tale. If you do want to contact a dead friend or relative or understand your past, present or future you do need to think carefully about who you call. Truly, it's a minefield out there.

In particular, I wanted to reach out to Alexis who sent me an email. She got in touch because she has, like a complete bellend, spunked more than £3k on countless hotlines, just like my mum did. It's torn Alexis's world apart. The only medium to ever get anything right was the one who said her grandfather had a missing middle finger. And all the psychics told her that romance was just around the corner. One even insisted that she would marry a man called Dave. I don't like to state the bleedin' obvious but: *it's a fucking scam, Alexis!* The sad thing was that from then on she only agreed to date people called Dave. Eventually she gave up and in her words: 'I've been single for seven, long, sodding barren, years.' Alexis, I feel your pain but that was a *really bad* game plan. Please, please stop before this gets out of hand, and I hope you don't have to phone a lot of frogs to find your Prince Charming.

But regardless of the charlatans the world of mediums and psychics is still a fascinating one. I mean, take the Hollywood

TV medium Tyler Henry. He's probably made millions out of his Netflix series *Life After Death*. I'm not for one moment knocking him. For all I know he could be a millennial genius with ultra-fast broadband to the dearly departed. But it is very strange that *all* of his clients are celebrities. And celebrities do loads of interviews and publicity and there's reams of column inches written about them and the details of their life. Isn't he just amazing at searching on Google?

On the other hand, I know some remarkable stories about psychic mediums, like the ones who contact the police and help them solve serious crimes. There's one guy from Bristol called Mike Baker who was working on a building site in 1974 when his spirit guide, Sukata, gave him information about the murder of a 10-year-old girl. Sukata was from the Sioux Nation and had died at the Battle of Little Big Horn, which in itself is nuts.

Anyway, the girl, Alison Chadwick, had disappeared from her home in Middlesex near where he was working at the time. Sadly, when he plucked up the courage to go to the police, they assumed he was a fantasist. But Mike persisted and persuaded the police to give him an hour of their time and a piece of paper. He wrote down information about the crime that turned out to be correct, namely he identified the underwear that Alison was wearing when she went missing. To prove his skills further he invited three police officers to a seance. During it, he gave the name Stanley Rogers. He also identified that a grey and red car had been used in the crime. Stanley Rogers was already a police suspect and it turned out he had been driving a grey Cortina. The week before the murder it had been resprayed red. He also told them the girl would be found in a fishing pond. Days later she was discovered at an angling club pond and Stanley Rogers did later admit to murdering Alison. How fucking extraordinary is that?

It is a high-risk strategy, though. Revealing specific clues like a car name or licence plate number or items of clothing that only select people would know could get you banged up for life. It almost happened to a clairvoyant called Etta Smith in California in 1980. She was imprisoned like a caged animal for four days after her psychic vision led her to the body of a missing nurse, Melanie Uribe. But instead of believing her, the LAPD arrested her on suspicion of murder. Eventually, three men with no known connection to Etta Smith were convicted of the killing and she was awarded compensation for being wrongfully imprisoned.

I don't know about you but I would be incandescent with rage that my special crime-fighting gift got wrongly interpreted by a bunch of dim-witted, disbelieving cops. I'd never help out again. In fact, it makes me pretty angry that the only thing fakes do is lead people to assume that everyone is winging it. I am absolutely positive that, despite my experiences, not all psychics or mediums are created equal.

Thankfully, some people have restored my faith. In particular, Jack, whose story I *fucking* love. He went to see a psychic after his first marriage ended in 2004 who told him that, one: he was going to use his mouth for work – okay, that's already bizarre; and two: he was going meet someone called Teri and that Tenerife would play a huge part in him realising that she was his soulmate.

Fast-forward ten years and . . . Actually, Jack tells it better. I'll let him take over.

In 2014 I was working in Fuerteventura in the Canary Islands. I was single and had been for three years. One afternoon I went down to the beach with my book, got myself a sun lounger and a bottle of wine. I was having a lovely time when I heard someone say: 'Excuse me, is this yours?' When I turned around a girl was stood with a newspaper in her hand. It wasn't mine but she took it, smiled and sat on a nearby lounger. She was beautiful. We exchanged glances and then began chatting. She was Scottish, as am I. It turned out that we lived in neighbouring towns. Her name was Teri. At the time, the spiritual reading I had had never struck me. But after Teri went home, we kept in touch. A few weeks later we agreed to go out for a drink.

Between then [meeting in Tenerife] and our date, I'd remembered about the spiritualist telling me about the name Teri and Tenerife. I laughed thinking how close she had been considering Tenerife is the Canary Islands, too.

The night of our date we hit it off amazingly well. I felt I'd known her for years. It was unreal. Later that night we got a taxi to hers and we were sat in her living room when I drunkenly told her about the spiritualist reading and how she'd told me my soulmate would be Teri and how Tenerife would play a huge part in it. Teri looked at me and said: 'Shut up!'

We ended up in bed together and, without any word of a lie, when I pulled her knickers off, she had a tattoo of the word 'Tenerife 2004' above her pubic area.

Excuse me, Jack, I have to interrupt. I've made some tattoo faux pas in my life (a now ex-boyfriend's name on my wedding finger wasn't the smartest move), but the words 'Tenerife 2004' on your cooter is fucking brave. Anyway, sorry, Jack, carry on . . .

Teri couldn't stop laughing and I was utterly stunned – really freaked out. I'd had the reading done in 2004. That same year, Teri had been on a girls' holiday and got the bad tattoo. We are still together. We aren't married (not doing that again) but we go to Tenerife every year in June for ten days. She's my soulmate.

I'm not convinced that spiritual stuff like that is 100% true but for her to get the name right, which isn't a common girls name, was good enough.

Awwwwww. That is *fucking amazing*, Jack! But what about the psychic's first prediction? The one about using your mouth for work. Please tell me it's clean . . .

As for using my mouth, we all do. I shout at fuckers all day.

☆

8

GHOST HUNTING

As soon as I suspected my home was haunted I logged into Amazon and began searching for equipment to help me investigate. But when you fear you are at the epicentre of a spectral shitstorm it is easy to get caught up in the moment. At the checkout, I reviewed my list:

1 x LED ultraviolet torch (£10)
1 x portable movement sensor (£25)
1 x thermal sensor (£160)
1 x REM pod (£250)

Did I need a voice recorder? Yep no harm in being over-prepared.

1 x EVP ghost-hunting recorder (£100)

Oh, and a T-shirt that flashed up in the 'frequently bought together' box. The one that says: *Ghost Hunting Mum: Fierce, Fearless and*

Fabulous. It's firm but friendly. Strikes the right balance, I reckon. Not every spirit is going to be malevolent. Some will just want to be mates.

1 x T-shirt (£20)

Did I want Prime next-day delivery? Fuck yeah.

Total at the checkout: £565.

Did I just spunk almost £600 on ghost-hunting equipment? *Fucking hell*...

Shopaholics be warned. I pressed 'Buy Now' even though I have always had a nagging feeling in the back of my mind about the effectiveness of most ghost-hunting paraphernalia.

When the boxes arrived I tore open the packaging, feeling a frisson of excitement. Hmmmm. It all looked great. It all looked like the real deal. But is it? I still don't know...

To be honest, I am dubious about whether much of it works. I mean, do real ghosts, poltergeists, funnel ghosts, orbs – any manner of paranormal phantasm – respond well to being hunted in the first place? Doesn't full-on phenomena appear when you least expect it, like those disembodied legs running around my bedroom? If I was a ghost, I'd want to retain an element of surprise. Surely, that's the reason why people who have never believed in the paranormal suddenly find themselves swirling around in a twister of transcendental turmoil: desperately searching, but failing, to find rational explanations for whatever has appeared in front of their eyes.

Without sounding too much like the Martin Lewis of the supernatural world: when it comes to ghost hunting, be on guard and maybe keep your debit card out of sight. There *are* plenty of sharks out there, ready to prey on innocent people's burning desire to see a ghost; to give false hope to would-be believers; to create connection to the spirit world even when BT has cut off the line after way too many unpaid bills; and to drink your bank account dry.

It's the same with ghost-hunting events. Believe me, I'm a sucker for a spooky ghost tour. Especially round a city I've never been to. Whenever I am in a place I don't know I always book one in. There's nothing more thrilling than being tapped on the back of the shoulder in a dark alley by an out-of-work actor with a pasty face, heavy black eyebrows and a Lurch-like costume. Of course, I'm not suggesting that all ghost tours or ghost hunts are fakes. But, think about it: if you were a ghost would you seriously want to reveal yourself in front of 40 hoodie-wearing hobbyists? Shy ghosts need not apply. And, if you do decide to step out from the shadows, isn't that just encouraging more people to turn up? There is a whole world of pastimes, from metal detecting to caravanning, that these people could try instead.

Then, there's the array of aforementioned equipment. In my view, some of it is pure gimmickry. For my appearance on *Uncanny* my REM pod detected *something* in my home that I do believe was not human. So to date, the REM pod gets my vote despite its inflated price tag.

But take the often-used Ecto-1. It's the radio-controlled ghost-catcher, with Slimer from *Ghostbusters* hanging out of the sunroof like a puked-on Eminem. Slimer lights up, whirrs and buzzes every time motion is detected. If I saw that weaving its way round the disused wing of the prison or the stately home I'd been haunting, I'd be fucking livid. Incandescent, in fact. *I'm being made an absolute mockery of here*, I'd think. *I'm not engaging with this bunch of jokers on principle!*

Through trial and error, I have come to the conclusion that most ghosts like to reveal themselves to the right people at the right time at the right place. Sure, the odd spirit might be a massive fucking show-off, playing to an audience, bringing the curtain down at every haunting with some over-enthusiastic furniture throwing, but I reckon ghoulish narcissists are in the minority. Most real spirits don't behave like that at all.

★

One story that fascinated me was that of the typing ghost of Tasmania as recalled to me recently by a man called Rowan, who still lives on the island, 150 miles off the south coast of Australia.

It all started in the year 2000. Rowan was ten years old at the time and often lay in bed during the early hours of the morning listening to the sound of touch-typing. It drifted up from the study below where a desktop computer sat. Both his parents worked from home, so at first he assumed it was his mum getting up early to begin work. Then something odd happened. One morning Rowan woke up and called out to his mother.

'I had assumed she was downstairs working. But there was no answer. No one was downstairs at all,' he told me.

At first, Rowan thought he was going crazy. But the typing carried on. It didn't happen every night, but at random intervals, typically between the hours of 3am and 8am.

'What did it sound like?' I wondered.

'Fast, manic typing. Furious clicking of a mouse as if someone was very frustrated,' Rowan said. As the study was directly below Rowan's bedroom he could hear it very clearly.

'On another morning, I was eating breakfast. I heard Mum at the top of the stairs shouting to me: "Rowan, you're not down there on that computer already?" She was convinced she heard typing too. And that it was me. Yet nobody was there.'

When Rowan did eventually tell his family about his experiences, his sister confessed she'd heard the same. Both of them had been too scared to talk about it for fear of what others would think. Despite Rowan's attempts to hunt for the ghost, the noise carried on intermittently for years. Every time Rowan tried to jump out on it or summon it, he came away disappointed. Until one time when he wasn't even trying . . .

'We'd learned to live with the noise,' he said. 'But one night I was in the room. Suddenly, the ceiling light in the centre began flashing like a strobe light. It exploded. Glass shattered across the room. When it started breaking I was terrified and ran from the room.'

Rowan's story didn't end there. Not long after the ceiling light incident, he was working at the computer when something happened that stopped him from ever being alone in that room again.

'I felt – and heard – a sharp intake of breath directly behind my right shoulder near my ear. Before then the typing had been some weird, spooky shit – never something sinister or dangerous. It still makes my heart race when I think about it.' To this day, Rowan doesn't know whether this was a vicious spirit wanting to lure him into the room by mimicking his mother's typing. I wonder whether it was just territorial about its space. (God knows, if anyone had come within 3 metres of my teenage bedroom or rifled through my collection of Pogs without permission I'd have gone fucking berserk.) Or maybe it was writing the paranormal equivalent of *War and Peace* and didn't want to be disturbed? But the fact that it only revealed itself when Rowan wasn't looking for it speaks volumes to me.

Children are highly receptive to spirits. They see and feel them at times when no one else can. I've read so many accounts of this happening. I think it's because they're fresh souls, as finely tuned as wild animals, picking up on noises, smells or sights that aren't on anyone else's radar. When I was a kid I remember sitting on the back seat of Mum and Dad's car mesmerised by every raindrop racing down the window, noticing every tiny little detail. It's as if children operate on a different frequency.

Not long ago, a guy called Steve wrote to me with a short but haunting tale that I'd like to think backs up my hunch. Some 20 years ago he was staying in Drumcharry House in Scotland – not on a ghost hunt or paranormal sleepover, but just as a regular guest. He was dressing his son for bed when his son peered over his shoulder and down the long corridor that stretched behind.

'What are you looking at?' Steve asked him.

'Man,' his son replied.

When Steve looked around there wasn't a soul in sight.

'There's no one there,' he told him.

At that, his son jumped off the bed and shouted: 'Man walking away.'

He chased after whatever he'd seen, disappearing around the corner to where there was a locked door to a separate closed-off wing of the castle.

'Man gone,' he cried.

'Gone where?' Steve asked.

'Man went through door.'

The next morning when Steve spoke to the mansion owners they confirmed that the grounds had been used as a grenade-testing base during the world wars. Several people had been killed there.

Two decades later, that night still puts hairs on the back of his neck.

*

When spirits appear naturally, there's scope to investigate. Coaxing them out like a bedraggled fox chased by a pack of hounds at an illegal hunt could be doing real paranormal researchers a huge disservice in my view. And I'm even sceptical about whether programmes like *Most Haunted* have helped or hindered the progress of real scientific discovery. I know, I know. For many people, scintillating TV would not be one hour of watching fuck-all happen in a darkened room. But if there's nothing to see, there's nothing to see. *Springwatch* doesn't exactly thrive on adrenaline-fuelled action for fuck's sake, and it goes on for an eternity. And personally, I'm never happier than watching hatchlings doze on a night cam for hours on end – no over-the-top drama needed.

Nevertheless, in the true spirit of enquiry I did book myself on to an official ghost-hunting evening. I wanted to put the sceptical part of my ghost-hunting brain to bed. In short, I wanted to believe that spirits do haunt old and empty buildings and will appear if you summon them.

The experience was confusing, to say the least.

The event kicked off at 6pm in a disused prison. We were welcomed in through the foreboding iron gates by the organisers – an unusual-looking duo named Cathy and Bob. Apparently they had worked there while the prison had been operational. Now it was closed, they hosted its regular ghost-hunting evenings..

'If you could make your way through the entrance and gather here,' Cathy instructed the group of 20 or so.

Like me, they had probably paid upwards of £50 for the evening. Some would be staying overnight, camping out in one of the cramped cells or on a wing floor. When I looked around I noticed some of them had brought their own sleeping bags and a few even clutched flasks filled with hot drinks. As I had an early start the next morning I wasn't staying over, but I planned to stay as long as I could. I wanted to get my money's worth, so I was eager to observe everything at close range.

I stepped to the front of the group. Immediately, I wished I hadn't.

'Are you . . .?' Cathy looked me up and down. Her eyes twinkled like fairy lights, before she clicked her fingers excitedly at Bob.

'Oh my God . . . Bob, look who it is. It's Maisie . . . Maisie . . . Day Cooper.'

'Daisy.' I smiled politely.

'Are you really her? I absolutely love your work, Maisie,' Cathy bulldozed on.

'Thanks. It's Daisy.'

'Bob, I can't believe it, can you? Well I never. Maisie Day Cooper. Great to have you here tonight.'

'Daisy,' I repeated. I didn't want to labour the point, but for fuck's sake.

Cathy gestured to the group to huddle in closer, while Bob stood woodenly beside her holding on to a large iron lantern. It had a fat wick burning at its centre and the faint smell of kerosene filled the entrance.

'Tonight, ladies and gentlemen, we've got someone here who you might recognise off the telly, so I hope the spirits come out to give her a big welcome,' Bob waved the lantern closer to my face as Cathy spoke.

Jesus Christ.

They stared blankly at Cathy, then turned to stare blankly at me. It was so embarrassingly awful. *Please ground, swallow me whole. Swallow me now.*

'Right, shall we let the haunting begin?' Cathy clapped her hands together. It was as if she was addressing a group of nursery school children rather than a bunch of adults.

As we began walking I couldn't help thinking how creepy the building felt. I'd never been inside a disused prison before. It smelled dank, like an old man's sweaty socks. In the lantern light I could also just about make out paint peeling across some of its walls. As far as atmosphere went, it got a ten out of ten.

As Cathy spoke, her voice lightly echoed around the corridor. So did the sound of her keys. As no prisoners were housed there, I thought it was strange she needed to unlock everything. I decided not to ask about it. *Ignore it, Daisy.* I didn't want to draw any more attention to myself.

Away from the entrance, we turned on to the main wing. In the half-light I could make out a sheet of netting above, presumably once used to stop prisoners throwing anything on fellow inmates or throwing themselves off. As we moved along the landing Cathy put her hands to her lips to quieten the low murmur of chatter.

'Shhhhhhhhhh . . .' she said. 'Oh . . . that's strange. Can you hear that? That's a bit weird, isn't it?'

To be honest, all I could hear was the sound of the old bloke next to me wheezing. It was subzero in that prison, and I was thankful I'd brought an extra-thick coat. Instead of listening out for ghosts, I'd become fixated on the rise and fall of the phlegm rattling around the old bloke's throat. The cold seemed to be playing havoc with his lungs.

'Sorry, don't want anyone to confuse me with a heavy-breathing spirit,' he apologised, bringing out his inhaler and giving it a couple of strong puffs.

When I looked over at Cathy she was throwing daggers at him.

'Are you done now?' she said, rather cuttingly.

'Yes, sorry. Name's Tony, by the way. So sorry.'

'Hi, Tony,' a few members of the group murmured.

'Let's move on, shall we?' Cathy said, now sounding very pissed off.

We shuffled on to B Wing. This was the largest open area in the prison, so long and dark that it was impossible to see to the end of the corridor. Suddenly, something moved. *Fuuuuuukkkk!* My heart somersaulted. There was a shadow shifting above on the atrium ceiling. Someone else saw it too.

'Did you see that shadow move?' one man said.

He looked remarkably like a Border collie I'd once seen on TV named Doggy Osbourne, who was the spitting image of the Black Sabbath frontman Ozzy.

Everybody's eyes darted upwards.

'Nah, that's just our reflection,' the woman next to him concluded.

'No, it was *definitely* a shadow moving,' he insisted.

'Not moving now,' the woman replied smugly.

Everyone stopped dead.

Cathy quickly waded into the ongoing debate. 'It's not uncommon to see shadows in this wing,' she said.

I did wish Cathy would stop trying to hype everyone up. It all smacked of wanting a positive review on Tripadvisor. Some of the group may have been there for a good scare. Maybe they didn't care whether anything was real or not. I, on the other hand, wanted to witness the real McCoy.

When I looked closely again, I was also sure it had only been the reflection of 20 gullible ghost hunters gathered in the corridor below. And unless the spirits shopped at Superdry one shadow was unmistakably Tony in his thick, black sports puffer jacket. I could even see the label, for fuck's sake.

Cathy explained that this part of the Victorian prison had housed the greatest number of inmates and that ghosts had often been seen suspended outside of cells. There were many reports of the heavy iron doors mysteriously banging without warning. Cathy reached into her pocket and rummaged around: she took from it three balls, which she tantalisingly turned over in her hands.

'There's high activity in this area, so we're going to see if any spirits will reveal themselves tonight.'

She gestured for everyone to step back and form a semicircle, then rolled the three balls some metres away. If I wasn't mistaken, they were the same balls I'd bought for my kittens Milo and George. They flashed whenever they batted them with their paws.

'Are you here?' Cathy called over at the balls. Absolutely nothing happened.

'If you would like to communicate, can you flash?' she continued.

'Huuuuuuuuh.'

There was a sharp intake of breath. One ball started flickering green. Then another red. Red and green LED lights rapidly winking and reflecting off the hard tiled floor.

'Bingo,' Tony called out. He screw-balled his fist in a mini-power grab. I sensed, like me, Tony was a serious hunter, not taken in by everything he was experiencing but trying to keep an open mind.

Admittedly, it was interesting. We all agreed that it could signal the presence of paranormal activity. One thing did concern me, though. I noticed the balls were still flashing a good five minutes later as we reached the other end of the corridor. Could it be a loose connection? It was impossible to tell.

Soon, we were edging our way towards a room that had been used for executions. Quite a number of people had been hanged there, Cathy explained. It was small with no window and a trapdoor at its centre. On entering I felt a shiver run down my spine. Horrible to think that this cold room was where people had met a grisly end.

Bob hovered the lantern near Cathy's face as she talked.

'So, there's many people who have experienced a poltergeist in . . .'

Cathy froze and slowly put her hand up to her mouth.

'Shhhhhhhh, can you hear that?' she whispered.

This time it wasn't Tony's wheezing but, honestly, I could not hear a fucking thing.

'I heard it,' one woman piped up. 'C'mon, yous, show yerselves, you bastards. We're not scared.'

Actually, I was feeling fairly on edge but also I wasn't sure a poltergeist would respond to that kind of verbal bait. I mean, poltergeists – or so-called noisy ghosts – are used to calling the shots. If they want to fling you around or send stuff flying, they will. They like to be the one that's in control. If I were one I'd put my foot down: *I'm not fucking coming out for you, or for anyone. My prison, my rules.*

By this time, Cathy was really starting to get on my tits. As we wound our way around, she continued to plant thoughts in people's heads. Some of the group genuinely said they heard and felt something, but I wondered how much of it was real. A person who wants to believe will join the dots. She also rushed through her questions.

'Is anyone here?

'What's your name?

'Why are you here?'

All right, all right. I wanted to step in. *Give the spirit a chance to answer!* Even I'd get performance anxiety with that kind of quick-fire round.

In the execution room we gave up hope of seeing or feeling the poltergeist. We had been there ten minutes and I was starting to feel weary.

'Before we break, we're going to try the pendulum test,' Cathy said. I had heard of this before, but I'd never seen it in action. Sometimes investigators use an actual pendulum but sometimes a person. If the person chosen is pushed one way or another, it shows a spirit may be present.

'If you could come forward, sir, that would be lovely,' Cathy said, pointing at Doggy Osbourne, who looked delighted to be picked.

We gathered in a semicircle around him.

'Now, stand with your back straight, sir. Can you feel anything?'

'Yup,' Doggy Osbourne shouted.

'What is it? What can you feel?' Cathy replied feverishly, ramping up the tension in the room.

'Shooting pain in me lower back,' Doggy Osbourne said, rubbing it hard with his fingers. 'We've been standing for some time.'

'Okay.' Cathy clicked her fingers, irritated. 'I think it's time for a break. I see some of you have brought flasks, but there's a coffee machine downstairs if anyone would like a hot drink.'

Doggy Osbourne grimaced like he'd let the side down but honestly everyone looked ready to wilt. The group dispersed, ready to meet back in ten minutes. As I walked out onto the landing, I couldn't help notice the cat balls on the floor, still flashing. *That's one persistent spirit or some temperamental wiring*, I thought.

Near the coffee machine, everyone sat around exchanging stories about the paranormal experiences they'd had in other locations. Lots happened in wings occupied by people who'd committed sex crimes, apparently. And there was a smattering of stately home stories too. People had made recordings of clearly troubled souls, others had seen videos. I didn't want to pour doubt on any of that, so I sipped my coffee. Quietly, though, I still maintained my hunch that ghosts of any integrity didn't reveal themselves like this.

I wandered out and got chatting to one of the security guards. He'd also worked in the prison for years when it was operational and now he patrolled it as a guard. He was tall and burly – a cross between an XL Bully and Tyson Fury but who'd let himself go a bit. If anyone was going to antagonise a ghost, it would have been him. I'm not sure I fancied its chances, though.

'Have you ever experienced anything here?' I asked.

'Nah. Lots of people have, though.' He laughed all-knowingly.

I found it hard to believe that someone who had spent so much time walking the prison's eery corridors hadn't heard a squeak, but people who'd paid the ticket price had.

'What? Seriously, nothing?' I checked.

'I have literally stood in the central courtyard and shouted: "C'mon, let's be 'aving you!" and there was nothing. Not a peep from those fuckers.'

'Right,' I said. The whole evening was becoming even more unfathomable.

Back upstairs there were a couple more rooms to enter before people were free to explore on their own and then bed down if they were staying overnight. I wished I could have joined them. If there was going to be any activity, I reckoned that's when the party might get started. Tony's worsening asthma sounded like enough to put anything off, though. I found him bent over and panting on the stairs sucking on his inhaler.

One final test was a sound experiment, done with a spirit box. These are used to detect spirits' voices. It's a radio that sweeps through multiple stations constantly to try to pick up spirit communication in between the channels. I'll talk about recording ghosts via EVP (electronic voice phenomena) more in the next chapter, but it was one method of ghost hunting that I did have some faith in. I had high hopes.

Back in B Wing, Cathy placed the radio-type device attached to a small portable speaker on a chair. She pressed a button and stepped back. Bob was still beside her, loyally shining his trusty lantern. A blue light illuminated and a noise kicked in like the sound of a distant train, chugging fast. This was the white noise in between frequencies where ghosts are often heard.

'Are the spirits here with us?' Cathy asked.

The group leaned in, straining to hear. There were definitely a couple of blip sounds but nothing decipherable.

Cathy raised her voice. 'Call if there's anyone here you want to talk to.'

Suddenly, Doggy Osbourne's arm shot forward and he waved his hand around like he'd heard something.

'Yes, sir, what is it?'

'It said my name!' he yelled, almost punching the air.

'What's your name, sir?'

'Philip Hunt!'

'Okay, okay. Sounds like we have something here.,' Cathy grinned. 'Let's play back a phone recording.'

Cathy gestured for us all to gather round. It hadn't sounded like 'Philip Hunt' to me at all. Something quite different, in truth. By now, I was finding it hard to keep a straight face and I stifled a giggle.

'Maisie, you're smiling. What can you hear?' Cathy said, while Bob swung the lantern in my direction.

'It's Daisy. Erm . . . I'm sorry. All I can hear is "fucking cunt".'

The group fell silent.

Should've kept your big mouth shut, Dais.

Then, Tony cleared the phlegm from his throat. 'Sorry, that's what I heard too.'

'Yup, sorry. I heard "fucking cunt" too,' one woman shouted from the back.

It seemed to be the one thing that most of us agreed on.

'It was *definitely* my name,' Doggy, aka Philip, insisted.

He was still protesting when Cathy parted the group and shuffled through.

'Let's move on shall we?' She tutted, leading us to the last room of the evening. It was nearing 11pm and soon I'd have to say goodbye to my new-found bunch of paranormal playmates.

The final room had been the location of the murder of an infamous inmate by his cellmate, Cathy told us. He'd been known to stalk the landing at night. After some time listening and watching, Cathy peered around the group.

'If you hear anything or see anything do put your hand up.'

Tony cleared his throat again, then had a quick puff on his inhaler. 'I don't know if I should say this, but I can feel the sensation of something being slowly inserted into my anus,' he said, a bit embarrassedly.

A few sniggers rippled around the room. Cathy's lips pursed and Bob almost lost control of his lantern. Then a voice trilled out from the group to break the stultifying, awkward silence. It was Philip.

'Well, we are in a prison,' he snorted.

☆

9

YOU HAVEN'T HEARD THE LAST OF ME

If you thought the haunting of my home in South Cerney was bizarre, then what I'm about to tell you defies all logic. It happened not long before I fell pregnant with my son Jack and before all the hauntings kicked off at my home. Honestly, I'm still trying to make sense of it.

One night, my temperature rose to scary levels. I began sweating. Every muscle in my neck felt stiff and my head was pounding. I took some Nurofen hoping it would relieve the pain, but by the morning nothing had shifted. That's when I got rushed into Swindon's Great Western Hospital. It was grim. Really grim. On arrival, I was taken to a mixed ward that felt like something out of *Day of the Dead*. The stench of disinfectant hit my nostrils immediately. This was combined with the smell of cabbage and canteen shepherd's pie, reminiscent of those fucking awful dinners we used to get at school. Eurrrrrrgh.

In the bay beside me there was an emaciated old woman lying among a spaghetti of tubes hooked up to several machines. As I tried to get used to my new surroundings, it became clear that she was on her last legs. People always talk about a death rattle, don't they? But I'd never imagined what one actually sounded like. *Jesus Christ*, it was relentless. Like water gurgling down a plughole. As the minutes ticked on it got louder, like a warthog snore, then softer, back to the endless gurgling. Part of me wanted to lean over, take her hand and tell her everything was going to be okay, even though I knew it probably wouldn't be. Another part of me wanted to leave. Instead, I put my earplugs in and drifted into sleep.

The next morning when I woke up, I looked over to find a solitary nurse clearing the white cotton sheets from the bed.

'What happened to the elderly lady?' I asked as I came to. Maybe she got moved or even discharged?

'She died,' the nurse said, pulling a sad face.

'Wow. I must have been out of it. Didn't hear a thing,' I said groggily.

'The old die quietly . . .'

Still, an overwhelming sadness did wash over me.

'Your job must be so difficult,' I said. I also felt bad for the lady. I doubt that she'd had any family around her in her last moments.

'At times it can be,' the nurse murmured softly before she padded back along the corridor.

While the doctors were trying to decide what was wrong with me, I'd also got chatting to a girl in the bed opposite. Stacey was terminally ill with cancer. Soon, she would be moved to a hospice to see out her final days. She'd been told she had only a few months left to live. Six at best. Before then she was planning on marrying her long-term boyfriend and she had wedding magazines piled up next to her bed. Stacey was flicking through *Brides* magazine as we chatted briefly.

'I have a lot to look forward to.' She grinned from ear to ear.

Wow. How can you be so positive? I wondered.

She was so young, and now she was stuck on a ward with yours truly, propped up on a pillow doing a brilliant impression of a beached mammal and sweating like a seal in a sauna. It was like some fucked-up version of *Planet Earth*.

'I think you're *really* amazing,' I shouted over.

I sincerely meant that, though I didn't think it was the time or the place to tell her I didn't think the off-the-shoulder ruffle-cake dress would suit her at all. Who wants to go out looking like a trifle?

She beamed and said, 'Thanks.'

Despite Stacey's inspiring optimism, the bleak atmosphere was starting to gnaw at me. Who'd have thought in a hospital there'd be so much death? Then, when I laid back for my umpteenth nap of the day the whole world began spinning. Bright white lights flashed in front of my eyes. *Holy shit*. Was I having a seizure?

'Can someone call a nurse please?' I muttered feebly.

Before long, I was moved into a private room. Suspected viral meningitis, the doctor said as they were wheeling me along the corridor – the white lights weren't just dodgy wiring on the overhead fluorescent bulb, then. I was clearly highly contagious, so much so that they moved me out of the ward so quickly that I didn't have chance to wave a hearty farewell to Stacey opposite: *'Nice meeting you! Good luck with the wedding!'*

My new room was on the same floor and somehow was even more depressing. It had one window with a tatty blind that was bleached out and stained from the sunlight. Not that there was any sunlight peeping through that day. The blind was closed and the room felt boiling hot. *If I died here, it would be tragic.* I was also more bored than a pole dancer with broken legs. I needed something – anything – to occupy myself. I got my phone out.

☆

In all the research I'd ever done into the paranormal I'd read countless stories arising from my current setting. Hospitals, hospices and care homes are *the* places to be. The undead haunt corridors, wards and rooms like Z-listers do *Celebrity Big Brother*. There are some astonishing tales, so many creepy stories from current and abandoned places around the world.

I don't know why, but one story I read stuck with me. It described 'the lady in the blue dress' who haunted an old people's care home somewhere in Wiltshire. Patients in a certain wing would ring the bell to call for a nurse: 'Could you make the lady in the blue dress a cup of tea?' they asked. But nobody was there. Then, one day, a nurse on duty thought she spotted the ward sister. She called out to her, but the reply came from a completely opposite direction. When she looked again, the figure had vanished. All this time, nurses had assumed that the ghost must have been a previous resident, but she wasn't. She was a senior nurse who walked the corridors in a blue dress, black tights and black lace-up shoes, still doing her rounds.

A nurse called Amy also told me about several hauntings she had experienced while she was a student. She had been working on a ward filled with elderly people. In the dead of night, she was checking on one patient's IV drip in a side room when she felt a cold, firm hand on her shoulder. It gripped her tighter. Thinking it was her mentor checking she was okay, or pranking her, she spun around. The ward was empty. Everyone was sleeping and her colleague was nowhere in sight.

'Did you try to make me jump on my rounds earlier?' she asked her mentor when she finally caught up with her at the nurses' station.

Everyone stared at her with blank faces. Nobody had moved a muscle since she left to check the patient's drip.

I've also spent years listening to EVPs recorded in hospitals. That's electronic voice phenomena that reveals spirits talking, inaudible to the human ear but able to be picked up on a recording or specially fashioned spirit boxes (remember Cathy and her device in B Wing in the previous chapter?). Eerie messages like: 'Help me. I can't breathe . . .'

☆

In my hospital room that day, I felt more lonely than I'd ever been. The white lights had stopped flashing and I could feel my temperature dropping, but this place was sapping my will to live. The old lady who had passed in the bed beside me; the terminally ill girl: those faces taunted me like a horror film on repeat. Doctors had also been in to prod, poke and test me, and I was still waiting on confirmation of my suspected meningitis. People die of meningitis, don't they? I was sure *a lot* did. I figured that if I was going to peg it then a half-decent spirit might prewarn me.

So, I lay in bed, phone in hand, pressed record . . . and waited.

'Is anybody here?' I asked.

I listened for a reply, but all I could hear was the hum of the machine next to me and the radiator gently hissing.

'What's your name?'

Again, the room was still.

'If anyone is here with me, give me a sign.'

There was no word at all . . . then, *FuuuuuuuuuuuuuuucK!*
Suddenly, my heart leaped. There was a sharp knock at the door and
a nurse glided in.

'Everything okay?' she asked, moving round the bed to top up the
water on my bedside cabinet.

'Uhhhhh-huhhhh,' I groaned, quickly shoving my mobile under
the sheet. My pulse was working overtime. *Fuck. Fuck. Fuck.* I was
pretty sure I wasn't allowed to use my phone in hospital in case the
signal messed with any life-saving equipment (I know, I know, please
don't judge me). To hide it, I attempted to wedge it under an arse cheek.
Don't mind me, just recording my arse. As the water slowly poured, my
nerves jangled again. My phone started to vibrate. Fucking hell . . . of
all the times, why was someone trying to call me now? I rolled to the
side and tried to ram it between my arse crack. I held it as tight as I
could until I could feel the voicemail kick in. I squirmed around a bit,
pretending I was busting a gut to manoeuvre out a silent fart. The last
thing I wanted was to have my mobile confiscated bang in the middle
of a paranormal experiment. The nurse looked at me confusedly,
frowned a little and glided back out.

'Just press the bell if there's anything you need.'

'Sure,' I said weakly, my arse cheeks still clamped together like
a vice.

The moment I heard the door click shut, I exhaled. I reached down
and prized the phone out. I did have the good grace to give it a quick
once-over with a baby wipe after I'd pressed stop on the record button.

Then I played it back. I wanted to hear something. I wanted to hear a voice so badly. Even if that voice said: 'Daisy, you really are a twat.' At least that would be some kind of reassurance. I can be a real twat sometimes.

There was nothing on the tape until . . . I heard a faint whisper. *What was that?* I played it back and listened to the sound again. Was my fever getting worse? Was I now having delusions? I'm sure I heard: 'Don't Be Afraid.' I played it again. 'Don't Be Afraid.' It was definitely a woman's voice. I kept playing it over and over. The words were muffled but they were also unmistakable: 'Don't Be Afraid.' *What the actual fucking fuck?* This was unbelievable! It was the first time I'd ever tried an EVP so it was more than unbelievable – it was fucking mental.

Later that day, Charlie and Mum and Dad came to visit. It turned out that it had been Chaz ringing from within my arse cheeks to check when the hospital visiting times were. When he arrived I couldn't wait to play him the recording too.

'Can you hear anything?' I asked eagerly.

I didn't want to plant any ideas or words in Charlie's head. I wanted to hear his honest reply. If I was hallucinating I needed to know. Charlie listened a couple of times.

'Don't Be Afraid,' he confirmed.

I knew it. I fucking knew it was real.

In fact, Mum, Dad, everyone who I played the tape to heard the same whisper and the exact same words. *Wow . . . this is extraordinary.* By now people would usually be telling me I was crazy or imagining things or making stuff up, but no one was.

As well as the many EVPs I'd listened to over the years, I had heard and read a lot about how electronic voice phenomena *must* be fake. Lots of people try to debunk it and say it's just white noise or background noise – that if a spirit was there, then why do none of them speak clearly? There's even a suggestion that it could be stray radio transmissions (hence the spirit box) and that we hear human language in the sounds because that's what we *want* to hear; it's not what's actually there. The doubters say it's just our minds playing tricks and that this must be the case because not everyone hears the same message. One person's 'I love you' could be another person's 'Fuck you'; which could turn into a nightmare if you were trying to have a long-distance relationship with a ghost.

Konstantin Raudive, the Latvian doctor who first reported EVP in the late 1960s, even claimed to have established contact with Hitler, Stalin, Mussolini and all sorts of 20th-century leaders. And he had the tapes to prove it. Apparently Hitler spoke to him in Latvian on one recording. To be fair, he said some pretty nonsensical things: phrases like 'kindle willingly' and 'You are a girl there or else you are thrown out.' Weird, huh?

When questioned about this, the doctor said that there was every likelihood that the voice may not be Hitler's at all, but rather a ghost who'd been trying to get through for ages but had probably got pissed off that no one had taken any notice – a bit like when you're stuck on hold trying to get through to customer service at Virgin Media. Frustrated, the ghost may have stolen Hitler's identity to get noticed. A bold and cunning move! Personally, though, I would have chosen someone a little less universally despised. Maybe someone a tad more popular? From the world of light entertainment maybe? Surely mimicking an icon like Marilyn Monroe would have bumped a spirit up the queue far quicker? What call centre worker, who's probably already been yelled at a gazillion times that morning, wants the fucking Führer, fake or otherwise, talking bollocks at the other end of the line? *Jesus Christ, it's Adolf again. Way above my pay grade. I'm putting him through to my line manager. I don't care if I don't get my bonus.*

Apparently, another voice came through that Raudive thought was definitely Winston Churchill's. He was reciting words from 'Land of Hope and Glory'.

Before my own EVP experience, I was prepared to question whether any of this was true or just an elaborate hoax by a massive show-off who'd built a recording machine for no real reason and had to justify to his wife why he'd spent so many hours in his garage. I ran through the finer details of the evidence in my head. In between sending millions of innocent people to their deaths, would Hitler have had the time to learn Latvian? Now, though, in light of my own experience, everything did seem more plausible. While there *must* be so many fakes out there clouding proper investigation, I'm also convinced there are many bona fide recordings.

Later, when I was eventually discharged from hospital and was recovering back home, I wanted to mark my momentous discovery. I had the words 'Don't Be Afraid' tattooed just underneath my right wrist. It's there to remind me that this did happen and that the paranormal does exist. And whenever I feel stressed or anxious that voice is there to guide me.

☆

EVPs make perfect sense to me. Why would a 21st-century spirit want to be stuck in a darkened room hovering around through endless hours of Ouija (unless it was just nostalgic for the past) when it could gab away and be heard? Ghosts aren't idiots. They probably know how to work new technology before most humans get the hang of it.

One man called John wrote to me with a spooky but touching tale about his great-nan. By the sounds of it, she was an early adopter of EVP. Even from the other side, she was way ahead of the game. These days I bet she'd be an influencer, probably throwing shade on Twitter (or X or whatever the fuck it's called these days). Maybe going viral on TikTok. When John was a teenager, though, she'd mastered the walkie-talkie.

John's bestie, who lived next door, had been given two handsets for his birthday.

'They had a limited range, but it was fine as our bedrooms were only 30 feet apart,' he told me.

Of course, this was in the days before mobile phones. John described how one night he was lying in bed when his walkie-talkie beeped. He assumed it was his mate, but when he listened it wasn't his friend's voice at all. It was a woman's. After a couple of words he recognised it as the voice of his great-nan.

'She asked if I was okay. I pressed the talk button and replied that I was fine, but that I was in bed and trying to sleep. She said: "That's good. Goodnight then pet," which was how she always referred to me.'

The next morning when John got up, the first thing he did was run downstairs and tell his parents that he'd spoken to his great-nan on the walkie-talkie. They both looked gobsmacked.

'Great Gran passed away late yesterday afternoon. We didn't get the call until after you'd gone to bed.' John's mum broke the news to him. Her death had been completely unexpected.

How fucking awesome is that? I can barely work out how to reply to emails. Yet his great-nan, while in the midst of crossing over to the other side, had the time to check that her great-grandson was tucked up in bed using a kid's walkie-talkie. What a fucking legend.

And what about Karen, whose nan June made contact around 12 years ago? Apparently, she was a very heavy smoker and spoke with a thick Cardiff accent, so her voice was unmistakable. Two weeks after she died, Karen's auntie received a voicemail on her landline. All the voice said was: 'I told you, Mal. I told you.' A very cryptic message and one that got everyone intrigued.

When the family called BT to enquire where the call had come from, there was no record of it ever taking place. Thanks, Karen, and I do hope your nan is up there somewhere chain-smoking fags and knocking back a glass of her favourite tipple like Patsy from *Ab Fab*. I also hope she's mastered *WhatsApp* and plans to leave a voice note soon.

✦

10

PICTURE THIS

Imagine seeing something so inexplicable that years later it still blows your mind whenever you think about it. That's exactly what happened to a woman called Amy. She was a teenager and had been out with her friend Dobby. (Thank you, Amy, for confirming that Dobby is human and not the house-elf of the Malfoy family from *Harry Potter*.)

The pair were walking at night through Astley Park in Chorley in Lancashire. Within the park is Astley Hall, an extraordinary 15th-century mansion with four wings that overlooks a large lake and Victorian walled gardens. Ornate oak panelling adorns its rooms and there's also high plastered and painted ceilings. After the First World War, the hall was handed over to the people of Chorley to be used as its war memorial. Inside its main hall is a special remembrance room where all the names of the fallen from the town are listed on wooden panels.

'The hall is famous and locals have plenty of spooky stories about it. Our history teacher also worked on the War Archives late at night, and he had some stories to tell. But I will never forget what we saw that day,' Amy confessed.

For years, stories had circulated about Astley Hall. The English Civil War hero Oliver Cromwell is said to have stayed there after the Battle of Preston in 1648 and the beautifully carved four-poster bed he slept in sits in an upper bedroom. In the courtyard, there have been sightings of a lady in Tudor clothing, children have been heard giggling throughout its rooms, a man and a boy have been spotted walking through the main hall and drifting up the staircase. Even the sound of Mozart being played from a piano when no one was there has been recorded. But, that night, it wasn't any of those things that Amy and her friend Dobby caught sight of.

The pair walked on in the darkness, up the pathway towards the hall.

'Only as we got closer did we realise what we were witnessing. There were lights on. At first we thought that maybe a group of people had snuck in and what we were seeing were torch lights. Then we thought it might be a security guard doing the rounds. As we approached, Dobby and I could not explain it. There were lights, but they were like little round glowing suns floating around inside the hall.'

Amy recalls around three or four lights. As the pair got closer to the bay windows and peered in from the outside, they watched the orbs calmly moving.

'Two seemed to dance around one another in figure of eight loops. I was in awe,' she said.

One step closer and suddenly the lights vanished.

'Go on. Go up and knock on the door, I told Dobby.' Amy recalled what happened next. 'I can't remember whether he did knock or not, but I stayed by the bay window. Then, I heard him shout, "Piss off!" to me. I was nowhere near him. He said that I touched him on the back of the neck.'

Dobby felt a hand sweep across his skin but no one was near him – not Amy or any other person.

Here, I must point out that Amy swears she and Dobby were not off their faces on cheap white wine. Neither had they smoked a massive spliff while ambling through the park. They weren't the teenagers me and my mates were – out after dark thinking we were the fucking bomb, necking Lambrini and setting our fringes on fire while trying to light a cigarette in a northerly wind.

But if Amy wasn't drunk or stoned, then what the hell does she believe she saw?

'I will not try and tell you that these were spirits because they could have been and they could still be anything, but I remember them often. Now I question things far more than I did before,' she told me.

As soon as Amy contacted me, I remembered a series of pictures I'd seen ages ago. They were of Arlington National Cemetery in Virginia in the States, where photographers had captured similar orbs above the graves of dead soldiers.

There's another story I also knew of from Colorado. The town of Silver Cliff was part of the silver boom in the 1880s. One night a group of miners were walking back from a party when they took a shortcut through the cemetery. Above the gravestones, balls of blue and white light began to appear. There were no further sightings until 1956 when teenagers were driving near the cemetery. Suddenly, numerous balls of light started moving between the tombstones.

Of course, there have been many attempts at scientific explanation since: light bouncing off the tombstones is one theory; the effect pitch darkness has on a person's eyes that makes them see small dots of light is another. Other explanations for strange lights and apparitions – sometimes called spook lights or will-o'-the-wisps – are dust pollution or condensation or just lighting anomalies. But is there a chance they could be supernatural? As yet, no one has been able to prove or disprove that they are. Yet there's photographic and film evidence of all of these. So, is photographic evidence real or not? Can we trust all those films and photographs of shadowy figures trapped in our human world that abound on the Internet? Silent spectres opening doors, hovering around windows like stragglers at a house party as 'Die for You' by Ariana Grande gets stuck on repeat.

★

What's really annoying is that capturing ghosts in photographs and on film has had a chequered reputation over the years. Personally, I blame the Victorians. Although photography was invented in the 1830s, it took a few decades for cameras to be used by the masses. When the technology did start to become more widespread, most people didn't have a fucking clue how to use it. (Like when DVDs replaced VHS and complete and utter twats tried to rewind the disc ready for the next person to use.)

Suddenly, there was an epidemic of spirit photographs being reported. Ethereal figures on roadsides or in graveyards or drifting above people's beds as they lay sleeping. Strange lights that danced above the coffins of the recently deceased. What most people didn't realise is that because of the camera's long exposure times, anything that moved while the photograph was being taken created a shadowy figure when it was developed. While lots of people were just too new to the technology to understand, others did know. But instead of just fessing up, one lie tumbled into a bigger lie and then into a monstrous whopper. It's a bit like when my daughter Pip swears blind she's seen a ghost and when I question her about it (I mean, *really* interrogate her) the ghost is always wearing a ridiculous polka-dot bow-tie. And a waistcoat decorated with stars. And he has a painted-on red nose like a pissed-up Rudolph, and he always behaves like a cunt to his supposed loyal friend and butler Robert the Robot.

'Did you *really* see a ghost, Pip, or was it just Mr Tumble?'

'It was definitely a ghost, Mum.'

'Are you sure?'

If I let that kind of behaviour get out of hand, who knows what batshit craziness could be unleashed in my house. And speaking of batshit craziness, this is exactly what happened when two girls were left alone with some paper, pens and a camera more than a hundred years ago.

The truth of the story which took place in the Yorkshire village of Cottingley is known throughout the world now but when it happened back in 1917 it was extraordinary how an entire nation was fooled. Two girls – Frances Griffiths, who was nine years old at the time, and her sixteen-year-old cousin Elsie Wright – came in from playing one day. They'd been splashing around in the stream at the bottom of the garden and their shoes were soaking. When their parents asked how they'd got wet, Frances said: 'I go to see the fairies.'

Of course, no one believed them. You can imagine the conversation:

'The fairies, huh? I don't think there are fairies in the garden, darling...'

'No, we saw them. They are real.'

Determined to support her cousin in the face of such withering incredulity, Elsie asked to borrow her father's camera. She took some snaps on an early camera that used glass plates and developed the pictures. Lo and behold, there were four little people beside Frances prancing across a mossy stone, like something out of *Peter Pan*. A couple were playing flutes. Another picture was taken weeks later of Elsie conversing with a gnome on some meadowland.

When I think about this whole sorry episode now, it beggars belief that anyone thought that these were real spirits. And I suspect that what truly went on may have been an entirely different version of the established story.

It always happens, doesn't it? One, proud, over-enthusiastic parent wants to encourage their child's imagination. All of the other parents there probably humoured them along the lines of: *'Oh fairies are they, darling? I bet you've got snaps of Bigfoot trying to buy shampoo in the local shop too! Anyway, run along now, time to wash your hands ready for supper.'*

And that would have been the end of it. But, no! Instead, one utter moron made the mistake of indulging the girls, saying something like: *'Oh my goodness, that's incredible! Fairies? At the bottom of the garden? And you've got the proof! How wonderful!'* In that half-hour window when the girls could have admitted that the fairy photographs were a deepfake, they chose not to. Dizzy with the buzz of having fooled everyone, they kept quiet. And the lie kept going . . . and going . . . and going . . . and the whole fairy mania began.

In the hysteria one parent told another, then that parent told the village gossip then the village gossip told the priest. *Fuck me, not the priest.* If ever there was a man who wanted to believe God worked in mysterious ways, it was him. Never mind that some of the finer details got blurry as the Chinese whispers passed along the line. Some people had telephones in their homes, so it would only have been a matter of time before someone got on the blower. It spiralled way out of control, as out of control as Elon Musk suddenly finding himself buying a social media platform he never wanted for billions more than most countries' national debt then unrepentantly trolling every fucker on it.

And when the news of the fairies reached none other than Arthur Conan Doyle, all hell broke loose. Arthur wasn't just the illustrious creator of the character Sherlock Holmes (bizarrely the biggest arch-sceptic on the planet), he was also a self-confessed Victorian spiritualist who believed that modern science could be used to prove the existence of ghosts.

Arthur lapped it up. He had several experts look at the photographic plates, who concluded they had not been tampered with. They couldn't prove the fairies were real but neither could they prove they weren't. So Arthur went ahead and published the images in his famous *Strand Magazine*. Funnily enough, he didn't seem that arsed to visit the girls himself or the site where the photographs had been taken. I suspect that he may have tried to but had met with some fierce resistance from parents who knew it was all a massive fucking lie that had got way out of hand. By that time, though, it was too late to backtrack. Whenever he rang, wanting to arrange a time, there'd be an excuse . . .

'Hi Arthur, yes, you could come tomorrow but unfortunately both girls have been struck down with a terrible case of something or other. Highly contagious . . .'

'Arthur. So sorry, any chance we could rearrange this week? It's the village fete and the girls are just a little bit busy making fairy cakes.'

'Arthur, apologies again. Wednesday is completely out. Something's come up. The neighbour's mother's cousin's brother's pet hamster has died. The girls are completely devastated.'

One time, he did manage to get his assistant, a man called Gardner, through the front door. But, honestly, his methods were hardly scientific. He appears to have possessed all the investigative powers of Scooby Doo. My guess is that Conan Doyle was a tight-arse and Gardner was probably working for below minimum wage, glad to be out from the clutches of the big boss for the day. Afterwards, all Gardner banged on about was how he'd been 'struck by the transparent honesty and simplicity of the family'. Because of that, he believed the photos were genuine. Bit patronising, no? I reckon he sniffed around for 15 minutes tops, scribbled something in his notebook, bid a hasty farewell and then spent the rest of the afternoon knee-deep in flagons of real ale at the Sun Inn before reluctantly heading back to the Big Smoke to file his 'report'.

During the whole of this supernatural mayhem what is most

extraordinary to me is that not one person thought to check either of the girls' bedrooms. Under a floorboard? Behind a bed? The back of a drawer? In any of those places I can guarantee that an eagle-eyed parent would probably have found a pair of scissors, some paper cut-outs, some pens and the remnants of some old hatpins that the girls used to attach the fairies to their surroundings before the photographs were taken. Not exactly rocket science! Instead, the hoax went unsolved for more than 60 years. *Sixty. Fucking. Years.* Eventually the cousins admitted their lie in 1983. Did they give a shit that they'd duped the whole country? Nope. They never saw it as fraud – just two girls having a laugh. Did they feel ashamed that they'd made very important people look like utter tossers? Nope, those people wanted to believe, they said.

Admittedly, part of me is wildly impressed. Hats off to any woman under the age of 18 who can make a mustachioed pompous twat from London look like a cock in front of his mates. The reality is that Conan Doyle wanted to believe, not necessarily in fairies, but in spiritualism. He'd converted to the new religion only a few years before. And, at the time, he'd been getting a slagging-off for being gullible and unscientific by his critics. He *needed* the fairies to be real. Plus, he was writing a book about spirit photography which eventually got published in 1923. Let's face it, he needed the money!

At least Conan Doyle was trying to prove something possibly world changing, however shoddy his technique. This was in contrast to Victorian commercial photographers who were far more unscrupulous and preyed on the vulnerability of innocent people gripped by loss, longing and grief.

All the rage in Victorian times was the practice of photographing the dead before they were buried or cremated – a kind of fucked-up family snap. A macabre market created because mortality rates were so high, especially among children. But some of these photographers also practised spirit photography and they offered to pop round soon after someone had died to capture their spirit for posterity. Adverts appeared in newspapers as brazenly as dick pics on Hinge.

KEEP YOUR LOVED ONE'S SPIRIT ALIVE

Freshly dead? Knocking on heaven's door?

Watch faces light up with this personalised gift.

2 shillings per photograph*

* As the spirit is not guaranteed we operate on a no-kin

no-fee basis. If two family members have died,

enquire about our buy-one-get-one-free deals.

In addition to these 'barely dead' shoots, photographers would invite people who had lost loved ones in for portrait sittings or turn up to seances where they'd set up their tripod. When the photos were developed the spirit would often be hovering above a family or a person's head or photobombing them for a laugh. The tragic thing is I would have wanted to believe this. I would have wanted to believe this *so badly*. Unfortunately, though, once the masses did get the hang of the new technology, photographers were exposed and found to be using lots of tricks: double exposure; blending two photos together to look like ghost pictures. It was all to make loads of cash out of the bereaved.

But just because the Victorians got over-excited, does this mean we should dismiss all unexplained images captured on film as fake? Despite Frances and Elsie's highly successful attempt at forgery, no one has yet been able to prove or disprove the existence of fairies. And there are plenty of photographs taken by people who swear blind that the headless horseman or the face-in-the-church-pulpit shot has not been tampered with or added to later.

One picture that's stuck in my head was taken in the ruins of Egremont Castle in Cumbria some time in the 1970s. I love it because it's so fucking ordinary. A girl was happily snapping her boyfriend in his flares and denim jacket. Seriously, he looked like a reject from Slade. But when the photograph was developed he was not alone. Behind him and to the left-hand side is the unmistakable impression of a skeleton. Its fashion sense wasn't much better than his. It was dressed in an orange dress coat like Widow Twankey and appears to be waving a ghostly wand in its hand.

Of course, that could have been explained away as a fake or some other unexplained phenomenon, except for one massive bombshell: the snap was taken on a Polaroid Swinger camera – one of those instant cameras you load the film into and each wallet-sized print is developed as soon as the snap is taken. How could anyone tamper with that?

Another of my favourite snaps is a photograph of two children playing in a garden in Stafford in the early 1990s. When it was developed there was a strange shape to the right-hand side that looks like a fuck-off massive doughnut. What's unclear is whether it's trying to eat them or it wants to be eaten. Whichever way, the children are completely unaware. Could this be a so-called hungry ghost? The soul of someone who's done something unspeakable and is being punished by insatiable hunger in the afterlife. If so, why did it come back as a Krispy Kreme Party Sparkle glazed ring and not the Nutty Chocolatta?

There has been some investigation into this photograph by paranormal investigator Dr Melvyn Willin. Sceptics had dismissed the shape as a hairband in the frame, or the thumb or finger of the photographer that somehow got in the way, or the camera strap dangling in shot. But, as Willin suggests, the shutter button was on the right-hand side of the camera so it's unlikely to be any of those explanations. The hairband theory may be plausible if it flew into the frame, but when does a hairband fly around a garden? To date, the case remains unsolved.

And there are loads of instances of pareidolia (the human ability to see shapes or make pictures out of randomness; think of the Rorschach inkblot test) that have also gone unexplained: the figures we see in clouds or stones or just in random household places; the image of Jesus Christ our Lord and Saviour on an ultrasound scan; the Madonna and Child in a rainbow; the Chuckle Brothers in a Babybel cheese.

Some followers sent me their own pictures – surprisingly few dick pics for once. Thanks to Lauren who sent me a very interesting picture of what could be a headless monk or maybe a soldier. Her boyfriend, who was a delivery driver, took the photo (as evidence of a delivery) in the garden of a couple he'd delivered some outdoor furniture to. It's hiding in the bushes. Also, full marks for not believing everything you saw, Lauren. In her unwavering commitment to uncovering the truth, Lauren called the homeowners to ask them if this was just a random, headless statue shoved under a birch tree beside the barbecue. Or whether it was something far more sinister. The world needs more serious investigators like you, Lauren.

'I could feel the woman going cold as I told her the story,' Lauren told me. 'I sent her the picture on WhatsApp, and when we spoke again I could hear her call her husband over. They were amazed. There was no statue there, but they said it all made sense because of the weird stuff that had been happening around their property.'

Spooky, huh? So, it seems, the case for photographic ghosts is very complex. Impossible to draw any real conclusions within the confines of this chapter, to be honest. Personally I have never seen an unexplained image in any of my own snaps. And I don't think that Darren Smith's penis accidentally hanging out of his trousers in the Primary Four group photograph really counts, although when I realised what it was, it was shockingly purple.

But plenty of people have seen strange things on film and photographs, with no reasonable explanation whatsoever. I have to conclude: the jury is out. But I do still keep thinking of those orbs that Amy described looping around in figures of eight in the room at Astley Hall with her friend – definitely not an elf – Dobby. Fuck me, I would have loved to have been there.

★

PART THREE

THE SPIRITS IN YOUR LIFE

11

LET'S PLAY HOUSE

If you had a choice, what type of ghost would you come back as? It's a question that's often rattled around in my brain. There are so many out there, each with their own unique way of operating. Personally, if I was to come back and haunt the living, I'd plan on being a ghost with a bit of va-va-voom. I'd want to be the kind of ghost who rummages around in someone's sexy drawer and lines up their dildos on the dressing table in descending order of height. Opening cupboard doors and randomly knocking over chairs is soooo 20th century! I'd want to be a ghost with a sense of humour, for fuck's sake! But there's always that point when any joke can go too far. A ghost who publicly displays someone's bank details on their Facebook status probably tips over from what seemed like a hilarious idea into seriously unfunny.

But, I guess if we can't always choose the course of our life, or our life's end, then we can't choose what the afterlife will bring us either. Will we be smoothly ushered through to the next world, gliding up on a star-studded escalator with no return ticket? Or stuck at the sodding barriers forced back by heaven's henchmen in their fluorescent orange tabards?

'Ticket's not valid, love. Now, fuck off out of it, and come back when you've sorted yourself out.'

'All right, but I will get across eventually, won't I?'

'Nothing's guaranteed. You'll have to pay the extra then reapply to the guv'nor, see what he says.'

'But I've spent a fucking age in the queue. And I've also got a Groupon voucher for a two-for-the-price-of-one cocktail on entry!'

'Sorry, love. As I said, not valid . . .'

'Well, fuck you!'

I read about a woman who died but, at the eleventh hour, had been brought back to life (more about near-death experiences later). On her brief tour around the underworld, before she got resuscitated, she drifted down to the gates of hell before beginning her ascent to gawp inside the pearly gates. Apparently, though, in the inferno she caught a glimpse of an emaciated Stalin repeatedly banging his head against a wall next to the wrought iron gates screaming: 'Okay, Okay. I'm sorry, I get it!'

It's stories like that which make me think that there's room for personal growth and change in the paranormal world. But it throws up other questions too. Does your passage to the other side always determine what kind of temperament you'll have if you are forced to trudge back to the land of the living? I mean, how long can a ghost stay pissed off for? Believe me, I can stretch out a monster sulk for days – weeks, even – but it does get exhausting after a while. And people start to ignore you, which is frustrating. And this leads me on to another question: what behaviour could you accept in a ghost, especially one that you had to live with day in day out? What are the rules for cohabiting? And can ghosts comply? If they have been given a second chance at life then why can't they attempt to at least *try* to achieve some kind of happiness? Of course, what you'll tolerate is a personal thing. Surely, it can't just be me who's made a note of cast-iron red lines?

- *Red line number one:* Scare my kids and you're out. No ifs, no buts, no second chances. I don't want to hear any excuses about how you were tortured, made fun of, bumped off before your time.
- *Red line number two:* Breaking stuff is an absolute deal-breaker.

★

The only reason I was able to live with my ghosts is that they seemed reasonably polite. Civilised, even. The picture mover neatly leaned the canvases up against a wall. They weren't punched through, or kicked in or chucked around. The saucepans that my friend Sarah heard rattling around in the kitchen had all been tidied away by the next morning. No smashed plates or frying-pan-shaped holes in the wall.

For that reason, I believe it is possible for ghosts to make perfectly compatible house guests. And many of you out there seem to agree. A woman called Sarah (yes, another one, not my friend Sarah) took the time to write to me to tell me how she'd grown up with a ghost in her parents' home in Cumbria. He was by all accounts a gentle old man who simply wanted to sit by her, usually on the end of her bed, while she was sleeping, or he'd hover over her quietly.

'I was never scared of it and it felt quite protective,' she said. To this day she still senses he's there whenever she visits her parents' home. It's as if he drops by to make sure she is okay.

Sarah went on to tell me about the ghost that recently visited her son. He wasn't scary or threatening either. He serenely glided past her son's bedroom. A week or so later Sarah found out that her elderly neighbour, John, had passed away around the same time as her son reported the sighting.

'He'd been a bit of a recluse and he didn't have any grandchildren himself. I immediately felt the ghost must have been John popping by to say goodbye to my son on his way to whatever the next life holds. I love that the man in our house was John, and not some creepy burglar!' she confessed.

But the ghostly experience is not the same for everyone, and my heart does go out to anyone whose domestic life has been turned upside down by extreme hauntings.

Not long ago reality star Katie Price invited me on to her podcast and she and I had an extraordinary conversation about everything that had been going on in her (now former) Sussex home, Mucky Mansion. Katie described spending years wrestling a demonic infestation. Normally, Katie, I'd advise a trip to your local GP and some strong cream, liberally applied to the affected area. We've all been there! Seriously, though, anyone's home being overrun by demons puts a real downer on things, especially those cosy winter nights curled up on the sofa watching *Strictly*. And Mucky Mansion does sound fucking dreadful when it comes to the paranormal. Katie was drowning in the critters: it'd gone way beyond flickering lights or icy cold spots, bad smells or random missing objects. Her ghosts had been appearing in the dead of night. Heavy footsteps outside her kids' bedrooms had left them petrified and screaming. And, creepiest of all, was a young boy who stood rigid on the top floor of her house, wearing a black jacket and a white shirt, his eyes just staring out into the pitch dark. Some years ago she also woke to find a demon with a large face and long black dress staring at her in her mirror. Katie – all power to you for sticking it out (she lived there for nine years). You're a far better woman than I am. I would've been crapping my cacks and a 'For Sale' sign would have been erected immediately.

Before I bought my new house, I even made a point of asking the owner whether there had been any reports of paranormal hi-jinks. I wanted to be 100 per cent sure that I was not entering the domain of a vengeful spirit. Of course, she looked at me like I had two heads and had landed from Pluto, but thankfully she confirmed that she had not experienced any visitations. I suppose it's a bloody unusual question to ask. Personally, I think it should be a question on any home information form – up there with a building's energy rating or whether its got rising damp or noisy neighbours.

★

The fact is that ghosts do inhabit many people's homes, given that it is the place where many people die. Yet being a natural empath, I try to see things from the perspective of the undead. I've come to the conclusion that being a ghost is a *seriously* tough gig. Most people want their homes to be an oasis of happiness and calm – a place where they can feel safe in their own beds, not constantly looking over their shoulders or jumping out of their skins at the slightest creak or bang. But even if as a ghost you mean well, you're probably going to fall foul of that.

If you've ever watched the film *The Others*, you might understand what I'm talking about. It's a movie from 2001 starring Nicole Kidman as mother of two Grace Stewart. In it, her home is seemingly overrun by ghosts. But, spoiler alert: it transpires that she and her family are the deceased living there. They are the ones now having to coexist with a perfectly normal, living family who have moved in.

Forget any of the blood-curdling classics like *A Nightmare on Elm Street* or *The Exorcist*, *The Others* is *the* film that stresses me out the most. Honestly, I can barely watch it. Imagine being in the house you'd lived in for years, not only to find other kids playing with your kids' toys, but a whole programme of redecoration had taken place that you never sanctioned. And stuff moved around so you can't find it. It would be like existing in a constant state of dementia. Maybe the living room's suddenly been painted hot pink and a bright yellow sofa placed along one wall? And the coffee table? What was wrong with the lovely rectangular oak table you had with the neat shelf for magazines? How could this family have bought a circular coffee table? In shabby chic, for fuck's sake?! I'd be absolutely raging, especially if I'd gone to all the trouble of picking out a muted beige colour scheme and coordinated it with a matching rug and curtains.

So, if you are a ghost who finds yourself in that position, do you stay angry? Or go with the flow? Do you at least make an effort to move with the times and embrace Wayfair and its, quite frankly, dizzying array of interior decor solutions? In *The Others* Grace Stewart stubbornly refuses to believe that she isn't still in the land of the living. Finally, the mortal family are forced to move out with Grace staking her claim.

And when ghosts start putting their foot down like that, that's when the shit hits the fan. Thank fuck I've never been confronted by a poltergeist, but I can guarantee one would do my head in. And there's a theory that poltergeists are mostly found in kitchens and bathrooms because these are the places where there's the most energy swirling around. Think about it: every kitchen is a seething hotbed of electrical activity. In bathrooms there's bucketloads of water – a massive source of kinetic power. And there's that saying, isn't there? *Energy can neither be created nor destroyed only converted from one form to another.* I've thought about this *a lot*. It reaffirms my belief that we don't just disappear into thin air when we die and that some restless ghosts seek out places where there's high levels of energy in the atmosphere. Poltergeists feed off these environments so that they can do their worst damage.

Chucking stuff around is just attention-seeking bullshit, though. But what can you do? It's a knotty paranormal catch-22 scenario. If you indulge a poltergeist by fearing it then it's got you right where it wants you: it's always going to try and get the upper hand by being an arsehole. If you ignore it, you do that at your peril. It will only demand more and in the process suck you emotionally dry like a needy partner. And it's not like you can ever force a ghost to cross over into the light. But I reckon you can be assertive. Show it who's boss.

These days, everyone is desperate to bring in a paranormal team to investigate and sort the problem out. In my view, this is only going to further antagonise a ghost. And when the team leave, you'll be left picking up the pieces. Remember the cat balls? The Ecto-1 Ghostbusters car? Besides, there may be a perfectly rational explanation for what's been going on at home that could get overlooked by some thrill-seeking Velma who wants to justify their very existence and the exorbitant hourly fee. My advice is to resist that urge.

If the problem persists, you could try fully cleansing the space. I thought about this when I was first confronted with my ghosts. The thought was fleeting. For starters, it would have meant I'd actually have to clean and probably declutter. I could not be arsed.

I didn't venture down this next route, either, but you could attempt a practice called smudging. This involves wafting an all-purpose, herbal spiritual cleanser around. Think of it like a Glade PlugIn for the paranormal world. The scent of sage is usually recommended, but lavender, rosemary and peppermint are also supposed to do the trick.

If that hasn't nailed it, try talking to the ghost. Tell it: 'This is my house.' Tell it: 'If you're not going to behave properly then I'm going to bring out the big guns.' Tell it you're going to have to resort to drastic measures. For God's sake don't threaten it with a torch and a vacuum cleaner – it will only piss itself laughing. A slightly more aggressive tactic is to sprinkle some salt around: windows, doors, those kind of areas that act as transitional spaces. Don't quote me on this, but I think the Saxa table salt variety may suffice – don't bother using that expensive Maldon sea salt. Especially as you may have to do this several times over and in the midst of a cost-of-living crisis there's a £1 difference and you get loads more. If the ghost is still there, with its fingers in its ears shouting la-la-la like a fucking five-year-old, start praying. Or bring in a priest to pray for you.

A follower called Zoe told me about a formal exorcism she was forced to carry out in her flat in Clapham in South-east London. This came after months of hearing footsteps when only she was at home. Her radio kept switching itself off and on of its own accord and in the kitchen, cupboards started to fall off the wall leaving piles of broken crockery.

'After this had been happening for a while, I went straight to the local vicar. He came and sprinkled holy water in every room. He opened the windows so the spirits could leave and not be stuck for an eternity in Clapham. He put the sign of the cross on my forehead and recited prayers. By the time he left, he'd sorted it,' she told me.

A good plan of action, Zoe. I, for one, could not imagine anyone wanting to be stuck in Clapham for an eternity. I'd be on the first train out.

Misbehaving domestic ghosts can be annoyingly persistent, though. And it may take several attempts to eradicate them. Sadly, the instances of paranormal crime have never been carefully documented, which I think is a massive shame. Though it's also fair to say that the circumstances around some goings-on are vague and, in some cases, wholly unreliable. Around a decade ago, there was one former police officer, Joseph Hughes from Ohio, who swore blind that the stolen goods stockpiled underneath his house had been stashed by a ghost. 'We believed that there was some kind of paranormal presence in the basement,' he told a court jury while mounting his bonkers paranormal defence. *Come on, mate. Even I can see through that one!* And, seriously, what would a ghost want with umpteen air conditioners, a 6,000-watt generator and some knock-off welding equipment?

Other cases have been less clear-cut, though. Back in the UK, at roughly the same time, a couple from Nottingham, Lisa and Phil Rigley, set up a CCTV camera outside their home after a spate of vandalism on their Volvo estate car, which was parked in their driveway. They assumed it was delinquent kids mucking around in the early hours of the morning. But what they captured on camera truly shocked them. Instead of catching vandals in the act, the recording picked up something far more other-worldly and inexplicable. In the pitch darkness a glowing white orb flew into their driveway and clambered over their car, before vanishing and reappearing on the opposite side of the road. The footage is extraordinary. And when the couple confided in a neighbour, she also revealed that she'd had ornaments go missing from her garden. Although they were natural sceptics, the couple couldn't find any rational explanation for the white apparition on the recording. After that occasion there were no further signs of damage to the car so the couple took the case no further. How do you even pursue a ghost for criminal damage inside or outside of your home?

As I said, though, I do believe that we can live side by side with the spirit world. I'd like to think that you can befriend a ghost even if it's badly behaved. It sounds crazy but whenever I walked through the front door of my haunted home I shouted, 'Hi there!' This was just so they never felt startled or caught off-guard. It's good to set those kind of boundaries: I respect your space, you respect mine. Let's just get through this until we can work out a better arrangement longer term. If I'd stayed in that house then I may have even considered attempting to train my ghosts.

I am convinced that encouraging ghosts to perform random acts of kindness could really help them in their quest to be happier. And there's a whole host of things a ghost could do for you, especially if you live alone. I've made a list of ten things I'd fucking love in a ghost, but you probably have your own wish list.

1. Scrub your back in the shower or bath.
2. Squeeze spots in awkward places.
3. Massage your feet.
4. Move heavy objects.
5. Bring down items from the loft so you don't have to go to the bother of fetching a ladder.
6. Do up or undo the zip on a dress or back-fastening top.
7. Sing a duet.
8. Play Frisbee in the garden.
9. Bring you Nytol in bed.
10. Turn the downstairs light off when you've forgotten.

Failing that, ghosts can simply make good protectors, like the one Sarah described sitting at the end of her bed. Or they can warn you of dangers or of unexpected things that are about to happen. To illustrate exactly what I'm talking about, I want to leave this chapter on a ridiculously positive note with one story sent to me by Keith. It's so fucking touching it could be made into a Richard Curtis film.

When Keith was a child on the Isle of Wight his mother told him of a female spirit who lived alongside them. 'She's a little old lady, who is never to be feared, only loved,' she said. Keith's mother had seen the old lady on many occasions, as had his sister. He hadn't but had always felt that someone or something was watching over the family.

One time when he was 16 years old, his family went on a foreign holiday and he was left at home. Being deaf, he couldn't hear what was happening around the house. One night he was woken by someone shaking his shoulder. When he finally came to and looked up, a vision that took the form of an old woman dressed in a black net curtain was talking to him. He watched her lips as she mouthed the words.

'She told me to go downstairs and check the water. Eventually when I did I found that the washing machine had flooded. When Mum phoned from her holiday the next day, I told her what had happened. "It's okay. It's the old lady, she was looking out for you,"' she reassured him.

It wasn't until some years later that Keith's family got one step closer to finding out who this woman was. 'We were renovating an upstairs bedroom when we found an unsigned Victorian death card and a ring with black ribbon tied around it. This confirmed to us that it belonged to our lovely old lady.'

But the real revelation came just before Keith's mum herself passed away. 'Before she died, my mum said she needed to share something with me. She had a brain tumour but in her final days I sat on the end of her bed giggling with her. She said that she believed that the old lady had always been her spirit in another dimension, constantly there to watch over her and us. Now, it was time for her and the old lady to move on and look after a new family.

'A few years later the house was sold to a friend of a friend who had a young family. After a while she asked if Mum had died in the house and that she could feel a warm presence there. She said she never felt alone.'

Keith, I hope that lovely old lady is still with all of you, keeping you safe from exploding white goods and other domestic catastrophes.

★

12

GHOSTS THAT GIVE ME THE ICK

As the previous chapter shows, no one can choose the ghosts in their life, but I'd like to put this wish list out there just in case any ghosts are reading this book. If they are thinking of haunting me, then I hope the following may make them think twice or at least force them to examine their behaviour and change. My red lines remain red lines, but this gives ghosts an opportunity to change.

Ick No. 1

If you are a male ghost who's died in a mountaineering accident, a freak camping accident or just on your way to the office, it's almost certain that I will want to exorcise you. That's because there's a high chance you'll be wearing a backpack and backpacks are my pet hate. Small or large, I cannot stomach the way they jiggle up and down, particularly when someone runs. *Eurgh!* Personally, I think any kind of man-bag is an abomination, but backpacks are the worst offenders. I don't care whether it has life-saving equipment in it. I don't care that it carried your trusted MacBook Air in the moments before the e-scooter crashed into you and spontaneously combusted. In death, as in life, I will have no truck with bastard backpacks.

Ick No. 2

I once read about a guy who died in a motorcycle accident and began haunting a pub near to where the fatal crash happened. Not satisfied with sitting by the bar and quietly nursing a pint and munching on a packet of pork scratchings, he decided to touch-up innocent girls on a night out: tit-groping, hand-up-the-thigh, arse-pinching levels of touching-up. For fuck's sake – it's bad enough when someone tries this in real life. And it shows so little imagination. (Perv: *'If I was a ghost I'd hang out in the women's changing rooms, hahaha.'* We get it, you're a perv.) Pervy ghosts are not even mildly amusing. And it's frustrating, too, because who or what do you slap? Fresh air? And the thought of a pervy ghost turning up at my home and eyeing me in some voyeuristic fantasy while I'm in the shower also gives me the ick. Especially as I wear a shower cap with water babies on it.

Ick No. 3

I completely understand that most ghosts will have had an untimely, violent or difficult death, but that's no reason to be a mood hoover. Skulking around, keeping everyone awake, crying in a corridor – it's ridiculous, grandstanding bullshit. I mean, even the maker of Cluedo realised that a corridor was a feeble place to die, which is why you never hear: *'Professor Plum in the corridor with the lead piping!'* People die tragic deaths in studies, billiard rooms, conservatories.

And, with some consideration, they don't suck the lifeblood out of the living when they return. If you're coming back as a ghost, have some fucking balls. Haunt an actual room or hang around somewhere lively like a nightclub or the Zombie ride at Ocean Beach Pleasure Park. Have some fun! You only live twice . . .

Ick No. 4

For me, one of the most irritating ghosts was Sam, the spirit guide of the late psychic Derek Acorah. This makes 'assistant spirits' also high up on my list of ghosts that give me the ick. Sam smacked of desperation, like the weird kid who hung out with the school bully – the kid who never had it in him to be the front man. Similarly, Sam hovered around Derek like a bad fart wanting to bask in the sweet scent of celebrity. I cannot comprehend why any ghost would be willing to inhabit working men's clubs, random church halls or auditoriums with a middle-aged medium every night and not even get paid. And where is he now that Derek himself has passed on? Out of work and nowhere to be seen! And these ghost helpers always have pathetic names like Pete or Alex or Sam. Stop chasing the coat-tails of the living – if you're that shit-hot, reveal yourself and get your own hit show!

Ick No. 5

I've never met a greedy ghost, but I reckon one would do my head in: the kind of ghost that would think nothing of hogging the reduced counter at Tesco. Everyone knows the type: the vulture that tries to get in before the assistant has even finished stacking the shelf and adding the yellow labels; the kind that manoeuvres their giant arse around to block entry to anyone trying to get a look-in; the type that would gather up the entire four legs of lamb at half price, denying anyone else a chance. It's not as if this ghost would even have a freezer to store them in! Ghosts consumed by endless wanting are devoid of any human goodness, in my view. If you are a hollow, selfish creature, not even moved by other people's plight during the cost-of-living crisis, then do one.

Ick No. 6

I don't know if ghosts have a say in what clothes or get-up they are going to come back in, but ghosts that dress badly are a massive no-no. Who would choose to come back to haunt people in flares and a bad 1970s hairdo? Who would choose to haunt anyone in leg warmers and pixie boots? Surely if anything is possible in the spirit realm, can't they at least be fashionable? As a bare minimum it should have flicked through the pages of *Vogue* or *Cosmopolitan* to see what's trending. I'm not pretending to know what, if any, rules govern this. I mean, what happens if you die at a fancy-dress party and end up returning as an ancient Egyptian or a Cavalier? That would be so fucking confusing. Does this also mean you have to think carefully about how you dress whenever you leave the house? Mum drummed into me the importance of wearing nice knickers in case I ever got run over by a car, but this adds a whole new dimension to the problem. Nevertheless, a ghost who hasn't thought through his or her post-death attire shows an utter lack of effort.

Rant over.

13

THE PARANORMAL AT WORK

It's 2011 and a taxi driver is picking up his first passenger of the evening. She's a woman alone, dressed in an unusually thick coat for the hot summer weather. At the city's main transport hub, she climbs in.

'Where would you like to go?' the driver asks.

'Minamihama.'

'Are you sure?' he checks.

The district is in the Japanese city of Ishimakishi. But the area that the woman wants to be driven to is virtually empty. Few houses remain standing and rubble and burned-out cars are strewn across every street. It's all but been destroyed in the devastating earthquake and tsunami that hit Japan several months before.

'That area has been lost to the waves,' the driver stresses, as he leans over and starts his meter running.

The woman's reply is chilling.

'Have I died?' she says, her voice trembling.

When the cabbie turns around again to answer, she's no longer sitting on the back seat. She's vanished into thin air.

This driver is not the only cabbie in the city to report such spine-chilling happenings in the months after the disaster that killed more than 16,000 across Japan and 3,000 people in Ishimakishi alone.

Another driver reported a young guy who disappeared en route to a formerly popular tourist spot in the city, Mount Hiyoriyama. Another passenger ceased to exist, evaporated like a will-o'-the-wisp, the moment he realised his home had been destroyed.

In the years that followed, a total of seven accounts were gathered by a student from a Japanese university who had started investigating unusual sightings in the region. At first, no one wanted to admit what they'd seen, but gradually some of the city's workers started to open up to her.

Each report had a similar thread running through it. All of the passengers were young, a fact that the researcher thought was important. Her hunch was that of everyone who had lost their lives, the young might feel the most bitter about having their existence snuffed out prematurely and being separated from their loved ones.

At this point, though, you have to ask: what the actual fuck? First of all, what strikes me as odd is how well behaved these young passengers are. Maybe it's just me, but most young people picked up late at night in the UK are so pissed they can barely remember their own name. One look in the rear-view mirror and you'll see their heads lolling around, repeatedly swallowing down the next wave of sick that could erupt at any time. Either that or they're trying to have a drunken fumble on the back seat.

Honestly, there are some mornings in the past when I've woken up and I don't even know how I got home. All I know is that there's £40 missing from my wallet and I'm haunted by the vague recollection of singing Britney's 'I'm a Slave 4 U' at the top of my voice while spraying rip-off Jo Malone Peony and Blush Suede up my miniskirt for good measure.

One cabbie I absolutely love who operates around my area has a full suite of onboard entertainment, including a virtual-reality headset for PS5 gamers. What a fucking legend – although it is a high-risk strategy to mix cyberspace with passengers about to projectile barf a bottle of Chardonnay and five vodka shots all over your divider screen. Whenever he picks me up I always give him a fat tip just to congratulate him on the utter lunacy of his business model.

'It's the fucking future, trust me, Dais,' he tells me every time I jump in.

Anyway, I digress. As far as Japan goes, it is perhaps wholly understandable why there would be so many tormented spirits wandering around, randomly bumping into the living as disorientated as Snoop Dogg at a garden party. After all, in the aftermath of the earthquake and tsunami the tiny nation had undergone one of the worst traumas that had befallen it since the Second World War. Non-believers would say these experiences were the result of that trauma – that survivors were imagining these figures as a way to process all the terrible grief they were going through.

There is no proof one way or the other. But the cabbies' recollections did seem very plausible. Pretty damn sweet, actually. All those interviewed had covered the non-existent fares, and one even said he'd be happy to pick up these so-called ghost passengers again. I don't know about you, but there's something about this story that tells me that these people were telling the God's honest truth. Why else would they fork out like that for fuck's sake? If they truly believed their passengers were ghosts and experienced their passengers as ghosts, then I am erring on that version of events.

In the same city, although there were no other stories of ghosts fare dodging on other forms of transport, there were equally strange reports of people seen queuing for shops that were once open. Tragically, some were headless, others missing hands or legs. The main street had been reduced to rubble but the queues still persisted – ethereal figures that could be seen standing then fading into thin air, inexplicably dropping out of the universe like socks in a tumble dryer.

☆

The whole idea of people encountering ghosts while at work fascinates me. And I believe it does happen far more than people realise. For those bearing the brunt of lost fares, missing takings, stocktakes that make absolutely no sense whatsoever, it can be wholly unnerving. And its always staff who get the blame. Random bag checks put in force. But what if other forces are at play?

Sensibly in my view, ghosts have been haunting pubs for donkey's years. And when you think about it, it's a smart choice. One: there's alcohol. Two: it's warm. Three: you can probably get a seat if you time it right during the week. Friday and Saturday night might be a bit trickier, especially if there's a shit band taking up a whole corner, but there's usually a spot hovering by the bar. And I reckon ghosts are bloody brilliant at pub quizzes, especially the history round.

But it's ghosts that inhabit other workplaces that can be unfathomable. It was particularly strange that several people wrote to me with reports of paranormal activity in Claire's. I find this an odd choice for the undead, unless they had been eyeing up a bats deely bopper or the cute skeleton drop earrings.

A woman called Vicky contacted me with an even stranger tale of a ghost she learned to work alongside during her time at Superdrug.

Poor Arthur. Vicky had been warned about him before she began working at the shop despite the fact that only a few people employed there had ever seen him or heard him; but, as Vicky explained, she got to know him quite well. 'I didn't believe the stories, however scant they were, but pretty soon after I started working there weird things started happening,' she told me.

Arthur seemed to pick his haunting times very carefully. He began his activity around closing time, when no one else was in the store other than Vicky and her manager.

'Products from the other side of the room would somehow end up behind me while I was tidying. I'd hear whistling in my ear, and a man's voice, even though no men worked there.

'One night my handbag had been taken from my locker. I couldn't find it anywhere until, as a last resort, I went into the men's toilets and found it placed perfectly in the middle of the room.'

Most extraordinary to me, though, is Arthur's apparent love of hair products. Sadly, it's as if he lived in completely the wrong era. Maybe all he desperately wanted was to be a contestant on *RuPaul's*

Drag Race or host *Queer Eye for the Straight Guy* but never got his big chance. If you don't mind me saying, Vicky, I think rooted in your ghost Arthur's mischief lies some deep-seated frustration about his sexuality, like a pound-shop Elton John.

Vicky continued: 'The middle aisle right by the door was filled with hair products. One night, I was pulling all the products to the front of the shelves. There was one can of hairspray that fell off the shelf every time I pulled it to the front. I picked it up and put it back but as soon as I walked away, it would fall off again. It happened three or four times before I said: "Nope, I'm not putting it back again." Eerily, when my manager came out and put it back on the shelf it stayed.

'Then I turned to the other side of the aisle and started doing the same with the hair dye, pulling it all to the front. One box of hair dye kept falling off the shelves. Again, this happened three or four times until I had had enough. I pulled up a stool and sat by the front door and recorded the aisle on my phone. I was so scared. At first nothing happened, but as soon as I spoke three boxes of hair dye flew up into the air and onto the floor.'

Hmmmm. The handbag placed neatly in the middle of the men's toilet; the hair dye; the hairspray. I may be way off the mark here, but I wonder whether Arthur was just trying to find a quiet space, undisturbed by the general public, where he could do his self-care in peace? Maybe his behaviour was a hint for you, Vicky, to hurry up and go home. And maybe he wasn't dormant all day at all? Maybe he was off drifting around Topshop before the tween rush to try on that lime green maxi dress and the belt with faux amber gold stones? All he ever wanted to do every evening was crank up the in-store sound system, bang on Nicki Minaj and slut-drop to his own reflection in the Superdrug loos.

I have to admit to having a massive soft spot for Arthur already. I don't think he was acting like a total arse-wipe. To me, he just sounds like a feminine ghost trapped in a man's body with a man's name. And I hope his chosen brand was L'Oréal: because Arthur sounds like he's worth it.

A woman called Laura also told me about a ghost she'd experienced when she worked at Caffè Nero in Doncaster. This sounds to me like all the classic hallmarks of a fucking entitled ghost who wants to impress his spirit mates with a large iced sugar-free vanilla latte with soy milk served with a pain au chocolat on the side.

This ghost may have been trying to do Laura a favour, though. Either that or it is entirely a figment of Laura's overactive imagination designed to get her out of doing any work whatsoever. And I feel well placed to say this, Laura, because what follows is exactly the kind of shit excuse I would have given when I worked in a department store.

Laura's ghost apparently haunted the top floor of the Caffè Nero building, which once upon a time had been used as an orphanage. There were still children's beds and old furniture and fireplaces littering the rooms and corridors. Laura says:

At the end of my first week I was in the building alone doing a stock take and catching up on some paperwork. Part of my job was to check the fire alarm panels were working. One of the panels that needed to be checked was on that top floor which meant I needed to walk from my office, through a fire door and up some stairs to the floor I knew was creepy.

Fuck. Fuck. Fuck. I have a bad feeling about this one . . .

It was dark by this point. And as I opened the door to walk up the stairs, I froze. What can only be described as an invisible force field began pushing against me. It was the strangest physical sensation of something pushing me back. Every instinct told me not to go up the stairs, so I decided to fuck off the last fire alarm panel check and just signed the sheet as working. I never dared open that door again.

I don't blame you, Laura. But I would like to point out one rather obvious element of this story that does concern me. I hope to fucking God there was never a fire because I do not fancy your chances at explaining that you sacked off a major health and safety check just because an unexplained spectral force was holding you back from completing it.

'Yeah, nice try, love. Ever heard of gross negligence?'

☆

Totally bewildering to me is a ghost who loves to hang out in an office block – you can barely get the living into offices these days. At least in a taxi you're going somewhere, you can take in a few of the sights. In a shop you can make shit jokes about starring in your own *Little Shop of Horrors*. But offices? To me that's like dying over and over and over again in the longest fucking meeting about a meeting, the theme of which is some action points to be discussed in . . . another fucking meeting. Oh. My. God. Why the fuck would you choose to stay here?

Theories abound about why the undead may choose to haunt these types of spaces. Some say that all workaholics may want to do is stay in the place they spent the most time in because they feel a deep affinity with that location. If that is the case, then I can guarantee I will end up haunting a bedroom, refusing to give over my bed and duvet to the living and fending off anyone who tries to separate me from my remote control.

Lots of people die at work too. Mainly from boredom would be my guess. Although I suppose there is some fun to be had as a ghost in an office if you were the light-hearted type. I've read loads of reports of random photocopiers switching on and spewing out reams of paper by themselves. Could this be a ghost amusing itself by photocopying its own arse cheeks? Whoopee cushions on people's chairs could also be quite a laugh, and it does give a whole new meaning to the term 'graveyard shift'.

★

I'll end the chapter with a story of a ghost at work that was sent to me by a fellow West Country dweller called Tamsin that I have become completely and utterly obsessed by. I cannot get it out of my head at all. I'll let Tamsin explain:

Between my undergraduate and master's degrees in London, I returned to my parents' to recover from academic trauma and postpone pursuing some kind of soul-destroying corporate job. During this time I worked in a clothes shop in Stroud, which sold almost everything for £10. Imagine the place swarming with middle-aged and elderly ladies who varied from delightful to horrendous (apparently £10 per garment isn't always cheap enough!).

On this particular day, it was unusually quiet in the shop. A middle-aged woman with blonde hair ventured in with her friend. I greeted them politely as I did all customers and they looked around like everyone before them had done that day.

The blonde woman then told her friend that she wouldn't be a minute and her friend should go outside without her. Already, this struck me as odd because the woman didn't seem to have any intention of buying anything. As soon as the dinging bell indicated that the door had closed behind her friend, the woman darted to the nearest standing clothes rail and swiftly ducked behind it. My blood ran cold. Was she trying to steal something? It was such a sudden and unexpected movement that felt . . . urgent. She clearly wanted me to look.

Before I had a moment to register whether I had a bizarre robbery on my hands, her head popped out from behind the clothes rail, protruding from a serpentine neck that was extending and contorting unnaturally. Her eyes seemed crazed; her long tongue flicked and hissed. The moment was over as soon as it had begun. She immediately switched back to normal, stood up and left the shop like nothing had happened.

Fuck me. I've seen some mental things in Stroud – apple hurling in January; the bovine tourist trail. Both weird and unnecessary. I've even attended a big cat support group set up for traumatised survivors of supposed big cat sightings where I aggressively eyeballed a man with a *Lion King* T-shirt (just don't ask!). But this is off the scale! Demonic possession in the bosom of a quaint market town in the Cotswolds?

But . . . but . . . but . . . hang on a minute. Before I get carried away, Tamsin did do her degree in medieval demonology, magic and witchcraft. According to her one of the typical manifestations of demonic possession is unnatural body movements and contortions. But can this happen? Seriously? Maybe it was just Tamsin's mind playing tricks, picturing the images she'd probably seen in numerous textbooks. And any self-respecting sceptic would ask whether this was a vision brought on by extreme stress or a hallucination caused by zero sleep – we've all been there, haven't we? But Tasmin has considered all of these possibilities and remains convinced that this is not the case. Over to her:

It could be argued that this was simply an encounter with one of the local eccentrics, or perhaps a more distressing manifestation of someone's mental illness. However, what I can't explain was the woman's neck length and movement . . . a human neck simply cannot move or extend like that.

This also happened during the day, at work – I guarantee that I was 100 per cent awake and alert. I have since experienced hallucinations as a symptom of Covid and subsequently long Covid. This experience was very, very different.

I have also read and listened to many accounts of encounters with perceived evil. Witnesses often recall a palpable, primordial presence; a sense of dread like no other. And perhaps, most disconcertingly, a feeling that they are in genuine danger. That day I felt threatened in a way I never have felt before.

Tamsin, I am shitting myself on your behalf. And I cannot thank you enough for sharing your story.

☆

14

THE SPIRITS OF INTIMACY

I was afraid I was going to veer off track – well, crash and burn off the road entirely – when I typed into Google the question: can you have a relationship with a ghost? Seriously, I'd never thought about it before. Sure, I felt a frisson as a clay-spattered Demi Moore got her pottery ruined by clumsy lover Patrick Swayze's inability to handle wet clay in the film *Ghost*. Who didn't?

And I felt rising irritation at Jamie, the ghost who came back to haunt his girlfriend Nina in the film *Truly, Madly, Deeply*. It left me with the niggling question: who the hell turns the central heating up that high unless you're in an old people's home?

But, I'd never *seriously* thought about a relationship with a ghost in the real world. The question threw up some mind-blowing answers. Unbeknown to me, there's a parallel universe of ghostly trysts going on that has been an absolute revelation.

Here's a small taste of what I found on a variety of online forums.

'I'm dating a 35-year-old man who was born in 1820. He's sweet, caring and considerate and I love that he calls me Princess.'

'Why didn't I find my ghost girlfriend before? She's so pretty and very stylish. She was born in 1920 and I really love her fashion sense, too.'

'This spirit is the best thing that's ever happened to me.'

'When I dated a spirit, it didn't go well and it took many years for her uneasy and uncomfortable presence to leave me.'

'Dating a spirit is a whole world of pain. Been there, done that, worn the T-shirt. Won't be doing it again. Still gives me the willies.'

So, dear readers, I'm sure you will appreciate that once I had opened this batshit crazy Pandora's box, I had to keep researching. Whether these souls are *actually* dating a ghost or simply believe they are dating a ghost I will never know – and, as the saying goes, never say never – but it has spewed up some interesting questions about ghost love, ghost dating, ghost marriage and . . . yup, strap in for the ride, because we're going there . . . the murky world of supernatural sex.

Admittedly, there's been times in the past when it has felt as though I've been dating the undead or a lead character from the zombie apocalypse. Though my one minimum requirement in any boyfriend is that he must have a pulse. No matter how hideous the relationship (believe me some have been dreadful – read my autobiography) it did not once occur to me that I could turn my attention to the spirit world. I mean, how the actual fuck do you go about finding a ghost partner, anyway? And if you do find one, should change your Facebook status to 'In a relationship'?

DESPERATELY SEEKING GHOST BOYFRIEND

38-year-old woman seeks the pleasure of a ghost for candlelit meals, weekend walks and imaginary sparkling conversation. Would prefer a head and torso, but is willing to compromise. While not specifically seeking a poltergeist, a ghost who knows how to lift and operate a sex toy will be considered. The Viking period is of particular interest to me – fit, muscular and able to provide when needs be. Stone Age – don't bother.

But I reckon dating a ghost comes with as many upsides as it does downsides. In the age of Internet dating being ghosted has become commonplace – that gut-wrenching moment when a complete and utter bastard cuts off all contact with you and doesn't have the balls to give you a reason. At least if you were dating an actual ghost this wouldn't feel weird or rude, even. Implicit in the relationship would be the understanding that your partner would disappear all the time. You'd learn to get over it.

I think ghosts could be amazingly low-maintenance partners too. You wouldn't have to worry about a ghost snoring in bed, hogging the bathroom in the morning, not doing their fair share of housework or childcare. And, if they had really bad fashion sense or an unsightly facial mole that sprouted gargantuan amounts of hair then being invisible means they would never show you up in public or embarrass you in front of your mates.

Even the mighty Madonna has reached out to the other side, as documented in her 1989 song 'Supernatural'. She really got into her ghost boyfriend – he wasn't demanding, was obsessed with his hair and he didn't care that she came home late. The American singer Kesha has also dabbled with the supernatural and claimed to have a haunted vagina after a ghost got stuck there. According to her, she waved a paranormal detector around her nether regions and it just kept beeping. I feel Kesha's pain. There have been occasions when my own cooter has felt like a gateway to the recently departed.

If I could choose my ideal ghost mate they'd be a dreamboat mix of liberated and gentlemanly. The kind of guy from a bygone era who would be happy to pick up the bill for dinner or throw a coat over a puddle for me to step over if it was raining but would equally think nothing of supporting the suffragette movement. Or if you got your arse pinched on market day, he'd have no fear in challenging the culprit to pistols at dawn.

Dates could be more fun too.

'Fancy a local execution this evening, my darling?'

'Oh, why not? And it's only Wednesday! You do spoil me!'

'Special treat, my love.'

Hanging out with his undead mates might get a bit tedious after a while but it's probably a small price to pay.

But according to my research some ghosts don't make ideal partners *at all* – one woman, Amethyst, who I sat glued to on *This Morning*, found herself catapulted into a fucking appalling relationship with a ghost. It's sad because it sounded as if it was all going so well. She'd met Ray on holiday in Australia and it was love at first sight? Or first . . . sense? Who knows? Anyway, they'd been dating for a while and she'd been planning on marrying him. But Amethyst was forced to call off her big day after a later holiday went completely tits-up. In 2020, she and Ray embarked on a trip to Thailand together, which did sound amazing. But Ray changed beyond all recognition while they were out there.

Previously he'd been loving but now she accused him of falling in with the wrong crowd, disappearing for hours on end, drinking and taking drugs, then bringing back all kinds of random spirits to their hotel room. What a fucking oafish idiot! In the end she had to kick him out and cleanse the room with sage. I shit you not, I sat on the edge of my sofa. My mouth was agape.

Another woman I watched with the same fascination on a particularly touching episode of *Say Yes to the Dress* was also due to marry a ghost. His name was Eduardo. According to the bride-to-be, he'd been a Victorian soldier but she also sensed he was a 'bit of a rebel' and had possibly been a rock star in a previous life too. At that description, I had high hopes for Eduardo.

And the way they met sounded *incredible*! He turned up on a stormy night, not in any physical form, but Brocarde, the bride, suddenly felt an intense burning in her chest. I get that after a chicken tikka bhuna. Disappointingly, he ended up showing his true aura too. Honestly, he started swinging his cock around more than Ray. He turned out to be a coercive controller, especially when it came to what he wanted his bride-to-be to wear.

Apparently he didn't approve of Brocarde wearing low-cut tops or any item of clothing that showed off too much flesh. He was from the Victorian era, after all. But the male entitlement still really got to me. The worst thing was that poor Brocarde went along with all of this. He was the love of her life, she said. She didn't ever want to piss him off for fear of losing him. Cue yours truly screaming at the telly: 'No, Brocarde, no! Don't do it! It starts with the dress, but next he'll be telling you what mates you can or can't go out with. He'll stop you from having that last vodka tonic because apparently you're too tipsy and behaving like a complete arse-wipe. Or you'll be constantly looking over your shoulder in Tesco while he tells you what food you can put into your trolley!' As I watch the scenario unfolding I feel like I've lived this relationship already in the human world.

Goes to show, if you could choose your ghost partner why would you willingly opt for a controlling Victorian ghost? Because of this, part of me thinks that Brocarde's ghost boyfriend was not a figment of her deliciously nutty imagination. Wouldn't an imaginary ghost be supportive of whatever you wore? If he's dreamed up, why put in place those kinds of restrictions? Why create problems in the relationship when there doesn't need to be any? That's like throwing a massive tantrum because your ghost boyfriend doesn't do enough DIY when you know full well that he can't even hold a hammer.

I fear for supernatural relationships like this one. As soon as I gained a deeper insight into what was going on I predicted it would end in divorce, despite the gorgeous dress Tan France and his team conjured up for Brocarde. As I suspected, the marriage lasted all of a few weeks. Eduardo got fucking hammered on their honeymoon in Barry Island and apparently went from warm and intense to threatening. And that's the other baffling part of this story – Barry Island? *The* Barry Island in Wales? I'm not dissing it but surely there are more romantic destinations? Although I hear the pleasure park does have a ghost train and bungee trampolines.

★

Ghost marriages did get me thinking, though. Is it even legal to marry a ghost? Very disappointingly, in the UK it isn't. No priest will marry you. Not even a registrar will preside over your nuptials. But bizarrely, in some cultures marrying a ghost is a perfectly acceptable act.

In Taiwan the living can take part in a ghost marriage purely because it is believed that if one person dies then his or her spirit will feel lonely in the afterlife and should have a partner to restore balance and harmony to their life (back to the yin and yang theory) otherwise they may come back with unfinished business. I think that's pretty sweet.

In China, ghost marriages aren't technically legal but they are informally practised, especially if a son or daughter goes to his or her grave before a planned marriage takes place. If something isn't done about the situation, a spirit could wreak havoc on the family, particularly in the form of serious illness. If it's the man who dies before he's married, then his fiancée is permitted to marry his spirit. But this is where it gets fucking weird. In the ceremony a white rooster stands in for the groom. The cock (resist the urge, Dais) also rides in the same carriage as the bride after the ceremony and later gets to turn up to any dealings with the groom's family. I cannot even begin to imagine what the wedding photographs would turn out like or how the rooster conducts those all-important negotiations on who gets the house. Cock-a-doodle-doo for a yes? Shits a pellet for no?

Trust me, I did try to find a more accurate answer but I am still none the wiser.

Over in Japan a ghost marriage often involves the ghost of the deceased marrying a doll in a full kimono. However, if the marriage is between a living woman and a dead man, a photo of the dead man is also placed in a glass case with the doll during the ceremony to cement the union and to keep the ghost husband calm. He has 30 years to wait before it is assumed he has successfully passed into the next realm. *Fucking hell . . .*

And, I shit you not, France is one of the few countries where marrying a dead person is totally legal. For this to happen, the living must prove that the couple intended to marry before one half unceremoniously dumped the other by gasping their last breath. Other terms and conditions apply as he or she also needs permission from the deceased's family.

The law sounds like it's a hangover from ancient times, but it isn't. Unbelievably, it was only introduced in 1959. It happened after a vast dam on the French Riviera collapsed, drowning more than four hundred people. The story goes that when the then French president Charles de Gaulle visited the site, one woman pleaded with him to allow her to marry her dead fiancée. He said something along the lines of, *'All right then.'* Since then thousands of bereaved people, mainly women, have married their dearly departed sweethearts.

And you know what the best thing is? Before almost all of these ceremonies you can still write a wedding list. Just because your betrothed isn't actually breathing, it doesn't mean you have to miss out on the thick-slice toaster or cutlery set or George Foreman grill that will get shoved in a cupboard never to see the light of day.

Plus, there's often a party or celebration, so you don't forego any fun, either. If you want glitter cannons and a three-tiered cake with penguin toppers you can fucking have it. The hen or stag do beforehand would be a sight to behold, though. I have a vision of lap dancers grinding on empty chairs.

How you manage the honeymoon is another level of entirely mystifying decisions to make. Do you book an extra seat on the flight or let the deceased hover near you? Do you pay the extra and book a double room? Do you book for two at the hotel restaurant and order for your deceased partner, then scoff it all yourself? Personally, I would stash the cash and insist on him hovering nearby – that's what a real gentleman would do.

Then once the honeymoon's over and reality kicks in, that's when a ghost partner is going to have to step up. It's so easy to let the rot set in. At the very least he or she is going to have to know how to haunt considerately. Turning a shower on now and again and walking around at weird hours probably isn't enough to dump it. God knows, we've all got our faults. To really make it until death (again) do you part, your ghost partner would have to be amazing in the sex department to hold your interest. And this dovetails neatly into my next topic: orgasmic ghosts.

★

Despite Amethyst's disastrous marriage to Ray, she is on record saying that when it comes to sex, spirits leave her more satisfied. She won't go back to a human, ever. But from what I've seen and read, it's not all red roses and poems on the pillow in the ghostly Garden of Eden.

Take the incubus, for example. I'm not going to beat around the bush here. He is an animalistic, predatory demon who mainly visits women in their sleep. Thankfully, no one who contacted me reported any such visitations and debate does rage about whether reported experiences are real. Psychiatrists will say that it's the result of something called sleep paralysis, that weird state between sleep and consciousness when you're having a vivid dream but are unable to move. Or it's the result of hallucinations brought on by madness or boredom or something like that.

Some accounts are fucking dreadful. It goes without saying that sexual assault of any kind is a clear red line and needs instant exorcism, but if you're going to be seduced or temporarily possessed in a consensual rendezvous you'd want to be awake, surely? I don't pretend to be overly energetic in that department, but I'd have to be comatose to say: 'Don't mind me, wake me up when you're done.' But the incubus is also clever and has been known to try any tactic to have its wicked way. Some have even promised women eternal youth and power, for fuck's sake. No matter how forceful or sexy he is, don't fall for it, girls. If Garnier anti-ageing face serum can't deliver that, I doubt an incubus can.

Then there's the succubus – the female equivalent of the sex demon. These can just turn up unannounced to haunt the object of their desires or can be summoned. I'm not a hundred per cent sure how people go about calling a succubus. And, let's face it, like so may other festishes, Internet porn has probably filled that gap in the market.

(Yes, in the spirit of investigation I have checked and paranormal porn is an actual sub-genre.) But if you can be arsed to pursue the old-fashioned route I don't think a succubus demands credit card details or has names like Elvira Roze or Lady Deliverance. That said, you summon a succubus at your peril.

Both in their male incubus or female succubus form these manifestations are there to do you harm. Quite literally some will fuck you to death. Before the thought crosses your mind, just think of Sigourney Weaver in *Ghostbusters* and that fucking dated orange dress and Eighties hair. It should be enough to put you off.

According to other accounts, sex with a household paranormal entity rather than an over-excited sex demon is a better prospect. And surprisingly its very, very common. It's even got a name – spectrophilia. But it still feels like a massive paranormal taboo to talk about it – of course, that's part of the reason why I am talking about it.

According to lots of mediums, completely sane people report being visited by the ghosts of dead lovers or just strangers – not in a vengeful or threatening way, but in a good way.

Some people are able to manifest the ghost of their dreams and have a fucking great time with them. Can you see where this is going? Yep, please, please don't judge me. In another 'spirit of enquiry' moment I attempted to get jiggy with a ghost.

Admittedly, it was hard to know how to set the mood. And when you're a busy working mum it's difficult to fit in an encounter with anyone, let alone the other realm – amiright? I decided a weekday mid-afternoon rendezvous was probably my only chance, squeezed in between a Tesco shop and banging some turkey drummers into the oven ready for when my kids came home from school.

Did I need to wear anything sexy? Probably not. I figured that a ghost would be able to undress me and pass through me any way it wanted. Wasted effort to get out my plunge bra and matching knickers. Besides, I didn't want to look desperate. I opted for my pink Barbie sweatshirt and cotton lounging shorts. It was 3pm, and I was feeling a tad nervous. Too early for a glass of vino? Probably . . . but what the hell. I needed something to loosen me up a bit. I sat in the kitchen for half an hour with a glass or two . . . or three listening to 'I'll Make Love to You' by Boyz II Men on repeat. Then, it was time . . .

Upstairs, I drew the curtains and a lit couple of candles – cinnamon is supposed to be an aphrodisiac, so a cinnamon candle was lit, making it more like the bakery section of a Morrisons than a sexy setting. That would do – nice soft lighting. I didn't want to give any spirit the excuse of a headache. Shit . . . what next? I had taken some notes from mediums I'd read online. They advised lying on my back and doing some yoga breathing. Not one described how I should I lie. Legs akimbo in an open-all-hours kind of way? Was that too forward? Maybe . . . Or clamped shut? Was that too straight-laced? Fucking hell . . . this was turning out to be a minefield. Again, I figured that a ghost probably wouldn't give a flying fuck. It might not even make a beeline for my cooter anyway. Do ghosts do foreplay? No idea! And if I did get a visitation, I hoped to God it wasn't a ghost with a weird kink. I've been there already and it didn't end well. That particular boyfriend loved being an inanimate object – a coat hanger, a footstool, a human rug I'd have to walk over in Primark stilettos. It did give him a massive boner, but it got tedious after a while. Besides, pretending to ping a human microwave is not remotely attractive. Not even if he has got an automatic defrost setting.

Back in my bedroom, I placed my thumb over one nostril. Breathe in for the count of five . . . then, slowly exhale for the count of ten. Jesus Christ . . . it was then I realised that the half-bottle of Chardonnay probably hadn't been a good idea. I felt dizzy . . . *really* dizzy. At this rate I wouldn't even be able to give my ghost boyfriend a half-arsed blower. I lay for a while, trying to focus on a spot on the ceiling until the room stopped spinning.

Many of the online articles I'd read also suggested that I imagine my ghostly lover. I shut my eyes and tried to conjure up my ideal ghost. The Viking idea was one I flirted with for a while, but I stopped myself. On balance I wasn't sure I wanted to summon someone who considered plunder, rape and pillage simply a warm-up on a weekday afternoon. All the advice was: keep it light. *Think, Daisy, think. Yes! Yes! Yes!* Eventually, I got it. I don't know why I hadn't thought of him before – Ben Shephard. My ideal imaginary fuck. He'd be a real gent too. Now I felt embarrassed I'd got a bit pissed. If anyone would understand, though, it would be Ben.

Some mediums recommended some light chanting. *Fucking hell* . . . What do you say? I closed my eyes again and took a deep breath.

'Ben, if you can hear this . . . come to me . . .'

I felt absolutely nothing other than creeping humiliation and rising anxiety. Suddenly, I heard a weird crackling from the corner of the room. *Fuck*. It was the cinnamon candle. When I looked over the wick had burned right down. Any longer it could leave a massive scorch mark on my dressing table and possibly set fire to my curtains. I leaped up and blew it out immediately. Hmmmm . . . Then it dawned on me. Ben Shephard is very much alive. Why would he want to visit me in a ghostly form?

Back to the drawing board. I searched the recesses of my mind remembering my dreamboat Victorian – the women's libber but also the man who was courteous and caring. Plus those sideburns the size of a small rodent and a hat could really do it for me – Dick Van Dyke to my Mary Poppins. At last I was in the zone.

'Spirit come to me . . .'

Suddenly, I felt a tingle on the back of my left foot. Could this be the way my spirit lover announced himself? Maybe I'd conjured a ghost with a foot fetish . . . I felt the tingle again. No. It was in the exact spot where I'd Bazuka'd a verruca the night before.

I lay there for a further five minutes. I don't know why but every time I tried to focus on the hot Victorian, a bloke that had an uncanny resemblance to *EastEnders*' Phil Mitchell kept popping into my head. My fanny recoiled. I tried to banish the vision, but the more I stamped it down the more it reappeared.

Sadly, I still wasn't feeling anything. Apparently, one of the barriers to experiencing ghost sex is if you don't believe enough. But I did and I still *do* believe. I *really* believe. Ten minutes after that, I felt the sudden urge to get up and go for a piss. It seemed to interrupt the magic and as I sat on the toilet I realised that the moment was probably over. I couldn't help feeling a weighty pang of rejection, though. *Jesus* . . . not even a ghost wants to fuck me. Is it my nose?

Or my choice of sweatshirt? Was the stench of cinnamon too much? Surely if you were dead this would be the offer you'd jump at? Bastard. I guess I'll never know . . .

   Since then I haven't tried to summon a sex ghost again, but I'd like to if I knew one would come. Maybe I'll just wait until the ghost of my dreams knocks on my door. Just like everything in the paranormal world, I remain open . . .

☆

15

DAISY TRIES TO JOIN
A WITCHES' COVEN

'So, Daisy, thanks for coming on the call with us today.'

'Absolutely fine.' I smiled politely.

It was not as fine as I was making out. In fact, I was feeling pretty perplexed by the whole rigmarole, but we were in Covid-19 lockdown number fuck-knows-what and I understood the request for a Zoom call. The problem was I felt like a contestant on *The Apprentice* about to be grilled by the female equivalent of Alan Sugar – half-woman, half-wolverine. Although the screen was a little pixelated, I couldn't help but clock the verdant forest of armpit hair sprouting out from each side of her vest top. There was zero bra in sight and I became mesmerised by the outline of larger-than-normal areolae pointing southwards.

Don't judge, Dais, I thought to myself. After all, I'd never conversed with a witch before, let alone a High Priestess witch. Maybe they don't do underwear? Or lady topiary? And part of me did feel pretty damn impressed by her wild abandon of the shackles of 21st-century womanhood. I mean, who can be arsed shaving unless the promise of a shag is at least 80 per cent in the bag? But it also made me barf slightly. The witches of lore I'd read about were hairy-lipped and snaggle-toothed, and I couldn't help thinking this woman was living out her own stereotype. Aren't modern witches allowed a little self-care? Maybe a spot of lip filler? As for the bloke sitting beside her, he was supposed to be the High Priest. Fuck me. I'd seen toilet brushes with more charisma. This was not what I expected at all.

'So, Daisy, it's great to meet you.'

'Likewise,' I said, hesitantly.

There was an uncomfortable pause as the pair eyeballed me.

'We're going to be frank with you, Daisy. We're a little concerned . . .'

'Oh, right. Why?'

'Well, we know who you are and we just need to check that you are here for the right reasons.'

'Okay . . .'

Shit. Shit. Shit. What *were* the right reasons for wanting to join a witches' coven? What the hell should I say? One: I was hoping I might be able to hang out in a forest – just for a couple of hours. Maybe take a breather from my kids. I love them, but the forest is *really* tempting. Two: I have replayed howling at a full moon over and over in my head. I don't even know if witches do this, but if they don't they should. Cathartic, I reckon. Three: I want to learn how to throw a few hexes on some particularly crap ex-boyfriends. That would definitely hit the spot. Also, it's lockdown and I've been going out of my mind. I've been baking banana bread like a coked-up Mary Berry and balancing random household objects under my tits and posting the videos on TikTok just to relieve the aching boredom.

I felt this almighty brainfart of reasons about to tumble from my mouth, but I stopped myself. I didn't think any of those reasons would land well with Glinda and the Wizard of Oz.

I smiled again and took a deep breath. *Think quickly, Daisy. Think quickly.*

'I'm very interested in becoming a witch, meeting like-minded witches and exploring my inner relationship with the natural world. I want to bring more meaning to my life and focus on joy.'

Bit far-fetched but I nailed it I thought. I did want to bring more magic into my life.

'OK, it's just we're concerned that you might want to use your experience with us as material for a TV series . . . or a book . . .'

For fuck's sake. I had gone to the trouble of applying to a witches' coven some distance from my home just to narrow down the chances of being recognised, but I guess the name Daisy May Cooper may have given me away. And, I couldn't 100 per cent promise not to use *anything*. After all, I'm a writer and an actress. Once I see, I can't unsee. Honestly, though, it *really* wasn't why I was there. Anyhow, the questions on the online application form were more difficult than trying to bag a membership to Soho Farmhouse – which is just Center Parcs for celebrity cunts. If I had been gathering material for a TV series I probably would have given up ages ago.

'This is not professional. It's purely personal,' I reassured them.

'You want to focus on joy . . .' the High Priestess repeated, her eyes narrowing suspiciously.

'Yep . . . joy,' I said, shrugging, as if I couldn't believe it either. Then, my words started to run away with me. I could hear myself talking anxiously, filling in the silence.

'I've also just been filming for the part of a witch called Thomasine Gooch in an upcoming BBC series called *The Witchfinder*, but I didn't think much of the depiction. I know there's far more to witchcraft than a ten-parter comedy series starring me and Tim Key. And . . . and . . .'

Shut up, Daisy. You've said enough.

'Okay, thank you,' the High Priestess replied flatly. At that, the Wizard of Oz nodded, then scribbled down some notes on an A4 pad in front of him. I was itching to read what he'd written. I was sure he would have jotted and underscored: 'DEFINITELY NOT WITCH MATERIAL' several times with his ballpoint pen. When he finished, he looked up, faintly grimaced and pushed his thick-rimmed glasses towards the bridge of his nose. Then, without saying a word, he turned to look at the High Priestess. She clearly ruled the roost. Even I felt intimidated by her. She was slightly overweight with hamster cheeks and peroxide-blonde shoulder-length hair which stood out against the dark walls of what I assumed was their dining room. Some of the walls were lined with shelves packed full of fusty-looking books. There were dream-catchers dangling in the background and a red chiffon cloth draped over a low-lit table lamp. And on one wall behind I could just about make out a pencil-sketch nude, hands outstretched, which looked vaguely like the High Priestess. *Is that really her?* I wondered.

'Personal. Not professional,' she repeated.

'Absolutely. Cross my heart. Hope to . . .'

Best not, Daisy.

✫

The bit about my personal interest was true, even if 'finding joy' was probably about as improbable as Severus Snape discovering mindfulness meditation. I have always been interested in witches and witchcraft, and I did want to explore this mysterious world. I wasn't promising I'd be any good at it. Getting too close to nature was already giving me the ick, but I was open enough to try exposing myself to it for an evening. If it freaked me out I wanted the option of going home to a bottle of wine and an episode of *Tiger King* on Netflix. And if these people were to be my guides then so be it. Maybe all witches are this serious? How would I know?

Until then, I'd only made half-arsed steps into the world of Wicca and the magical arts. I'd read gazillions about old-school witches. I'd become well versed in the stories of the Salem witch trials in America during the 17th century when mostly innocent women (and the occasional man) got accused of sorcery and were hanged. Plus the witch-hunts that swept across this country during a similar period of persecution. A pretty brutal way of ditching your spouse in my view.

And witch swimming? Who the fuck thought that one up? It makes no sense whatsoever. If suspected, witches were placed in a body of water. If they sunk to the bottom, they were innocent; if they floated, they were guilty and killed. Either way, they were dead! Drowned at the bottom of a lake or decapitated then melted like a marshmallow on an open fire, which makes the rule of law in 17th-century England an absolute fucking joke.

Thankfully, witchcraft has moved on since then. And it's this modern witchcraft that I've grown up with. Take Sabrina, the teenage witch. In the 1990s she was as close to a 'woke witch' as you could get. I bloody loved her! She was the half-witch I always yearned to be: born of a warlock father and mortal mother, she deftly kept one foot in this world and one foot in the other realm. She was a fearless fighter of injustice – a girl who always helped out her mates with a fleeting spell. Plus, she had a very fit boyfriend called Harvey but who was a bit thick. It took him until season four to even clock his girlfriend was a witch! Nevertheless, Sabrina was a girl who refused to commit 100 per cent to the dark side for fear of losing her independence. Girl power on steroids! *Yes! Yes! Yes!*

Another guilty pleasure of mine was from around the same time: the teen horror movie *The Craft*. In this story four outcast girls are drawn to each other at a Los Angeles high school, then unite in a witches' coven to fight duplicitous boyfriends, racist bullies and cruel step-parents. Over time, they become consumed by their own power, which spirals out of control. I remember watching it on repeat, quietly in awe of this coven but also making a mental note that if I was ever schooled in the dark arts, never to unleash this beast. My narcissism does not need to be fed like a greedy goblin. But I did find the idea of getting off my face on power very, very intoxicating.

Admittedly, my most recent fascination with witchcraft – the reason I was on this Zoom call – didn't stem from the purest of reasons either. Sure, in my more generous moments I'd love to cast spells to save the whole of mankind. I would love it if horrendous, powerful people could wake up to an infestation of rats or snakes or suddenly lose all the wealth they've amassed through dodgy dealing and insider trading. I'd love to cast a spell so that the local animal shelter win a grant from the lottery and are able to look after as many injured hedgehog as physically possible.

I wanted to be a righteous witch. Of course I did! But I was also going through a divorce. I wanted to know how I could get the best settlement. A good barrister was probably the answer, but what if there was a better, cheaper way? Some serious break-up hoodoo.

As a first step I bought a book. Pathetic really, but it was the definitive encyclopedia of spells. Five thousand of them. The 'Ultimate Reference Book for the Magical Arts' it said. As soon as it arrived from Amazon I ripped open the cardboard box and flicked past the introduction with all the restraint of a vampire bat. Yeah, yeah, I know all the stuff about using magic responsibly. I know I'm not supposed to be overly mean or let it go to my head or practise magic simply for my own gain . . . But once I got passed these snooze rules – *fuck me*! – there was some really good shit in there.

There were divorce spells that banished all trace of a partner from a home if that person's aura had been lingering around. There were even spells to protect women's financial independence: one involved dressing a green candle with Jezebel oil and burning it, rolling the wax into an egg shape, then pushing Jezebel root into it using a penny. All that I could do but placing it inside a nest fashioned with twigs and burying the nest egg at a crossroads all seemed like a lot of effort. Still, it was a spell I was willing to try if it saw my earnings increase and it gave me some security.

There were even spells for gamblers which, honestly, I found hard to get my head around. Apparently, if I wanted to win big on an each-way accumulator at the Grand National or place a bet on Swindon Town FC climbing their way out of League Two, all I had to do was bowl into Betfred with a drawstring bag containing a devil's shoestring (whatever the fuck that is!), a sprinkling of patchouli oil and a pinch of vetiver. Again, WTF? Then, I needed to spit into the bag and hey presto! I'd win and I'd win big.

★

'So, we'd like to go through your application form, Daisy,' the High Priestess interrupted my thoughts.

Eurgh! The application form. I'd filled it out once. Did I really need to go through it again?

'Sure. Took me an age to fill out!' I joked.

Glinda didn't even crack the faintest of smiles. Nothing. Instead, she elbowed the Wizard of Oz, who rifled through some paper stacked on the dining table. He pulled out my carefully crafted replies and handed the sheets to the High Priestess. He still hadn't uttered another word.

'Thank you, Brian,' she said. *BRIAN? Fucking BRIAN?* Granted, I realised I was a complete novice in this world but surely a High Priest had a better name than Brian. In the Bible, high priests are called Joshua or Eli or Zadok. At the very least I was hoping for a Benedict or a Tarquin.

Brian slinked back to his A4 pad like a burrowing mole.

'So, Daisy, we asked if anyone close to you knows of your interest in Wicca. You wrote "No". Could we explore this a little?'

'Erm . . . okay . . .'

'So, you've never spoken to anyone about wanting to join a coven?'

'No, definitely not.'

'Why is that?'

'I'm not sure my family would understand. My brother Charlie would piss himself laughing. My dad would roll his eyes. And I have a husband – sorry, an ex-husband – who I'm divorcing so I wouldn't want him to jump to false conclusions . . .'

'What kind of "false" conclusions?'

'Well, that I'd lost the plot.'

'I can assure you, Daisy, that no one who is interested in becoming a witch has ever "lost the plot",' the High Priestess said between gritted teeth. Her eyebrows buckled like she'd morphed into Miss Trunchbull.

At that Brian furiously scribbled down some more notes, then slowly raised up his oversized Sports Direct mug, took a sip of tea and stared at me. Quite menacingly, actually.

'So there's no family history of Wicca?'

Are you kidding? The nearest my parents got to witchcraft was naming the cat Abracatabra. Mum was far more spiritual than she was into magic. I decided to keep that to myself.

'Nope. My mum loved Halloween and was a dab hand at turning bin bags into costumes, but that probably doesn't count.'

'No. It doesn't. So do you have anyone who you could provide emotional support as you embark on this journey? A boyfriend perhaps?'

'Yeah, I have a boyfriend but, to be honest, his days are numbered. Bit of an RIP-marriage-shag that's snowballed. Must. Get. Rid.'

'Right . . . thank you, Daisy. But, would he be open to you taking an interest in the occult, in paganism, in Wicca?'

'No idea. It's none of his business. Besides, I'm a strong woman. I'm doing this for myself, so I don't think I need to confide in anyone.'

'Training to be a witch does take dedication, Daisy. There are study groups to attend and each witch is on their own spiritual journey. We do meet as a coven, but everyone is at a different stage of learning. How do you feel about study, Daisy?'

Fuck. Another hard one. Now is not the time to tell these people I have the attention span of a gnat on Ecstasy. Just ask my secondary school teachers. My ADHD is so extreme that the chances are I'll get bored halfway through the first lesson and want to take up macramé or golf.

'Yep, really looking forward to the study,' I offered with a pained smile.

'The study is very exacting,' Glinda said slowly, which seemed to provoke a violent head nod from the Wizard of Oz. '*Very. Exacting*,' she repeated. 'Physically and mentally.'

Hmmm . . . physically? I wasn't sure what that meant! I could dance round a fire a bit, give it everything I've got. But she was making out like this was some kind of boot camp. If I wanted that level of exertion, I would have applied to join Sweaty Mama – the all-female exercise class for mums in Stroud. All the physical effort, minus the magic.

'Well, no pain, no gain!' I tittered nervously. I still could not raise a smile from either. In truth, both of them terrified the shit out of me, but maybe this stony routine was to show me who was boss. Maybe in the study sessions they would soften up . . . be more, well, human.

The questions kept rolling. Did I practise meditation? Actually, I had tried it often but struggled with it as my shopping list kept popping into my head: *Must remember to get crumpets for breakfast. Oh and I'm out of pasta . . . again!* They also wanted a full rundown of books about the subject I had read. Embarrassed, I mention the book filled with the five thousand spells. I looked at Glinda hopefully. *Please, please make me feel just the slightest bit welcome,* I thought.

'A start,' Glinda replied, rather sarcastically.

We limped on to the end of the interview. I couldn't help thinking it was one of the worst auditions I'd ever been to. It was more painful than the time I tried to be an exotic dancer and my tits tumbled from my badly fitted frock while pole dancing to the track 'Ghetto Romance' by Damage. Tragic. Do they like me? Do they want me in their coven? I had no clue whatsoever.

'As you will have read on the form, Daisy, not all applications are successful, but we want to thank you for your time today. We will, of course, inform you of our decision in due course.'

'Thanks. I look forward to hearing from you,' I said. I genuinely did mean that. I did want to be accepted, to be part of this secret group doing secret things even if these people didn't seem like my tribe at all.

*

Days rolled by and I hadn't heard back from the High Priestess. Thankfully, lockdown was drawing to an end so I knew I could get cracking with other projects, but in the back of my mind, I did feel a deep well of rejection. Daisy May Cooper – can't even be a witch. I'd almost given up hope when an email dropped.

Dear Daisy,

Thank you for your time last month. We have now fully reviewed your application and we are pleased to inform you that we feel you would be a suitable candidate to join us.

However, we would like to discuss the study sessions with you. As we are still in lockdown, would you be available for a second Zoom session? We anticipate that by the time your first session is booked, we will be able to meet in person.

Yours sincerely,
Karen and Brian.

Yes! Yes! Yes! I didn't know why, but I was as giddy as a helium balloon. In that moment, all the weirdness and apprehension I felt about Glinda and the Wizard of Oz had melted away. It felt really fucking good, as if I was standing on the cliff edge of a whole new chapter in my life, ready to dive in. What have I got to lose? Excitedly, I started googling appropriate witches' attire. If I was going to be turning up at a study session I wanted to look the part – confident, like I owned this shit. And these days, witches can be goddam stylish. No one is wearing black capes or pointy hats unless it's to a fancy dress party.

When I searched around I discovered Witchcore – an aesthetic that incorporates everything witchcrafty from fashion to interior design to spell casting. It made my inner emo sing. TikTok seemed to be the place where witches or self-identifying witches hung out. There were pictures of girls in cheeky leather tops and skirts, lacy tights, customised vegan Doc Martens boots. Also, several sexy corset dresses did not escape my notice, one in a gorgeous vampy purple, but I decided that was probably a bit much for a first meet. Besides, I still had to get through my second interview, booked for the following evening.

'Daisy, nice to meet with you again.' I heard Glinda's voice echo out from the black screen.

'Thanks. You too. But I can't see you. Can you see me?'

'Yes, we can see you, Daisy.'

' Ah . . . I think your camera must be turned off. You're the meeting host, so I can't—'

'*Brian*, Daisy can't see us. What aren't you pressing? I thought you had the camera switched to on!

'Hold on a minute, Daisy. *Brian, it needs to be on!*'

'Okay, okay, Karen. Give me one minute. Look, here, the camera is here.'

'Yes, you said it was on.'

'No you . . .'

It occurred to me that Karen was probably the least witchy name I could imagine. But maybe that's the point. Being a witch isn't extraordinary any more, it's a path lots of ordinary people want to tread. I listened to Brian and Karen passive-aggressively bat back and forth. It sounded more like a crap sitcom than a witches' coven. Then, both their faces flickered up on to the screen. They were sitting in exactly the same spot with stuck-on smiles. I noticed that Glinda's hair seemed a bit more tussled this time around. And she also had on some ruby-red lippy. Dare I say it, she looked . . . almost . . . alluring. On the other hand, nothing short of a full face transplant could have improved her sidekick.

'Daisy. Congratulations on getting this far. We're excited you want to join us, and we wanted to discuss what you can expect from a first study session.'

'Great!'

'The first of these sessions always takes place at our home. We like to meet people one on one, get to know them a little better. Within time, you will be introduced to others in the group.'

'Amazing.'

'It's all very informal. We like to put people at ease so we do enjoy a bottle of wine. Do you drink, Daisy?'

Do I drink? Erm . . . at the moment, as much as is humanly possible. When I do, I'm like a racoon in a garage, but they don't need to know that. And I'm suddenly warming to this pair. Maybe they are my kind of people after all . . .

'Yes, I like a glass or two . . .' I lied.

'Great. We ask that you bring a bottle.'

Cheapskates. I know there's no membership fee for the coven or any upfront payment but an introductory slug would have been a nice touch.

'Okay . . what colour would you prefer?'

'Red. We drink red.

I'm more of a Chardonnay girl myself, but I didn't want to incur Karen's wrath.

'Sure. I'll bring a nice Malbec. Tesco Finest okay?'

'Whatever you choose.'

'We must also discuss the issue of nudity.'

'I'm sorry . . . what?' I said, almost spitting out my mouthful of tea.

'Nudity. We'd like to explore more about how you feel about your body.'

This was a massive curveball I had not anticipated. The conversation had taken an almighty nosedive, and I noticed a weird look come over the Wizard of Oz's face – a glazed look as he gripped his pen tighter.

'Okay . . .'

'How comfortable are you with your body? Your naked body.'

'Erm . . .'

Well, after several lockdowns, I'd become a human dustbin, munching down Jaffa Cakes like I was Oscar from *Sesame Street*.

'I could lose a stone or two . . . but . . .'

'Not your weight, Daisy. How comfortable are you expressing yourself while naked? With other people . . .'

I wasn't entirely sure what Glinda was getting at, but I've never held back on an under-the-duvet fart regardless of whether a partner is lying beside me if that's what she meant.

'Okay . . . I guess . . .'

'And orgasm?'

'Or . . . ga . . . sm?'

'Yes, we use orgasm to connect us to our energy source.'

'En . . . er . . . gy. Source . . . Right . . .'

I felt myself stammer and a wave of nausea rose up from the pit of my stomach. Then, my vagina started to freeze over.

'It helps us to focus. Direct intention. Achieve our goals.'

Fuck me.

My brain went into reverse thrust as the realisation dawned. Karen and Brian were swingers . . . or doggers . . . or maybe both. Daisy, Daisy, Daisy, how did you not see this coming? The whole application thing. The interview. The whole reason I was there was so they could work out whether they fancied me. How did it get to this?! If I'd wanted a threesome I wouldn't have feigned an elaborate interest in witchcraft – easier to put a call out on Stroud Swingers! I felt duped, like Edward Woodward in *The Wicker Man* about to be burned as a sacrifice. The thought of being spit-roasted by this pair appalled me. And, let's face it, if I wanted to 'connect to my energy source' I could do it on my own, in the privacy of my own bedroom, day or night, thank you. Still, I decided to see where this kinky pair were taking this conversation.

'I'm . . . erm . . . fine with orgasm. Really . . . fine,' I said.

Glinda explained further about how they worked their way through the Kama Sutra like some kind of DIY manual, while I nodded slowly. Throughout, I could hear the Wizard of Oz's breath rise and fall more heavily. Either he'd become significantly aroused or the dust from his library had exacerbated an existing asthma condition. When I look back on this now, I cannot believe I stayed on the call. Not only that, but at the end of it I even arranged a date to go to their house. What was I thinking? Was my life that empty?

As the day of the study session rolled around, however, I got cold feet. When I checked it out on Google Maps, the address the High Priestess had handed me looked like it was in the middle of nowhere. She had also instructed me to tell only one person where I was going. Everything seemed so odd that in the end I bottled it. I didn't turn up for the study session. And I didn't ever speak to Glinda and the Wizard of Oz again, despite them emailing me several times to ask where I was and what had happened. Had I changed my mind about joining a coven? I couldn't bring myself to reply.

One of the saddest things about this whole experience was that I never did get to wear my new leggings and glittery black lace bell-sleeved dress I'd ordered from H&M. Nor did I get to howl at the moon. I am, however, still working my way through my book of spells and filling my head with tales of witches from the past. And I do still want to join a coven. I *really* do. But a legit one. Not one where I have to get my kit off and sip red wine while being connected to my energy source courtesy of a couple of sexual deviants. When I think about it now, the whole thing had been so unprofessional and I should imagine broke a number of rules from the witch code. So witches . . . *real* witches . . . if you're out there somewhere, give me a sign . . .

★

16

PARANORMAL PETS

Believe it or not, your pet pooch, pussy or any other animal you keep may be one of the best weapons in your armoury to alert you to paranormal activity in your home. And, of course, pets can also come back to visit you after they've passed over. *Yes! Yes! Yes!* We've reached the final chapter in this utterly random examination of the ghosts in your life: paranormal pets.

Ask any bona fide paranormal investigator and I can guarantee they will all say the same: if you have ruled out the rational and believe that there is still a ghost or unexplained paranormal activity happening in your house, watch the behaviour of your pets closely. It all goes back to frequency. Remember my earlier theory about children being able to tune into the finest of details – me watching the raindrops running down the car window? Well, animals actually do operate on a different level – they see and hear on a frequency perfectly placed to sense visitations from the undead when us mere mortals are drowning in the mire of psychic quicksand, grasping for answers.

I believe I have seen this phenomena for myself. When I lived in my old haunted home, I frequently watched as my new kittens Milo and George stopped dead in their tracks. They would stare out at something on the wall or on the floor or in a corner of the room. At first I thought they were being complete dicks, but gradually it dawned on me that maybe they could see what my cleaner Debs thought she could see – a cast of ghostly characters coming and going. A whole other world that I was not tuned into at all. Whenever I followed their eyes, there were no flies or daddy-long-legs or insects buzzing around. There were no mice or furry animals scurrying. There was nothing. Just two cats in my kitchen – frozen like Elsa stuck in an eternal winter.

As with all of the paranormal world, there's no scientific proof that pets have the ability to tap into it. Certainly the sea monkeys my kids used to keep would have the psychic ability of a brick. The only talent these shrimps had was to swim around their fish tank and multiply at a bonkers rate. We started with a few eggs and ended up with thousands. They had the brains the size of amoebas and yet the whole experience was incredibly stressful.

But many other animals are highly intelligent and do possess a sixth sense. Dogs are bloody awesome. They can hear stuff at a frequency a hundred times higher than humans can. They can see objects from far greater distances, especially in twilight or early dawn, that go undetected by the human eye. And they have a sense of smell one hundred thousand times that of a human that can practically detect a fart before you've even done it. This makes them brilliant at sensing impending disaster. If ghosts are real, dogs would definitely be the first to know. It's the same with cats. Just like their canine counterparts, they can also see and hear activity we can't and detect changes in the atmosphere, seismic vibrations and sense invisible electromagnetic force fields. This means dogs and cats know when there's about to be a thunderstorm or an earthquake or a tsunami – they're up there with the world's best early-warning systems. Yet they can't tell us or document a single thing about it, so sadly this avenue of scientific study is cut off.

When you think about it, these animals probably hold the key to every single paranormal conundrum on the planet. How fucking annoying is that? And this is where I think the scientific community needs to step up.

Imagine if Stephen Hawking had developed his theory of black holes but no one had invented the computer with the weird voice that he could talk through? Or if Einstein had stumbled on the theory of relativity and suddenly become mute? Or he couldn't write any of it down? If we could simply train a dog or a cat to press a large keypad displaying a ghost emoji for 'yes' it would be a fucking good start. I'll leave that thought out there with the boffins among you. *Come on* – there has to be a way!

Aside from pets sensing paranormal activity in our homes, there's also the animals that come back to visit us. Sadly, I've never experienced a ghost animal, but I was heartened to read that many people have. Not only that, but ghost animals do seem to be pretty friendly. I've not been inundated with reports of the kind you'd find in Stephen King's *Pet Sematary*.

I'm sure there is the odd bull terrier who comes back to rip someone's face off. Or a rabid bunny rabbit that was confined to its hutch all of its life that was never stroked could easily have unfinished business. Or the stray cat that lures you in like a honeytrap with its soft purring and gentle miaow before scratching the fuck out of a person. But I think this is rare.

Martin reached out to ask if ghost pets were 'a thing'. He has had numerous encounters with what he believes is a ghost cat over the past five years. A self-confessed sceptic, he's nevertheless certain he's caught sight of a large black fluffy animal skirting around the edge of several rooms in his house. It's got so common now that he just shrugs and says: 'Ghost cat's back.'

Martin, you are talking to the converted here, and Martin does live next to a graveyard. However, far be it from me to piss all over his paranormal ponderings, but I think some serious investigation needs to happen if Martin is to get to the bottom of this. I'm talking CCTV cameras in all the affected areas. Of course, I would *love* this to be a ghost cat, but it could also be a massive rat looking for its next meal, like the greedy and oafish Templeton from *Charlotte's Web*. Before any firm conclusions can be drawn all other possibilities do need to be eliminated from the enquiry.

Just as intriguing is a story I read recently about a ghost dog in Manchester. A couple had been driving to the cinema in the centre of town. Suddenly, out of the darkness, they spotted a creature bounding past them. When it turned, its body was that of a dog but it had no head. As the couple followed it, it disappeared through what they assumed was an archway, but when they drove past, it was a closed door painted blue.

If that wasn't weird enough, the couple began researching as soon as they got home. There were reports from as early as 1825 of a headless dog seen around the area of Manchester Cathedral. Could this be the dog that ran in front of their car? They'll never know. But they were sure that what they'd seen wasn't a real dog, and it did disappear through a closed door.

In fact, I discovered that there's an amazing database of paranormal activity that anyone can tap into and find countless sightings of ghost animals dating back centuries. In my own area of Gloucestershire there's been plenty of odd animal goings-on: sightings of fawn-coloured ghost cats, big cats, the inexplicable sound of horses hooves in some areas and – wait for it – a shower of pink frogs in Stroud. They were bouncing off umbrellas and pavements and hopped in their thousands to streams and gardens. It sounds insane! At the time, there were several theories about how they got there, including them being transported from the Sahara in a sandstorm. Again, all of these could have perfectly reasonable explanations. Yet to this day, the mysteries remain unsolved.

☆

As far as pets go there are also those people who say they can tap into animals – so-called pet psychics. And, true to form, I do have a sorry tale about a pet psychic. Let's just say, the punchline to this story is that I am still unpopular with one part of my family, even though it wasn't entirely my fault. In fact, I was only acting as an intermediary between my uncle and the psychic world.

It all began when my mate Lily contacted a very reputable pet psychic. Her tortoise had been missing for ages, way beyond the winter months. Secretly, I suspected that it had used its hibernation period as an opportunity to do a runner. The pet equivalent of faking its own death, like that man who staged a canoe accident but was actually living in a cupboard in the house next door to his wife and claiming off the insurance.

I didn't expect much from the pet psychic at all. But, I kid you not, this woman was like the Dr Dolittle of the South West. Minus the top hat and facial hair, of course.

'Your tortoise is under dead wood and behind some tulips,' she told Lily. The conversation was over the phone. It didn't even happen on Zoom (where she could have spied the garden set-up) and she'd never once been to Lily's house. *Extraordinary!* And when Lily went to search in the garden that's exactly where she found her pet tortoise. Disappointingly for me, it hadn't faked its own death. It turns out it was just a lazy bastard that had wanted to sleep way past springtime.

The story could have ended there but for me and my massive Daisy-shaped mouth. I made the mistake of telling my uncle's ex-wife the tale about the pet psychic and the tortoise. She was an actress and had been touring a play around the country. While she was away she'd asked my uncle to walk her dog. He did, but only to the pylon at the end of his street so it could have a shit. Then he walked it back. Bone idle does run in our family.

Intrigued by the pet psychic, my then aunt paid for a session. It was all going well, until the psychic dropped an almighty bombshell.

'Your dog wants you to know something.'

'Oh, and what is that?'

'He wants you to know that for weeks he has not had his regular walk around the park. Not even close. All he's seen is the pylon at the top end of the street.'

Imagine a pet psychic ratting someone out? Dobbing my uncle right in it for lying through his back teeth. It does serve him right, but what a way to find out. No one could have predicted that. He's never forgiven me for putting her on to the Mystic Meg of the pet world.

Another woman, Tomomi, also wrote to me with a cautionary tale. She made the grave error of visiting not a pet psychic but a *pet-loving* psychic. During the session a strong smell of mushroom kept wafting through the room. The psychic reckoned that the unusual stench was connected to one of Tomomi's past lives. At times it got very strong before fading away. But halfway through the session Tomomi heard something stir from the corner. She noticed a pet poodle on a cushion by the woman's chair. The penny finally dropped. It had been letting rip throughout the whole session and had sent the psychic completely off the scent. Tomomi – I do hope you asked for a discount.

☆

PART FOUR

GHOST STORIES

17

A SHORT HISTORY

What is it that we love about ghost stories? It's a question that has always fascinated me. And why do we love telling them? Like the complete idiot I am, I thought ghost tales were a relatively recent phenomenon. Sixteenth century at a push. As usual, I was wrong. It turns out that one of the first written recordings of a ghost story could date all the way back to 1500 BC.

And . . . the story is *a-mazing*! It's written on a tablet no bigger than my hand but apparently gives a full set of instructions on how to banish a ghost. Given the lack of writing space, I imagined that this might read as the pre-Christian equivalent of: 'Fuck off you big bastard and don't darken my door again.' I was wrong. Instead, the tablet calls for an exorcist to make figurines of a man and a woman, fill up two vessels with beer and at sunrise call on the Mesopotamian god Shamash. Apparently, he's the guy responsible for transporting ghosts to the underworld. There, the pesky spectre is transferred into one of the figurines. It's unclear who gets to neck the beer. But it's the last line of the text that I truly love the most. It says none other than: 'Don't look behind you!' *Yes! Yes! Yes!* Isn't that fucking insane? It's the phrase that anyone who's ever read a spooky story or watched a terrifying horror film knows . . . and that phrase could be more than 3,500 years old. Mind blown.

In Roman times, too, there's evidence of written ghost stories – chains heard rattling and the undead roaming rooms and vestibules. Roman ghosts don't show up to do people much harm but tend to be there to remind people to respect the dead, especially if they've been short-changed on a funeral and the gathering consisted of a less-than-Roman-standard king prawn ring and vegetable samosas from Iceland.

All this tells me is that stories about the paranormal are in our DNA, in our very bones. They are woven into the fabric of how we understand the world. Personally speaking, although I am itching to uncover the truth, there's also a part of me that loves that ghosts are, as yet, unexplained. (Readers, if you've made it this far, I'm three-quarters of the way through this book and I still haven't got a fucking clue.) Getting to the bottom of my own ghostly experiences has felt like a Sherlock Holmes detective story with twists and turns, surprises and dead ends. But who cares? As I said at the start, I believe the answer is out there somewhere, but do we even want to find it? If the investigation into the paranormal was closed, what the fuck would we have to talk about? Isn't there a weird comfort in ghost stories shared by the living?

To be clear, I've not read a ton of ghost stories. Anyone who knows me knows I hate reading, especially overly long books. I'd rather be farting around on the sofa, flicking through *Take a Break*, reading about the woman who's expecting a baby pumpkin or the haunted dressing table that saved another woman's cat. But I have watched a lot of scary films and documentaries, and I've scrolled through YouTube and watched people describing ghosts and classic ghost stories, which is almost the same as reading them. Right?

Take Shakespeare, for example. He loved a ghost. He was forever trying to squeeze one into his plays. (Believe it or not I did learn something from my fucking horrendous time at RADA). Unfortunately, no one knows whether Shakespeare had actually seen a ghost or believed in ghosts or whether they were just handy for his plots. I mean, without the ghost of his father popping up to remind him to avenge his death, Hamlet would never have had the balls to kill Claudius, the guy who poisoned him. Even then, it took Hamlet until Act V to commit this deed, by which time some theatre-goers must die of boredom themselves and come back to haunt the theatre.

In Shakespeare's *Richard III* (1592–3) there's no fewer than 11 ghosts who put in an appearance. *Eleven!* They do all happen to be the people he's killed and they only appear to tell Richard about the really shitty death he's going to have at the Battle of Bosworth the next day. If I'd have been him, I wouldn't have bothered going. If one ghost tells you something, it's probably best to be sceptical, but when there's a traffic jam of them with the same story then you do need to listen. Oddly, though, not a single one of those ghosts predicted Richard would end up under a car park in Leicester, discovered in 2012, likely with a parking fine dating back more than 500 years. Bastards.

Jump forward about 250 years to Charles Dickens's *A Christmas Carol* (1843), one of the most-told ghost stories of the modern age.

It's one of my favourite stories ever and Dickens was clearly writing for people like me who have a very short attention span. It's only 64 pages. Yes!

At its heart it's all about ghosts who come back to teach us something about life – educators without the boredom of school. Did some tight-arsed employer with a likeness to Ebenezer Scrooge ever get visited by three ghosts – past, present, and future – prompting him to change his penny-pinching ways? Unlikely, would be my guess. But bigger picture it is a story about the afterlife and what awaits us on the other side if we're not honest, decent people – just like Mum threatening me with Granny Bertie's ever-present eyes whenever I was naughty. Or the creeping guilt I feel if I don't round up my change for charity at the Tesco self-service till.

Is *A Christmas Carol* scary? Kind of. It is creepy? Yeah – especially Ebenezer Scrooge's foreboding house and the rattling of chains coming from the cellar – that feeling of dread. And the face of his business partner Jacob Marley that appears in a door knocker. In its heyday, it would have been top-notch fright-night material. In my view, though, the story only gets truly scary when you begin to imagine what your own modern-day ghosts of Christmas past, present and future would look like. It may not come as a surprise to know that mine are a fucking triple bill of horror.

Daisy's Ghost of Christmas Past

I told this story in my autobiography *Don't Laugh, It'll Only Encourage Her*. (If you haven't read it then I'm doing you a massive favour because now you won't have to bother.) But the story is worth retelling because it is probably the one instance in my past that I'm most ashamed of. And just so you can picture it more clearly, in this film remake of *A Christmas Carol*, I would like to be played by a young Kate Winslet (think *Titanic* Kate rather than Ronal in *Avatar* Kate), and all the ghosts will be played by Big Mo from *EastEnders*.

And . . . Action!

Daisy is at home in Cirencester with her brother Charlie. She is around 13 years old. Dad has hired a camcorder from Radio Rentals and Daisy and Charlie have begun making films together. To amuse themselves they are leaning out of an upstairs window and filming their neighbour. Elizabeth is a god-fearing woman who runs the B & B next door with her husband Stanley. Her house is terrifying – Jesus on the cross is hung on every wall. But Elizabeth also has the habit of sunbathing topless in her back garden, her saggy honkers on show for the whole world to see. Her areolas are so huge they look like dartboards. Charlie and Daisy think it's a great idea to aim mint chocolate Matchmakers at them: 25 points for the outer circle, 50 for the inner and right on the nipple it's a clear bullseye. But no matter how many Matchmakers land, chocolate melting and oozing down Elizabeth's red-raw skin, she doesn't stir.

Enter Big Mo, the Ghost of Christmas Past. She takes Daisy to see herself and Charlie laughing like hyenas, taking aim with a Matchmaker then ducking down behind the window before they get caught. But the real revelation comes when she and Daisy go inside Elizabeth and Stanley's house that evening. Daisy realises that she hasn't seen them as people at all, just objects for her own amusement. A Premier Inn has opened up nearby and the usual visitors to the annual air tattoo have relocated there. It's £29 per room including breakfast. Stanley has a terminal illness and this combined with their B & B failing is about to put them out of business. They are having to move to Wales, for fuck's sake. Daisy realises she has no regard for Elizabeth or Stanley. All she saw was tits and a dartboard. This, sadly, will shape the Daisy she is to become.

Daisy's Ghost of Christmas Present

Cut to the next scene: Daisy is at her kitchen table. She is on her mobile phone scrolling through Instagram. She's caught up in the moment, consumed with vengeance. She's outraged at a man she's seen on *Married at First Sight*. He's a gaslighting bastard and Daisy has taken to social media to troll him. She's so enraged by his constant lies that she types in: 'Your hair looks like a fucking mop' on his feed. Of course, she is operating under an assumed name and has the profile picture of a dead catfish. To be fair, his hair doesn't look like just one mop, but three Vileda SuperMops taped together. He even has a hairband to pull it back which also gives her the ick.

Enter Big Mo, the Ghost of Christmas Present. She takes Daisy to hover over herself at the table scrolling and spitting out her bile. Now, Daisy is on the BBC Good Food website trolling a complete random who has simply written under a recipe for lasagne: 'Great tip: I substituted cottage cheese for Bechamel sauce.' Consumed with bitterness Daisy writes: 'What do you want? A fucking medal?'

Big Mo takes her to the home of the gaslighting bastard. He's looking in the mirror almost weeping at how unmanageable his hair is. He's lamenting on how, deep down, his self-confidence is at an all-time low, more so now he can't manage his hair problem. Daisy reflects that she should have just made a comment about his controlling behaviour and not been personal about his hair.

Then Big Mo takes her to the home of a woman struggling to feed her family. Cottage cheese is on a buy-one-get-one-free deal in Tesco and she's bought two 500-gram pots. She's in the kitchen – moments before her children run through the door – desperately trying to make the topping stretch over the large Pyrex dish, which is far too big for the amount of lasagne she can afford to make. Daisy hangs her head in shame.

Daisy's Ghost of Christmas Future

Daisy receives a phone call. It's from the high street bakery chain Greggs. They have approached her in the past about a sponsorship deal. Back then they thought Kerry Mucklowe would be the perfect vehicle to promote their sausage, bean and cheese melt.

'We're sorry, Daisy, we don't want to pursue any opportunities,' the voice on the other end of the phone says. 'Elizabeth the human dartboard; the Instagram trolling. We just think you're a cunt. Any future deal is off.'

Big Mo lets Daisy witness this phone call alongside a slew of other cancellations. The BBC say they can't work with Daisy any more. A second series of *Am I Being Unreasonable?* is cancelled. ITV feel the same. She was due to appear on Ant and Dec's *Saturday Night Takeaway*. It's cancelled. She was also lined up to promote a local bakery's butter buns. They sent her 200 every week just so her love of them felt authentic. Cancelled. The worst thing is, the deliveries stop.

A double-ended dildo manufacturer also expressed an interest in having Daisy as the face of its campaign. It stops contacting her. *University Challenge* has even called to say they will never, ever consider having her on any team in any forthcoming series. Okay, that's a lie. That *really* is pushing reality!

After witnessing the slow, painful death of Daisy's career, Big Mo then takes Daisy to an alternate reality: one where Daisy sends the gaslighting bastard from *Married at First Sight* an apology – not about his behaviour, just about his hair. In this version of events she also buys the stressed-out housewife a year's supply of Tesco cottage cheese – not just the standard pot but Tesco Finest – and even tries the substitute recipe herself. Actually, it is delicious. The comment on the BBC Good Food website was *really* harsh! And she floats over Wales to find Elizabeth still sunbathing topless in her back garden. Sadly, Stanley has passed away, but Daisy helps Elizabeth improve her customer service thereby turning her B & B into a profitable business.

The last scene is Daisy running around the streets of Cirencester shouting: 'I'm back. And I'm *really* not a massive cunt. Promise.' Big Mo is watching on from the sidelines, smiling.

THE END

Scary? Welcome to my brain.

☆

Ghost stories, like *A Christmas Carol*, used to be a staple of Victorian life, especially around wintertime and on Christmas Eve in particular. Gothic fiction and gothic horror got a sell-out family audience.

With those long, dark nights, no electricity and fuck-all else to do throughout the holidays, loads of people – rich and poor – used to huddle round their fires and try to scare the shit out of each other.

As many of these stories were delivered by someone telling them, it didn't matter whether people could read or write. Plus, as winter was considered the time of the year when everything dies before it transforms and changes into spring, I'm pretty sure it was the actual law to be nice to people for a few days, even if you went back to being a complete cunt for the rest of the year. Probably why loads of ghosts turned out to be seasonal moral arbiters.

But it was when these stories started to be written down and published that everything cranked up a gear. By the time Dickens died in 1870 it was commonplace to see ghost stories in print. He was a bestselling author in the UK and across the pond in the US – kind of like the Stephen King of his generation, but with a beard more like a dead Yorkshire terrier and far fewer film deals. Loads of his stories were set in graveyards and creaky old houses, which nowadays would be considered tropes, but back then they would have been the creepiest places around. Besides, the carbon monoxide given off by gas lamps meant people were probably mainlining spirits 24/7 even when there weren't actually any around. (Hot tip: today, if you think you have seen a ghost then it's always a good idea to make sure you are not hallucinating first by checking if you've got a dodgy boiler.)

Around the same time as Dickens the reading of penny dreadfuls reached fever pitch. These were booklets, between eight and sixteen pages, costing one penny and were the Victorian equivalent of *Crime Monthly*. The great thing about them was that you didn't have to be rich to enjoy a good scare because these stories were affordable. And a lot of them were a hotbed of supernatural entities. The ghosts and bloodsucking vampires (one called Varney) and bogeymen within their pages were the living embodiment of our waking fears.

But at the time panic spread that these books were destroying the minds of the working classes and would cause a breakdown in society. One well-to-do commentator even said the penny dreadful was 'tempting the ignorant and unwary, and breeding death and misery speakable.' What an absolute twat. It reminds me of when, in the 1990s, the video game *Mortal Kombat* almost brought an end to civilisation as we know it. Though, at the same time, people managed to overlook the size of Lara Croft's tits in *Tomb Raider* – which were horrifying. In 1996, they prompted . . . erm . . . not so much of a panic among men but did cause girls like me everywhere to question: how the *actual fuck* does she run so fast with 36DDs and no bra?

Anyway, fast-forward to the advent of film and TV and stories of the supernatural went from creepy and spine-tingly to in-your-face, jump-out-of-your-skin scary – like *A Nightmare on Elm Street* and *Candyman* and all those big-budget (as they were back then) horror films I bloody loved when I was growing up. These featured malevolent spirits who had some serious beef back in the world of the living. But, let's face it, some were so overdone they became funny like *Jack Frost* and *Bride of Chucky*.

Then followed, of course, the home-movie style *Blair Witch Project* – which was basically some teenagers camping out and running around in a forest with a camcorder. It was pretty scary, actually. And in a quest to experience the same kind of terror,

Charlie and I did try to copy it. It turned out to be absolute bollocks. For starters, the tent was a nightmare to put up. We forgot our torch. It was fucking freezing, and the rustling in the trees a few hours into our sleep-out *was* petrifying until we heard the words:

'Jen, how do you expect me to get a boner when I've got a fern bush rammed up my bum hole?'

'Well I can't kneel on these leaves for ever, Steve.'

I was 11 years old at the time, so that was very confusing.

And now in 2024 we're talking about ghosts all over again. The ghost story is back with a vengeance. Sales of horror books and books about the supernatural have sky-rocketed. If I meet a celebrity, it's all they want to talk about. Tilda Swinton – she's mad for it. It's as if people have achieved fame, they've got the money and now all that's left is to turn their attention to the unexplained.

There's also a part of me that thinks our outlook on the world has changed too. It's as if we've peeked out from behind the heavy velvet curtain of our precarious existence and thought: *The planet's fucked, World War III is around the corner; world poverty is at an all-time high. But it could be worse – we could be ambushed at any moment by a spirit with a massive grudge. Fuck it, let's read more . . .*

And when you look at what happens to our bodies when we read or watch a ghost story, I think there's something life-affirming about ghosts and ghost stories. Our hearts beat that little bit faster. Our skin prickles. There's endorphins and dopamine firing round us like a pinball machine. We're taking that fight-or-flight response, owning it and riding that motherfucker like Hyperia at Thorpe Park – all without having to pay the entrance fee. We can do it all from home!

There's something amazing about ghost stories, hopeful even. Ghosts, friendly or not, whisper in your ear that there's more than just this life – that what we're doing down here is just a dress rehearsal for so much more . . .

★

18

THE SANDOWN CLOWN

There's a story that's hidden deep in a journal of paranormal sightings. It's a story that I've become mesmerised by and I want to share it with you. I've become more mesmerised by it than staring endlessly at pictures of Wayne Lineker's under-the-eye-bag-removal surgery – which, by the way, if you haven't seen the result, is fucking phenomenal. Anyway, this story happened on the Isle of Wight more than 50 years ago.

Two children were playing near an area of Sandown on the island's east coast called Lake Common when they heard the strangest noise in the distance, it was almost like an ambulance siren blaring. Curious, they set off in the direction of the source of the noise, across a golf course and through a hedge, ending up at a swampy meadow on the edge of the town's little-used airport.

Just as the children were crossing a wooden footbridge over a narrow stream, a blue-gloved hand appeared out of the water. Then a figure emerged. It splashed around, trying to retrieve what seemed like a notebook that it had dropped. Then the figure stumbled away, turning its back on the children and disappearing into a metal hut, the type you find on a building site. It moved slowly, almost hopping with one knee raised high, like a constipated chicken.

Terrified, the children legged it in another direction. When they glanced back and saw that the figure had reappeared, the wailing sound started up again. Now, the figure had in its hand a microphone and a flex. Was it about to burst into Gloria Gaynor's 'I Will Survive', the karaoke version? Disappointingly not, because that would have been bloody brilliant. Instead it boomed over at the children: 'Hello, are you still there?' At that, they moved closer, close enough to speak to the strange figure.

And this figure *was* out of this world. The girl, Fey, reported it as almost seven feet tall. It also had no neck. 'It's head appeared to be wedged straight into its shoulders,' the account says. It wore a yellow pointed hat which was attached to a red collar and green tunic, like something out of the *Wizard of Oz*. Then, on top, it sported a round black knob on its hat with a wooden antennae attached to either side. For eyes, it had triangular markings. Instead of a nose it had a brown square, and it had yellow lips that didn't move. Its cheeks were white and it had red hair that tumbled haphazardly on to its large forehead. Honestly, its fashion sense left a lot to be desired. Genuinely forgivable only because it was the Seventies.

As the children edged nearer, it wrote something in its notebook. It didn't write the words in the right sequence but pointed to them in the order that they should be read. 'Hello and I'm all colours, Sam,' they read as it pointed.

At this point, you might be thinking that this is all one big bullshit story that surpasses even the dizzy heights of bullshit previously described in Sir Arthur Conan Doyle's work and the Cottingley fairies saga. I don't believe it was. There's something about the detail of this story that fascinates me.

Sam, or whoever this creature was, could speak words even though it didn't open its mouth. Its blue-gloved hands only had three fingers and feet only three toes. The children asked it questions about itself. They asked about its ripped clothes, to which the creature didn't seem to have an answer. They asked if it was a man. It replied: 'No.'

Was it something else? A ghost perhaps?

'Well, not really, but I am in an odd sort of way,' it replied.

'What are you, then?' they kept on asking.

The only answer Sam gave was, 'You know.'

For fuck's sake, Sam, it wasn't the time to be a weird seven-foot man of mystery!

Sam went on to tell the children that they was not alone, even though the children reported that no one was with Sam. Sam then beckoned them into the hut. It was small from the outside but a palace inside, with two floors. The sort of gaff that looks like a garden shed but actually has three bedrooms and an en suite jacuzzi and would be featured on *George Clarke's Amazing Spaces*. There, Sam told the children that they fed on berries collected in the late afternoon.

And that's when Sam did the weirdest party trick ever. Sam took a berry and popped it in its ear. When Sam shook its head, it rolled out through an eye. Then Sam took the berry in its hand, popped it into its ear again and thrust its head forward. This time the berry appeared through its mouth.

When the children eventually left Sam and headed home they told whoever they came across on the way that they'd seen a ghost. Of course, no one believed them so they shut up. That is until three weeks later when Fey was clearly about to burst and ended up spilling the beans to her father. He wrote down the story and passed it on to the British UFO Research Association. Was it an alien? A ghost? A scarecrow with a fucking weird sense of humour?

But there's another element to the story that makes me believe that Sam wasn't human or an alien but a real ghost. While the children were talking to Sam, two workmen were nearby putting up a gatepost. They carried on working, seemingly oblivious to everything that the children were seeing and experiencing. They didn't raise an eyebrow at the sound of the siren wailing or when Sam got out the microphone and called the children over or when Sam led them into the hut to perform the berry trick, which would surely raise some concern.

What is it about this story that I can't get enough of? I think it's because it's just too odd to dismiss it as total and utter bollocks made up by children. And, yes, I've read the thoughts of many who do cast it aside as hauntological gibberish but, the fact is, the case of the Sandown Clown remains unsolved.

The account raises so many questions. Why would someone dressed like a seven-foot clown be lost in a swampy field when there was no circus in town? And if it was a hoax, it was a pretty fucking elaborate one. Why go to all the trouble of knitting gloves with three fingers? Are clowns known for their knitting skills? And why reveal yourself only to two children? And the trick with the berry must have taken a lot of practice. I can't even juggle (and believe me I've tried). No other sightings of this strange creature were ever reported.

Given the precise detail of the story, the only other theory that paranormal researchers have come up with is that this was what is called a *folie à deux*, which is a French expression meaning the 'madness of two'. Apparently, it's a very rare psychotic disorder where two people who are closely related share the same insane delusions.

Personally, I can relate to this theory.

It took me years to psychologically fuck with Charlie so much that he and I shared the same crazy visions. And I do know what it's like to grow up bored as shit in a small town where everyone has the same haircut and one pair of trainers. That can make you imagine all kinds of weird stuff. But a seven-foot creature? I don't think this would happen even in mine and Charlie's wildest fantasies. By comparison, our flights of fancy were quite tame! We reimagined WWE wrestling smackdowns in the living room with Charlie sporting a pair of blue Speedos as Kurt Angle and me, aka Trish Stratus, dressed in a sparkly leotard with square-toed calf-length boots. Once I persuaded Chaz to dissect a snail with a pair of tweezers, telling him it was dead when it wasn't (he still hasn't forgiven me). But a ghost that could technically have been done for kidnap and did a trippy thing with a berry? I don't think so. That said, at the time the Sandown Clown appeared kids only had space hoppers to play with so maybe their minds wandered a bit further.

And even if Charlie and I had agreed on the detail of this massive shaggy-dog story, it's unlikely that we'd ever be able to agree on the same version for long enough to stick to it. Writing *This Country* together was bad enough. That inevitably ended up with me calling Mum and crying down the phone.

'Charlie's behaving appallingly!'

Mum would act as the peacemaker and talk to Charlie.

'What did he say?' I'd call Mum later and ask her.

'He says he's sorry,' Mum would report back but all the time I knew he'd actually called me a massive cockwomble.

The idea that siblings or close friends could string this out for more than a few days is absurd. One or both would crack. 'She told me to say it!' would surely fall from the boy's lips under duress. Or was Fey an arsehole? Maybe she threatened him with having to chow down on one of his mum's favourite lipsticks and barf it up later. Or perhaps she tied his leg to the bed while he was playing *Earthworm Jim* on the Sega Mega Drive so that he broke the bed when he tried to leg it downstairs after his mum called him for tea. And Fey didn't say a single word when he got the blame for it. If you are reading this, Charlie (which I'm sure you aren't), then I am sorry. Not *that* sorry, though.

The point is that there are some stories just too peculiar not to hold a grain of truth. And maybe because no logical, credible, believable explanation has yet been found for the Sandown Clown that's why it's still spinning around in my brain.

★

19

THE MISCHIEVOUS PARANORMAL

Thank goodness that not every ghost or spirit wants to come back and give the living a hard time or teach imperfect humans like you and me – especially me – a valuable life lesson. Some are just here mainly for fun, to brighten up people's day and to step in when life is . . . well, just a tad shit. Just like the famous green fairy in *Moulin Rouge*, played by Kylie Minogue in the film. I have a particular soft spot for Kylie because she once said the rhubarb and apple chutney I made for the South Cerney Village Fete was, I quote, 'Beautiful'. *Fucking hell!* Kylie tasted my chutney! What's more she bloody loved it! And she is exactly the type of little creature I like to think of when I imagine the imps and piskies and sprites and fairies that have populated the British Isles for many centuries and remain rooted in our folklore. Even though Kylie is technically Australian.

I've never seen any of these little people, but I yearn for the day when I might be out on a windswept Exmoor or Dartmoor – quite possibly astride a donkey, lost and with dark blue storm clouds rolling in from the horizon – and one might reveal itself to me. I'd even be overjoyed if one sent me in the wrong direction, just for a laugh, if only I could catch a glimpse.

The actor and writer Mark Gatiss recently told me about something that happened to a friend of his when he was driving to Cornwall. He was on a winding country road, the night was drawing in and in the distance he thought he'd seen a small animal – maybe a rabbit or a baby badger – in the headlights. But when he got closer and slowed right down, a childlike figure with pointed ears and a gnarled, leathery face spun around, grimaced and hotfooted it into the trees lining the roadside. Isn't that extraordinary? And former *This Morning* host Fern Britton says she saw a whole family of similar-looking creatures in a hedgerow one time when she was filming a travel series in Cornwall.

What's even more amazing is that in the days before TV and radio and Amazon Prime, storytellers – or droll tellers as they were known – would wander from village to village and tell stories of exactly the same sorts of sightings. Every tale was told in exchange for bed and board for the night, so I can see how a droll teller might be tempted to make shit up. But the droll tellers collected stories from village to village too. In my mind, there's just too many witness accounts for these tales to be dismissed.

When I started to read up on it, it seemed clear to me that the creature that Mark's friend had seen had been a piskie. In Cornwall, it is said these creatures do not typically have wings, unlike in other areas. And there are lots of differing theories about what piskies actually are. Are they ghosts or some other entity? Some say they are the souls of pagans who weren't let into heaven: not bad enough for hell and not good enough to enter the pearly gates. Stuck in a sort of holding area, like Yorkshire. On Earth, they are doomed to shrink in size before they finally disappear. Other stories say they are the souls of babies who were never christened, which is also a theory given to the existence of fairies.

Whatever their origin, piskies are creatures after my own heart – just a little bit naughty. Joan the Wad, Queen of the Piskies, is shrouded in mystery, and there are accounts of her being both good and bad. She hails from the smugglers' cove of Polperro on the south coast of Cornwall. And as piskies are supposed to be brilliant at household chores, it is possible that she ran her own successful cleaning business. At some point, though, she branched out into supplying the area with tonnes of tourist tat. Honestly, you can't shit for lucky charms of her – key rings, jewellery, ornaments – some are *really* bad ornaments – all of which makes me think that Joan was both a miniature feminist icon and a massive narcissist. Apparently, if you carry a trinket of Joan with you then the gods of good fortune will shine down upon you. And I get that, I really do. Give me a compliment and I'm like a dog that rolls on its back and exposes its nipples. Buy some merch with my ugly mug on it and I'm drooling, licking your face off, promising the world – although even by my low standards the Kerry Mucklowe mask is a fucking horror show.

As for Jack O'Lantern, Joan's other half, it's difficult to get the measure of his character. Like Joan, he is a light seen by travellers at night – a will-o'-the-wisp (very different to the jack o'lanterns Mum and I used to decorate the front porch with at Halloween).

But this power couple were hardly Bonnie and Clyde. I think they were probably hardworking but got a bit bored with country life. Jack liked to attend to his apocalyptic veg patch while Joan deep-cleaned. And sometimes they liked to get a bit pissed to liven things up. They did petty stuff like riding farmers' horses, turning the milk sour, maybe some cow chasing now and again. And their *pièce de résistance* was leading people with their torchlights into swampy moorland bogs when all these weary travellers wanted to do was get to Falmouth before the pubs shut. Funny at the time – probably not so funny the next morning. At heart I reckon they were warm and decent, though.

Joan and Jack are renowned among the Cornish piskies. But it seems there's plenty of others around. Sophie wrote to me with a fucking brilliant encounter she had with a creature that she suspected was a piskie. She'd been out walking with her family almost 20 years ago when she spotted a gnome-like creature sitting under a tree. Was she scared?

'Yes, at first I was scared,' she told me. 'He had a brown, wizened face and he was just grinning at me. I remember him so clearly. He had twinkly eyes, a beard, a mossy green coat and a hat. He was all the same colours as the earth, but I noticed him immediately because he was so out-of-place in my reality.'

Was Sophie with anyone? Did any other witnesses behold this otherworldly vision?

'No. If they did they didn't say. I started to shout and point, but I quickly thought better of it. I felt completely daft, like someone was taking the piss out of me or playing a prank. Or maybe I was going mad or seeing things. Moments later when I looked again there was just a tree stump. If it was an animal, it didn't look like anything I'd ever seen before. In some ways I'd be happier to know that it was.'

Fuck me. I would have loved to have been alongside Sophie that day. More than the actual sighting, I wanted to know if the experience changed her? It's not every day a piskie pitches up under a tree and into your life!

'Yes, at first I felt really confused. I'd never seen a ghost or anything like that before and wouldn't have called myself a natural believer in any of that stuff. And this didn't feel like something sent from heaven or another realm, like an angel. But in a way it was profound. At the time, it made me think a lot about nature and how we should preserve things and look after the world. Since then, I've never been able to forget it.'

Wow. A tiny creature appearing to teach us about our tiny place in this gargantuan universe – and to remind us to do our recycling. What are the chances?

And there's an equally brilliant story I heard about a man driving through Cornwall sometime in the 1990s. There were hedgerows on either side of the road. He was going at around 45 miles per hour, eyes straight ahead, when something compelled him to look into the hedgerow. There, he caught sight of a tiny, brown, leathery-skinned and angry-looking man. He was completely undressed other than a loin-cloth and he described him as having a hooked nose and large ears. He was pointing with his index finger. The man braked suddenly. It was then he realised. In a haze of tiredness, he had been veering off the road and was in danger of falling sharply towards a seawall. Had he not caught sight of the creature, who had appeared to warn him, he could have hurtled over a cliff face, along with his wife and baby son. No wonder the piskie looked furious.

Closely related to the piskie is the knocker. While piskies are known in broad areas of the West Country, knockers are specifically connected to the old tin mines in Cornwall. They are named knockers because of the hammering sound they were supposed to make against the mine walls.

To me, knockers seem the perfect combination of swashbuckling heroes but with a brilliant sense of humour. They lived deep within the mines and these little fellas were pictured as a metre tall with white whiskers and wearing miner's clothes. Sometimes they just wanted to hide miner's tools, tangle up some ropes, break a few ladders, take a bite out of someone's packed lunch or simply extinguish torch flames. At the end of a shift, miners would throw food into the mine to feed the knockers just to keep them onside. I can see how their pranks could get quite annoying, but they might also have brightened up a miner's day. After all, most of it was spent in the dark.

Apparently knockers got particularly animated and mischievous if miners whistled or swore underground. Jesus, I would be fucking screwed seeing as every noun, pronoun, verb and adjective that tumbles from my mouth is a profanity. If you're easily offended, I am truly fucking sorry.

Some believed that knockers were the ghosts of former miners killed in the pits. So that's why as well as making mischief they also came back to warn the living of any impending disasters like avalanches. Their knocking could lead miners to rich seams too. One story I read was told by a miner in the 1940s. He heard knocking in a particular part of the mine before the ground crumbled in front of him. There, before his eyes, were glistening bunches of crystals, all colours of the rainbow, which covered the walls and floor of the hollow space he'd uncovered. When he peered in further, there were three knockers sitting together 'no bigger than a sixpenny doll'. They were dressed in mining clothes and the knocker in the middle had his sleeves rolled up and was holding an anvil.

'How are you?' he politely asked the miner, who replied he was fine and apologised for letting in a draft. Figuring the knockers were now cold, the miner turned to fetch his candle to warm them as they huddled. But as he turned again and peered in, the knockers were gone.

✦

There are so many other little creatures from Cornwall to Wales to Scotland that I don't have the space to discuss them in this opus. And there's also a great deal of confusion over what people believe they have seen. As an example, there are those who think they've spotted a piskie but they may have actually seen a spriggan as the two look quite similar. The difference is that spriggans mainly hang out in ruins and guard buried treasure, just like their distant relatives the Irish leprechauns.

To be honest, spriggans don't have a great reputation, but I think they've probably not done themselves many favours. It's a bit like the class clown. Once you've been naughty a few times – leaning back on your chair at the back of the classroom, showing your knickers to anyone who laughs, pinging Hubba Bubba off the end of your pencil, drawing a dick and balls over your textbook – you suddenly find yourself getting the blame for absolutely everything.

The crime list for spriggans is endless: they sent in whirlwinds to put the shits up travellers; ruined crops; stole children; they got blamed if a house collapsed even though it was probably just a dodgy builder; if anything got robbed, including cattle, their name did the rounds. I'd say as forces of nature go they are probably just a bit loutish and unmanageable rather than total cunts.

And then there's fairies, an entirely different subgenre of the diminutive supernatural and taken very seriously by fairy watchers. These mainly live in woodland communities or by lakes and hills in rural places. One extensive study took place between 2014 and 2017 carried out by the Fairy Investigation Society. It is a document to behold: awash with sightings dating back decades and from all corners of the UK. Unlike the profiles of Tinker Bell and the hoax Cottingley fairies – dainty, winged creatures with ballerina-like tutus and a wand – fairies actually take many (less Disney-like) forms.

There's reports dating all the way back to the 1930s that talk of furry-type creatures that aren't exactly animals but are not of this world either. Other fairies are dressed in clothes of leaves and flowers. One was the size of a person's thumb and wearing a green dress. And there's tree fairies that are reportedly up to seven feet tall – slim and with a trunk-like body and branches for arms. One woman saw exactly this creature casually strolling down the road! She had been on the telephone at the time and watched from her front window as it passed. She watched it for a full two minutes before next-door's hedge obscured the view and she lost sight of it.

And there are many reported dancing balls of light, not unlike the orbs that I mentioned earlier, that people often believe are fairies.

Other surprising aspects to these stories is that there are sightings of the same fairies by different people – it's not always one person on their own.

In Scotland, where everything is a lot more frightening, fairies have been called out as more banshee-type creatures. Their wail is supposed to foretell a person's death. The washer at the ford (the shallow crossing of a river), in particular, is the death omen, who is depicted as beautiful and who weeps. She washes the bloody garments at streams and riversides and turns to tell the beholder that they are his or hers. What a fucking dreadful job. I hope she gets paid holiday and is given a free gym membership or similar, just to relieve the stress. And just think of the havoc caused to shellac nails.

But I have to ask: are all these people who believe in fairies or who claim to have seen fairies mainlining deadly nightshade? Or are fairies like ghosts? Coexisting with us but on a different vibrational level and not always obvious to our limited spectrum? Has being glued to our mobile phones and computers meant that we notice so much less of this natural phenomena? And is calling these tales 'fairy tales' just a bit fucking insulting? Like all of the paranormal, we don't yet have proof, but that means we can't disprove anything either.

For me, it says a lot that supposedly fairy stories were first written down in around the 13th century in this country, but people had been telling stories of fairies way before that. And it's not just in the UK – fairy stories span the world over, which is probably why there's an absolute shit-ton of fairy variants, as dizzying as the choice of supermarket loo roll. And like a fart in the wind, no one can pin these creatures down.

And why are we still telling stories about these creatures? We're not banging on about trolls or mermaids or phoenixes with exactly the same enthusiasm. Vampires have made a bit of a comeback recently, along with dragons, but I blame *Game of Thrones* for that. If something endures to that extent, might there be some truth in it? I await my very own fairy godmother to guide me in the right direction . . .

★

PART FIVE

THE RANDOM PARANORMAL AND THE UNEXPLAINED

20

ASTRAL PROJECTION

It wasn't long after our friend Michael Sleggs died and we'd started filming the third series of *This Country* that I had another unexplained experience. At the time I was consumed with grief for Slugs and desperately unhappy in my marriage. One day I was lying in bed when a strange sensation spread through my body. Every pore in my skin began tingling, like a faint vibration running across me that became more and more intense. A voice started speaking in one ear. I had no clue what it was saying. It sounded like a woman talking in Spanish who'd not had the courtesy to switch on Google Translate. Her words were like a hail of bullets raining down on me, fast and distressed.

In my other ear, a man was speaking loud and clear. 'I'm drowning,' he said. He sounded like a Brummie, which was odd. The voice repeated these words over and over, boring into my brain. At first I wondered whether the pair had met on a Jet2 holiday in Benidorm, shagged each other and she'd turned out to be a total psycho.

Maybe they were trying to have a heated argument with each other and my massive head was getting in the way? I debated leaving them to it – don't mind me, guys – but then the voices started to fade out like they were slowly dying. *Fucking hell . . . this is insane.*

What I didn't know was that this was the calm before the storm. All of a sudden, I sensed two hands rising up from my body. In that moment I could feel myself being catapulted upright from my prone position. I was moving so fast that I had no time to stop myself and all around orange and red lights began flashing. Then, the two hands rolled me out of my body. Literally rolled me, like a slab of pastry being rolled by a giant rolling pin. It sounds crazy, I know. But I also know that what I experienced was real. For ages it felt as though I was just hovering above myself. And the moment I came back into my body, I felt constrained again – like being zipped into a tight wetsuit. After that, the feeling slowly disappeared.

I've had bad dreams before. *Really bad* dreams where the whole world has come crashing in around me. The 'I'm going to get cancelled from every TV programme I've ever appeared on' kind of scary. I've even had nightmares that have left me petrified with my eyes wide open – a form of sleep paralysis. One I had all the time as a child was where I was running through school corridors, as fast as I could. The florescent lights above flickered before cutting to darkness. A figure was chasing me, a finger's length away from touching me. And when I saw him he was tall with electric-white hair, like chalky waves. No matter how far I ran the corridor got longer and longer.

Those were dreams I recognised, but this felt completely different. All I know is that when I came to, I knew couldn't carry on with my life the way I had been. It felt like some kind of out-of-body awakening. But what the hell was it?

The only proper out-of-body experience I'd had was when I was 16. I'd drunk mushroom tea while listening to Bob Marley at the home of some random ex-military guy me and my mates had befriended after a night out. Only that time, there were no voices ringing in my ears. Instead my head morphed into Mr Potato Head – the toy with detachable features and one of the stars of the *Toy Story* films. In this vision I had an ear as a nose, a moustache as eyebrows and an eye for a mouth. Fucking ridiculous. And Mr Potato Head didn't tell me anything useful at all. To be fair, anyone with an eye for a mouth would have had trouble speaking anyway. Admittedly, Mr Potato Head had been helped along by a fair amount of cheap white wine and psychedelic substances. So the only lesson I ever took from Mr Potato Head was never to go near magic mushrooms again. Especially if they've been given to you by a guy who looks like a cross between Jason Statham and a red M&M dressed in military fatigues and who has a large dog on guard beside him named Subwoofer.

This time around, though, everything felt odd. How could it be that I'd just vacated my own body with no help whatsoever? It left so many unanswered questions. For starters, if I really had vacated my physical form and floated above myself why the fuck hadn't I bothered to dust off the cobwebs on the top of the lampshade?

The experience stayed with me for ages. At the time I'd also been pregnant with my son and so other distractions took over – and life took over. But that day did keep returning to my thoughts. I was so confused that in the end, not long after I'd given birth to Jack, I confided in a friend. Surprisingly she didn't tell me that I'd lost my mind.

'Let me put you in touch with someone who can help,' she said.

'A shrink?'

'No! Someone who'll introduce you to a different way of seeing things.'

'Erm . . . okay . . .'

And that's when my eyes got opened to a unique aspect of the supernatural: astral projection. Astral what? Yep, I had exactly the same reaction too. What the fucking fuck is that? Well, I was about to find out . . .

The woman my friend put me in touch with is called Jade Shaw. We ended up meeting for a coffee in Central London. Jade is young and super-pretty. I don't know why, but I immediately felt connected to her. But I was anxious. Really anxious. *Deep breath, Dais, just explain what happened. Hopefully she won't piss herself laughing!* I started on my story. As I reached the end, I looked at her hesitantly.

'What do you think? Do you reckon I'm mad?'

'What you've experienced is perfectly normal.' She leaned in, smiling.

'It is?'

I stirred my coffee and looked into Jade's eyes. She seemed totally sane.

'What do you mean?'

Jade told me that we all have a soul and it can detach from our physical body. It can go out into the world and explore.

'So, let me get this right. My soul could be at Ocean Beach in

Marbella, scantily clad in a bikini and sipping cocktails, pretending to be something out of *Love Island*? While my physical body is actually pushing a trolley around Tesco?'

'Not exactly.' Jade grimaced.

It was clear that my understanding of the astral plane needed some work. In any case, Jade said the places I could go to would probably be far better than Marbella. I know, hard to imagine.

Jade went on to explain that we all have what's called an energy body or an astral body and that we can use it to travel to other realms and meet people in other realms. Jade had had unexplained experiences herself as a child, but when she was older she had one out-of-body experience that changed her life for ever. During it she travelled to another dimension entirely. After it, she gave up her job running a dance company, travelled to a Buddhist retreat and studied astral projection for five years.

Although what had happened to me had been spontaneous, people can learn how to astral project and she can teach them.

'Learn?'

'Yep, you can induce it,' she said.

'What? Like how?'

'With meditation and techniques like hypnosis.'

'Wow. So it's not magic?'

'No, it's not magic. It's real.'

But that didn't explain what my out-of-body experience had been about. During it, I'd heard voices. *Miserable* voices. Voices that sounded like they wanted the one-way express ticket out of my head, not even super-off-peak.

'What did all of that mean?' I asked.

'The experience was trying to tell you something,' Jade replied.

'But one voice was talking in Spanish! I couldn't even understand her!' I pointed out.

'But she sounded like she was dying...'

'Yes, in so much pain! Like the poor woman was stuck on a delayed Ryanair flight minus the air conditioning and sat next to an English stag party belting out "Don't Let the Sun Go Down on Me". It was utterly heartbreaking.'

'And what was the other voice telling you?'

'That it was drowning,' I said soberly.

Jade and I talked some more and during that conversation I realised that I had travelled to another realm. This wasn't just a practice reserved for God, angels and that woman off the Netflix series *Behind Her Eyes*. Whatever I had tuned into had been trying to give me information that I could bring back to this world.

'So what happened in the days after you came back into your body?' Jade probed further.

'It was strange, like a peace had descended over me.'

By the time I met with Jade I'd already given birth to my son Jack. And everything *did* feel peaceful. What had also become clear – crystal clear – was that I needed to move forward with my life. I needed to end my relationship and go it alone. Painful, but true.

'So you had a wake-up call?'

'I guess so,' I concluded.

Weird that my mind had tried to make sense of all the dark things going on in my life by taking flight from my body. Now I was in free fall and I hadn't even bothered to pack a parachute. Granted, I've never been the best prepared. This was all a bit fucking terrifying. On the other hand, I'd got a mile-high view of myself and I hadn't been consumed by vertigo or vomited on anyone. Surely, though, the only way is down?

'Not at all,' Jade explained. In fact the experience could open up a whole world of possibilities. I just needed to be open, she said.

'So, it's kind of exhilarating?'

'More than exhilarating. It's life-changing.'

When I got back home, I fired up my laptop and began searching around. Astral travel . . . nope, that was an independent tour operator in . . . fucking Swindon of all places! Holiday packages, cruises, hotels, flights and so much more. Sadly, their 25-year business didn't stretch to out-of-body experiences. It would only be a matter of time, though, like sending people to Mars or the Moon. Ah yes . . . got it . . . astral projection. Fuck me, there was pages and pages of the stuff.

In fact, astral projection has been around for a lot longer than I imagined. There were accounts from all over the world, dating back thousands and thousands of years. Indigenous Americans believed they could travel to a spirit world then jump back into their bodies. Reaching nirvana in Buddhist culture is supposed be part of a similar voyage. The accounts went on . . .

Even the American military were interested in astral projection and in the 1970s and 1980s began researching it. There's one report that's a dizzying word salad of hypnosis, holograms, quantum subatomic particles and astral projection. I won't lie, I did intend to read it. But it felt like wading through treacle. Even the diagrams made no sense whatsoever. In a nutshell, though, the army wanted to find out if astral projection could be used to focus soldiers' minds and to gather intelligence – like sending the mind on satellite missions. They also wondered if it could be used to learn foreign languages and help people solve world problems, all while being outside of their bodies. In the end, the report got shelved and was not made public until many years later. And it's unclear whether any of it was ever used. Currently, world peace seems about as realistic as me getting to the end of that report – which definitely didn't happen.

Fast-forward a decade or so and another experiment took place on one woman who claimed that she could astral project on tap. In one of the first experiments of its kind, neuroscientists from a Canadian university scanned her brain while she was in the throes of an epic trip. And do you know what is remarkable? The brain scan showed that what she said she was experiencing was real. She wasn't telling massive porkies about seeing herself rolling in the air or floating above horizontal planes. Disappointingly, researchers put this down to hallucinations rather than the paranormal at work. Yet, there's still been so little research done into this. And if it does prove to be some kind of brain phenomenon then scientists still don't understand how a person can simply switch into this state. All I know is that it happened to me without switching on anything.

Jade had been spot on, though. The experience did change my life. I didn't feel trapped any more, choking and alone. I started making decisions that felt as though they could be good for me. *Really fucking good*. Even if there were a few relapses along the way, I would still be on the right road – I am human, after all. And I have tried to get back to astral projection since. Sadly, it's been without much success. It does take a lot of focus and learning, two things that I am fucking terrible at. And it also feels like quite a long way to go without being able to vape. If only it was as easy as logging on to Astral Travel in Swindon and booking an all-inclusive two-weeker to Corfu, entertainment thrown in too. I'd pack my bikini tomorrow.

★

Astral projection has made me far more open to other ideas about the universe, though. Whether they eventually prove to be an aspect of the paranormal or not, I'm willing to be receptive. I definitely believe it's good to be open to most things in life, except maybe housework and murder. And perhaps astral projection does force you to see your life from a different angle, like all other unexplained phenomena.

Recently I had a conversation with the TV superstar Rylan. What he told me was extraordinary. In 2012, just a few weeks before auditions started for *The X Factor,* which made him famous, he'd been on holiday in Ibiza. While he was sat on his favourite rock, he picked up two stones. He made a wish, then threw one stone out to sea and placed the other in his back pocket. His wish was to appear on *The X Factor*. Back in the UK, two weeks later, he got the call to audition. Every week he performed with the lucky stone in his back pocket. Rylan didn't win but he was asked to appear on *Big Brother* and the rest is history. And I absolutely love his story, because it feels to me like the power of the universe at work, like all its cogs and wheels are whirring away and we just need to tap into its life-changing energy.

What Rylan was talking about is actually a recognised practice called manifestation – the idea that if you think positive thoughts and focus on positive goals then they will happen. It was a term coined way back in 2006 by the author Rhonda Byrne in her book *The Secret* which is the book Rylan brought on to my podcast, *Educating Daisy*. At the time, loads of people laughed at her but the book became a bestseller and I reckon there's something in it. Plus Noel Edmonds is a devotee. In my view you don't get more of a ringing endorsement than Noel, although I suspect he adopted the practice after his ill-fated foray into the Mr Blobby-themed amusement park Blobbyland, which had a lifespan of all of three years during the 1990s.

It is hard to get your head around manifestation, but I believe it's like getting on the same energy level as your future self. It's the law of attraction. If you think positive things – they come to you. If you're a cunt – you become a giant magnet for bad shit. And as soon as I heard Rylan's story, I had a thunderbolt moment. Manifestation had already worked in my life, and I hadn't even realised it. The universe had already given me what I wished for.

In the run-up to having *This Country* commissioned, Charlie and I had setback after setback, disappointment after disappointment. While Chaz was on the point of giving up and/or killing himself, it turned me into a weird version of Wonder Woman – actually, more like the Hulk with tits. As far as I was concerned I'd cast my stone and made my wish and now all I had to do was reach my goal. Anything else would have been *really* bleak. Thankfully, I didn't rip off my shirt to reveal a luminescent green six-pack. That would have been hideous – and almost certainly illegal. But I did the mental equivalent. I wrote a shameless begging letter to the head of comedy at the BBC and put our dreams in motion.

Was that manifestation? Probably, when I think about it now. Although I did actually have to do something. But if I could do that once then I must be able to do it again . . . and again . . . and again.

That said, I do think there is a point when manifestation could go too far. It's mantra is: ask, believe, receive. But don't you have to be careful about what you wish for? What would happen if I was a fitness instructor who'd secretly yearned to be an elephant all her life. *Ask, believe, receive.* Even if I shut my eyes and pray really hard, with the best will in the world I'm never going to be an elephant, hanging out in the savannah with my mates, watching *Dumbo* on repeat, or becoming the star of nature documentaries. I'm still going to be Daisy, the human, albeit with unbelievably muscly abs. Isn't that setting myself up for a life of utter misery? Isn't that the exact opposite to casting my net into the universe to achieve lasting happiness and fulfilment? I did point all of this out to Rylan, who suggested I explore this with a professional who charges by the hour.

As for the closely related cosmic ordering, that's dangerous in the hands of someone like me. It's the practice of writing something down and placing an order with the cosmos. Although it's apparent lack of effort is attractive, if I asked the universe to give me everything I thought it owed me then I'd already have worked my way through the Argos catalogue and manifested a garage full of random exercise machines, a three-storey rabbit hutch and several life-size models of

Ben Shephard. The list would be endless. And all through the power of my mind . . . well, that's what I'd tell the bank anyway.

For the moment, I think I'll forget cosmic ordering and just stick to believing in a better future. And if, at any point, I once more leap out of my body and see the world from a different angle, then this time I'll enjoy every bloody minute of it knowing that I'm safe in the hands of the astral plane.

★

21

MY PAST LIFE

I've been utterly obsessed with past-life regression – journeying under hypnosis to the people you were during a past life – ever since I watched a documentary about a little boy whose recollection of his supposed past life made for one of the most chilling programmes I'd ever seen. Cameron Macaulay spent all of his life in Glasgow. Yet, inexplicably, from the age of two, he could remember precise details from a previous life. He talked of falling through some kind of portal from a tiny island in the Outer Hebrides of Scotland, called Barra, to his current life in Glasgow. But none of his family had ever been to Barra, which lies 220 miles off the Scottish coast.

In Glasgow, Cameron lived with his mum and his little brother. On Barra, Cameron had grown up with a different mum – who he missed terribly – and a dad called Shane Robertson who, as Cameron told it, died when he was knocked down by a car. He recalled the white single-storey house he lived in which overlooked rock pools on the beach and the sea. He had brothers and sisters and, from the window, they used to watch aeroplanes land on the beach – the only form of runway on Barra. He also owned a black-and-white sheepdog.

As imaginary friends go, that's absolutely mental. I thought I surpassed myself with the non-verbal relationship I developed with the school rabbit who fucking hated my teacher Mrs Canes too. Plus the hours I spent in my bedroom at the epicentre of my Sylvanian Families universe where the rabbits ran the local swimming pool and the badgers took charge of the post office. Then, of course, there was my telepathic relationship with The Borrowers: the little people who controlled my mind. They really were very naughty and turned out to be the forces behind my outright refusal to wear knickers at nursery school.

But was Cameron's past life just an open-and-shut case of a child having a crazy imagination? One psychologist who was interviewed thought so. In his view, children create false memories gathered from information they've seen on TV or stories that have been told to them. But Cameron's mum wasn't so sure. She had no contact with anyone who knew anything about Barra. And Cameron's flashbacks had begun when he'd first learned how to talk.

It wasn't until another less sceptical expert accompanied Cameron and his mum to the island to work out whether Cameron's memories were real that Cameron's story got a whole lot weirder. After some searching, the family found the exact house on the beach that Cameron claimed to have grown up in. They also discovered it had been owned by a family called the Robertsons who spent every summer there. However, there was no record of a Shane Robertson or details of any member of the family who had ever been killed in a road accident.

But it's the last sequence of the documentary that I've never been able to shake from my brain. After travelling to Barra and retracing his past life, a calm descended over Cameron. After that he didn't speak about Barra or seem troubled by it in the way he'd been before. It's as if he'd made peace with his previous existence. How strange is that?

I wanted to try to find Cameron. By my rough calculations he would be in his twenties by now. I wanted to know what he still remembered of his past life and what he thought about it now? Was he under psychiatric supervision? Or living a completely new life under an assumed identity? Or, like me, had he managed to forge a career out of talking utter bollocks? It turns out I was not the only person looking. On social media I did stumble across several Cameron Macauleys. Most looked far too young to be the real deal. And the only strong contender had written on his profile:

PSA: I am not the Barra boy who lived before.

That Cameron did look like he was having a fucking ball, though. His girlfriend was well fit and by the looks of it he was on a lads' holiday every other weekend, visiting somewhere scorching hot and clutching an ice-cold beer. He was a Manchester United supporter, though, so I guess no one is perfect.

★

My search for answers about past-life regression could have ended there. But then I received an email from a woman whose neighbour claimed to be having an affair with Jackie Kennedy. In case I was in any doubt, she confirmed that her neighbour was in his eighties, not off his rocker and not suffering from loneliness either. Apparently, he and Jackie had been an item in a previous life and now she often popped back to visit him. One night she even banged on his front door at 1 am to alert him to the fact that he hadn't locked it properly. *Yes! Yes! Yes!* I'd fucking love it if Jackie O, former wife to US president John F. Kennedy, then wife to the billionaire shipping magnate Aristotle Onassis and once *the* most glamorous woman in all of Christendom, turns out to be a highly active member of a local Neighbourhood Watch scheme. Shows she's down to earth, I reckon.

Another woman also wrote to tell me she'd been 'regressed' live on stage at Dorking Halls. However, she was still sifting through the evidence. During the process, she called out her past-life name and the name of the exact road she lived on. Throughout she began speaking in a different accent. She is currently trying to trace whether anyone of that name did live at that location.

The more I read, the more intrigued I became. Then I started thinking. *Did I have a past life? If I did, then who was I?* Deep down, I had probably always imagined myself as Henry VIII – a fat, bearded oaf gorging myself on lamb, venison and swan washed down with gallons of ale or wine, only taking a bath once a year and murdering my partners as soon as I was done with them. In the unlikely event that I did turn out to be the second reigning monarch in England's Tudor court it would explain a lot about my inflated ego.

I've also often wondered whether my kids have ever had a past life too – especially my daughter. Inexplicably, ever since she was born it feels to me like we've met before. She's an old soul, different to me in so many ways: Saffy to my *Ab Fab* Patsy. I do check in with her and Jack now and again in the hope that something from a former life might materialise.

'What do you remember before you came to this planet?'

'Nothing,' they answer, staring at me blankly like I've suddenly grown two heads. Every. Single. Time.

It was the moment to take matters into my own hands. I decided to book my very own regression. After a search through an online directory, I was taken aback by how many people actually offer this service. Were they all legit? Impossible to know. As yet, there's no Checkatrade for the profession. But I'd love it if there was . . .

> Awful experience. Totally botched the job. I ended up as a fucking lobster. Every waking hour was spent tapping against the window of the display tank in Mandarin Heaven in Coventry. Asked for my money back but didn't even get offered a discount. Will not be using again or recommending to anyone.

As the process does involve some light hypnotherapy, I did hope I would choose well. The last thing I wanted was to zone out only to come back brainwashed as a fully paid-up member of a doomsday cult or the dodgy one from the band Blue. I cast my eyes down the list, in the end settling for the man with the most qualifications after his name (I had no idea what the letters meant). He also had the kindest-looking face. Not exactly scientific, I know. There were some glowing testimonials too:

> My session with Henry was the best fun I've had in ages.

That sounded promising.

Henry showed me that my husband getting stuck in traffic for twelve hours was not proof he was having an affair.

That last one was the real clincher. I picked a time slot and pressed send.

The day before Henry was due to arrive he requested an online introduction. He did seem pleasant enough, although I couldn't help fixating on his ginormous ears, like Spock and King Charles had spawned a lovechild. He spoke in a wispy, New Age voice that I had trouble hearing at times. I leaned in and persevered.

'During the session you may regress to one past life, maybe more,' he explained.

'More than one?' I said, surprised.

'You could travel to several, Daisy.'

'Really?'

Fuck me. At this rate I could tumble off the space-time continuum completely. Would I ever make it back?

'Oh, and it would be great if you had in your mind an intention.'

'An intention? Like . . .?'

'Something that you might like to resolve in your life. Perhaps something that's weighing you down, playing on your mind.'

I did have a sizeable list. Things like why Tesco Clubcard deals didn't seem as good as they used to be. Or the fact that Caramac bars had suddenly been discontinued, sucking every last drop of joy out of my weekly shop.

'I'll think about it . . .' I promised.

'Oh, before I go. Do you believe in the afterlife, Daisy?'

I wasn't sure where Henry's line of questioning was going, but I kept with it. He didn't seem like a swinger, but as we know, I can't always spot 'em.

'Yes . . .'

'What does the afterlife look like to you?'

'Well, I'd like to think it's quite beautiful – a bright light on the other side.'

'Yes, quite beautiful,' he repeated.

Then, Henry paused before he dropped the D-bomb.

'How do you feel about witnessing your own death, Daisy?'

How did I feel about witnessing . . . My thoughts trailed off.

'Is . . . that . . . included in the price?' I asked, stalling for time. Quickly several scenarios flashed before my eyes. None of them were perfect, but if I had to make a choice . . .

'Well, gasping my last breath on a fragrant bed of rose petals would be preferable, I suppose. But if I drowned in a pit of other people's excrement after having my fingernails and toenails ripped out by a medieval torturer while being restrained in a vice, then I'd probably struggle,' I replied. Drowning in anything is my worst nightmare *ever*.

'Right . . . thanks, Daisy. Most people find they are calm observers of their deaths, even if those deaths are violent, gruesome or completely unexpected.'

Fucking hell . . . Henry did have a knack of trying to find the positive in everything.

'Right . . . well . . . I'll give it go shall I?'

'So I'll look forward to seeing you tomorrow?' Henry chimed.

'Yep . . . sure.'

I took a deep breath. A quiet voice in my head was now telling me that this was a *really* bad idea. On the other hand, I was unbelievably curious. *Nothing to be afraid of, Dais. Only your own hideous demise played out in real time. Yep, no biggie.* Plus, there could be some benefits. While hovering above my body I could perhaps finally make peace with my nose – see it from a different angle. I've always been self-conscious of its size, but what if it didn't turn out to be the beak I'd built up in my head? That would be good.

That night I was unusually restless. By then I had moved from my haunted new build to a 19th-century property and to help with my paranormal research, my boyfriend had erected a camera in my bedroom (not what you think, you dirty fuckers!). There were zero reports of hauntings there (not that the owner admitted to, anyway) but I did want to make sure. All the camera picked up that night, though, was me tossing and turning and stumbling out for a piss every ten minutes, like an incontinent Bigfoot.

By the time Henry arrived the next day my nerves felt like thin shards of glass jabbing into every pore. I'd had very little sleep. To distract myself, I tidied my living room several times over. I couldn't decide where I'd be more comfortable. I rearranged the cushions, lit some candles, then blew them out and rearranged the cushions again. I shut the blinds, then partially reopened them. Henry had suggested that I have some tissues handy, but I'd forgotten to pick up a box. Instead, I sat an unused toilet roll next to the sofa, hoping that it might soak up the thousands of tears I shed when I found out I'd come back as a fucking fruit fly.

'Lovely to meet you.' Henry held out his hand before I led him through.

He did seem very sweet. He'd even brought a blanket for me to huddle under to keep warm in case I didn't have my own. We sat chatting for a while. Overnight I'd been thinking and by then I had a multi-question pile-up.

I wanted to know whether people do actually regress to a past life or whether it's some kind of metaphor. Going back in time to solve current problems made me wonder whether it would just be my subconscious mind whirring away, digging up weird associations from the recesses of my memory. None would be real, just an imagined way of tapping into thoughts and feelings.

'That's a good question, Daisy,' Henry replied, shuffling in his seat. He did seem rather uncomfortable with my interrogation.

'Well, what do *you* believe?' I asked.

I noticed that Henry didn't answer my question directly. Instead he told me about a woman he regressed the week before who found herself in Arthurian times. In the realm of the Round Table she trusted people, whereas in this life she trusted no one. That she'd trusted people in her past life became a lesson she was able to bring back. She needed to have more faith in people.

'It's never happened to me but people don't always come back as something living or breathing,' he continued.

'Are you serious?'

'There are many reports of people regressing to rocks or gasses. So your question is complicated.'

I almost had to stop myself exploding. Daisy May Cooper: reincarnated as a raspberry fart. That would be a post-and-a-half on Instagram. I looked up at Henry. He didn't seem a fart joke kind of guy, so I downgraded my outburst of laughter to a weak smile.

'Did you think about your intention, Daisy?' he continued.

'Yep.'

Probably, that had been gnawing at me the most, keeping me awake. I wanted to understand my relationship with my daughter Pip better. Recently, we'd been clashing badly. And if we had met in a previous life, as I suspected, then I wanted to find out if I could take something, anything back to help us. I wanted to reach in and damp down the red-hot heat, the mum guilt, the turmoil of the situation and get back to being a harmonious duo.

After I explained my intention to Henry, his lips pursed tenderly and he nodded as if he understood. He really was an almighty tree-hugger but I kind of warmed to him, too.

'Ready, Daisy?' he said.

'Ready...'

Within moments I was in a half-conscious state. The strange part was I was aware of what I was saying but unable to control where I was going. As Henry talked gently, he asked me to invite a mentor to accompany me. I chose Slugs. The bastard still hadn't bothered to visit me in the afterlife but I was aching to hang out with him again. Then I panicked. What if he didn't turn up?

Good to have a Plan B, Daisy, I thought.

'I also call on Jesus and the Archangel Michael to help me on this journey,' I said quickly. Better safe than sorry.

'Beautiful,' said Henry.

Henry did say the word 'beautiful' *a lot*.

Soon I was walking down an ornate wooden staircase carved with love hearts and intertwined with flowers and leaves. When I reached the bottom Henry told me to imagine a beautiful place in nature. Admittedly, my garden wouldn't have been out of place in Enid Blyton's *Enchanted Wood*: moss, toadstools, frogs croaking under an overcast twilight sky. Where the flute music came from I have no idea. At least the Archangel Michael had put in an appearance. He was perched on a stone along the garden's pebbly path, grinning inanely and rocking gently like he'd just dropped an E.

'Thanks for guiding me,' I told him.

It was good to see him, but I did feel pissed off that Slugs or Jesus hadn't been arsed to come. Maybe their phones were switched off? More likely they'd had a better offer – a caveman being chased through a forest then ravaged by Tyrannosaurus rex or a gladiator battling it out with a lion. Who knows?

'Now, I want you to look up at the sky . . .' I heard Henry say. 'There will be some clouds and one in particular will draw your attention.'

He was right. A long, thin, dagger-shaped cloud drifted into view.

'Can you see it?'

'Yes,' I murmured.

'Don't worry, it will support your weight if you climb on to it,' Henry reassured me.

Honestly, I wasn't sure. Had Henry clocked my fat arse?

But surprisingly, when I attempted to climb on Henry turned out to be right. Within seconds I was lying back, luxuriating in all its royal fluffiness like the Queen of Sheba in a Radox bubble bath flying over deserts and oceans, meadows and valleys.

'When you come down, tell me where you land,' Henry said.

And this is where my past-life regression truly began. Suddenly, I had thrown off all the shackles of being Daisy May Cooper. I was a young boy wearing dark brown boat shoes and navy velvet culotte trousers. My shirt was starched white linen but, somehow, I'd lost my jacket. I must have been playing around coal too, as I was covered in soot.

'I don't want my dad to be cross with me,' I said.

Where I'd landed was slap-bang on a busy dirt road in a town. I was stood right next to a horse and cart. The local grocer, a man with a large moustache, was loading the cart with heavy sacks of potatoes and I stood watching him, trying to brush out the coal smears from my shirt with my hands.

Soon it was time to face the music and go home. I made my way along the road and through the wrought iron gate of the townhouse I lived in. It was the maid who answered. Her face contorted the moment she set eyes on me. She was clearly very angry.

'You ran off!' she shouted, dragging me to a tin bath so I could get clean.

My mum was dead, apparently. I don't know how, but I did know that she loved me. I also loved my little brother and my father, even though he was very strict. At that I couldn't stop my real-life tears from falling. Henry had torn off some sheets of loo roll which he handed to me. It was the strangest feeling.

Once I'd dried my tears, Henry asked me to move on in the story. The next scene appeared to me just as clearly. I was around 12 years old, at boarding school, brilliant at sports, especially cricket. And, as soon as my school years were over, I married. My wife was kind, artistic and very musical, whereas I was some kind of trader.

By now, my father had died. My wife and I also had a boy who died, but after that she'd given birth to a daughter called Polly. She looked like me and was very stubborn with a fiery temper. *Could it be Pip?* I wondered. She reminded me of her even if she didn't have Pip's flame-red hair.

Polly was as wilful, though. A few years later she eloped with a boy and was travelling throughout Europe. I'm not sure I liked the look of him. And she and I lost touch, until one day when I was 64 years old. Then, I received a letter from her from Zurich telling me that she was okay. What Polly didn't know is that the letter arrived on the last day of my life. I'd been ill for some time and confined to bed. My lungs felt as tight as a snare drum. And, as I took my last breath, I felt myself floating above my body. I hadn't realised how thin I'd got. I did look dreadful. And my nose . . . fuck. It really was massive.

But the only person I wanted to see was my daughter. In the next scene I was looking at her in her small apartment. I wanted her to know I was there, so I hit a pot in the kitchen that tumbled over. Polly cleaned up the spilled water, but I had no idea if she knew it was me. When I left the scene I was unsure if she knew I was dead. All I do know is that I loved her and that she loved me, and maybe my death would allow her to make her own decisions in life. That I couldn't control her, and I needed to trust her.

Soon, I was back on my cloud, soaring above the world.

'See where it takes you,' I heard Henry say.

But when I slowly came back down, I'd landed right back in my living room.

'Here,' I said.

When my eyes flickered open, it felt like I'd been to another planet. *Holy fucking shit* . . .

I was also desperate for a piss which made me wonder whether that was the real reason I'd landed back in Blighty.

'Could I have gone to another past life?' I asked Henry.

'You could have gone to several. You may have hundreds of past lives. You had only one today because that's probably all you could cope with,' Henry said.

To be honest, I felt as though I hadn't exactly done much. It's not as if my one past life had been packed with much drama. Most disappointingly, Henry VIII didn't show. There were no decapitations or anything. And my death? Fuck me, zero exertion there. It must have been the laziest way to kick the bucket ever. Just one last breath while lying on my back – and then curtains. No wonder Slugs and Jesus didn't turn up. It was hardly a thrill-seekers' paradise, like turning up to Alton Towers to find the Nemesis Reborn ride is shut. I suspect the Archangel Michael was just off his tits and took a wrong turn.

The experience was extraordinary, though. *Really* fucking extraordinary. While I was lying there, it all felt so real. If felt like looking into a crystalline pool observing another time fractal. Like 5D thinking compared to my 2D linear world.

'What do you think you learned?' Henry asked.

That was unbelievably clear to me too.

'In my past life my father was just grieving for my mother – that's why he was so strict. He didn't know what to do. Maybe parents never really know what to do but just do their best? And the fact that I was always in trouble . . . well, maybe that was about always being scared of fucking up, always terrified of being judged – an insecurity that always eats away at me in this life. Probably more as a parent. As for my daughter Polly, I learned I need to take a step back and let her make her own decisions, even if she gets things wrong. Maybe I need to do that with Pip?'

'Amazing what you can see,' Henry said.

'Thanks,' I replied, and I did mean that sincerely. I still was none the wiser about whether I'd actually travelled to a past life or just imagined one. Or whether Henry believed I'd travelled there either. I suppose somehow, it didn't matter. It changed something, changed my perspective on a tiny part of the living world I was struggling with.

'Do you enjoy what you do?' I asked Henry as we stood chatting as he threw on his overcoat.

'Oh absolutely,' he smiled. 'And the best thing is, I get to learn so much about history.'

'Right . . .'

It took a moment for the cogs in my brain to register those words. Other than the rocks and gasses, that was probably the craziest thing Henry had said in the whole two hours we'd spent together. The idea that me, Daisy May Cooper, would trot out anything that resembled historical accuracy was utterly insane. I have trouble remembering what happened yesterday for fuck's sake – sloppier than a fucking soup sandwich. And I'm not even sure what year I did end up in. During the Victorian era, by the looks of my clothing, but there was nothing more precise than that.

I opened the door and Henry vanished into the late-afternoon sun. As I sat down it did feel as though a weight had been lifted from me. I was happier than I'd felt in a while. I felt as peaceful as Cameron Macauley had looked the minute he landed back in Barra.

★

22

NEAR-DEATH EXPERIENCES

Years before I ever wrote *Am I Being Unreasonable?* with my friend Selin, I came across an unbelievable story. It was the story of a man who had been brought back to life – saved from the clutches of death.

It all happened back in 2006. It had been just another day when David Ditchfield had taken a friend to Huntingdon Station near Cambridge to see her off. While he was helping her on to the train with her luggage, giving her a kiss and a hug goodbye, the doors beeped and began to shut. What he didn't notice was that the bottom of his thick coat had got caught between the sliding doors. Unable to yank it free before the train started moving, he got dragged along, running to try to keep up. The train picked up speed, but he still couldn't wrestle free from his coat. It accelerated more. His eyes locked with his friend's eyes. She looked back in horror, frantically trying to open the door. Within seconds David lost his footing and got pulled into the gap between the door and the platform edge. As it picked up speed again, he got sucked under the full weight of the roaring train, each carriage thundering over him.

Weeks before his dreaded accident, David had watched a programme about a baby who had miraculously survived a fall from a block of flats without any injuries. Experts put it down to the baby's body being limp. Unaware of the danger ahead, it didn't tense up like an adult would. To survive, David relaxed like a rag doll and pressed himself deep into the tracks. In his book *Shine On* he describes how a strange calm washed over him. When the last carriage sped over him, blood was gushing from him and a searing pain shot through him. One arm had been ripped to shreds, severed from the elbow. Miraculously, he was still alive.

David's ordeal didn't end there. He was rushed to hospital, losing blood fast. As medics worked around him he lost consciousness. But instead of dying he says he felt more alive than at any time in his entire life. At first he entered a darkened tunnel, then orbs of multicoloured light danced around in front of his eyes. He could see that he was laid out on a huge slate of rock covered in a blue satin cloth. From his head to his toes he felt bathed in a bright white light. Warmth and love radiated across his body. An all-encompassing love that he'd never felt before. Then, when he got catapulted back into the land of the living, he was surrounded by doctors frantically talking and working around him.

David eventually recovered and that's when his story gets even weirder. Beforehand he'd been a factory worker. In his mid-forties he thought he was a failure in life. Financially he was about to dive off a cliff and be evicted from his home. Now, in the wake of his death-defying accident he rediscovered an artistic side that had laid dormant for years. He began composing and painting. Soon he was writing classical symphonies and playing to sell-out audiences. Eighteen years after his brush with death his paintings are now exhibited across the world.

Wow. Imagine staring death in the face like that then shoving two massive fingers up to it. Like the biggest 'fuck you' ever. And that entire train sequence stuck in my head. I could not forget it. So I wrote it into the storyline of *Am I Being Unreasonable?* Albeit with a darker comic twist . . .

★

Since then I've read whatever I can find about near-death experiences. Naively perhaps, I thought David Ditchfield's brush with the other side was unique. It isn't. All near-death experience stories have similar threads running through them. Lots of people find themselves swimming in light. A tranquillity descends over them like they've never felt before. Their bodies reach a stratospheric high like no other – better than any drug or Caramac bar on the planet.

I've even drummed this version of the journey to the afterlife into my kids.

'What do we do when we die?' I ask them.

With almost military precision they know the answer: 'We head towards the light!'

It's good to train them young, I think. I would hate it if any of my family took a wrong turn and never got to see something that fucking spectacular.

Of course, that doesn't mean we should all be skipping towards a bright new dawn with carefree abandon way before our time. But when we do check out, I'd like to think this does provide some comfort.

The funny thing is, there are many more extraordinary aspects to near-death experiences. Certainly, every person I've read about or listened to has said that once they started to pass over to the other side they didn't want to come back. In fact, most felt a tad pissed off when they had to re-enter the mortal world, like when you take the turning off to Chessington World of Adventures desperate to ride its new World of Jumanji but get lost on the A243 and find yourself back in bloody Surbiton like an absolute muppet.

Some near-deathers also got so immersed in this other realm that the past meant almost nothing to them: everything that they'd achieved in life, or hated in life, everyone they'd known, wasn't important any more. It's as if all the time during their life on Earth they were just acting in some fucked-up soap opera. They were busy having families and going to work and playing a role. David Ditchfield even began searching for his family over the precipice of his granite slab. But not in a sad, mournful, regretful way. He describes it as pure calm. In any case, he couldn't see them. Instead, he got hit by a massive Niagara Falls of stars cascading from the heavens with shooting stars plummeting through the middle. He was happy to leave it all behind. Weird, huh?

I always thought that on the journey to the afterlife you'd see whatever you believed in. It could be God or Allah or Shiva or Bradley Walsh. I have no idea what I would see. I do believe in a creator but I don't think that God is an old man with a mile-long wispy beard. Though I do believe that he or she or they – or whatever God self-identifies as these days – is the mayor of the universe and mayor of ghost-town. I don't reckon he patrols anything, though. Why bother? May as well sit back, have a cuppa and watch *Line of Duty*. And I do believe that Jesus existed, too, even though I have my doubts that he was the *actual* son of God. In reality, I think he was the David Blaine of his time – a guy who was just brilliant at magic tricks and word got around. *You have to see this dude, it's fucking bonkers.*

For me there has to be something else out there other than pure, hard rational science. There *has* to be. Think about the intricate design of a tiny acorn and how it grows into a majestic oak tree. And all those people in the world who do utterly mind-blowing things – the selflessness of sacrifice that surely goes against much of human instinct. I can relate on some level, like the time when I was in Swindon and there was an old woman aimlessly wandering around, scouring the shop floor of Sue Ryder.

'Have you lost something?' I asked.

'Yes, dear. My bank card.'

Mum was with me and we were a bit pushed for time.

'Don't get involved, Dais,' Mum whispered in my ear.

But I couldn't help myself, especially when I found out this woman's story.

'I've got £200 in that account. It's to go towards a holiday with my daughter,' she confessed.

At that, my heart melted like a large dollop of raspberry ice cream under a blasting hot sun.

'I'll be back in a minute,' I said.

Quickly, I legged it to the cashpoint, drew out £200, returned to Sue Ryder and handed it to the old lady.

'I can't take that, dear,' she said, staring up into my eyes.

'You can and I'll get you a taxi home too.' I smiled.

When I think about that now it's probably the kindest thing I've ever done for anyone. If it had been a scene in *Doc Martin* there would have been a full orchestra playing. When I finally caught up with Mum I really was a bit pissed off, though. I'd set my heart on a gander around Home Bargains that afternoon. So had she. And dealing with that bastard old woman and her lost bank card meant we didn't have the time.

'I told you not to get involved,' Mum reminded me.

I digress. But sacrifices like that do reaffirm to me that there must be something more to life and the universe. And that God or Allah or Shiva or Bradley Walsh isn't an outside force. My belief is that 'God' is really just a gargantuan big ball of loving energy. And that energy vibrates through us. And people do say that during near-death experiences they are hit by an overwhelming feeling of perfect, all-encompassing love. And maybe what you see at the end of life isn't connected to anything earthly, but some entirely new phenomena.

Whoah! Fuck me, this is all getting a bit deep. Run with it, Dais, run with it. My publisher did say they wanted something profound in this book, because I would be wrong to mine death simply for its comic potential . . .

The thing about near-death experiences is that no two are exactly the same. And they have been experienced by people whether they are religious or not, adult or child, scientist or artist.

Gary wrote to me with his experience. I'll let him tell the story:

I was on a day out with my best friend and his Mum and Dad at North Wales' premier water park, Rhyl Sun Centre. I say premier but I use the term loosely as it was a shit hole.

As it is in these sorts of places they announce over the loud speaker that there will be 'WAVES IN THE BIG POOL!' My friend and I rushed to the pool and swam to the far end where the waves are at their biggest.

It turned out that this periodic thrill ride in the big pool wasn't as much fun as we'd anticipated. My friend swam back to the shallow end, but I decided to stay a few minutes longer. When I realised the big waves were a bit of a let-down too I made my way back. This was, however, no easy task. The pool was now absolutely full to the brim with partially naked holidaying Scousers and North Wales locals.

Gary – this sounds filled with foreboding. Full to the brim? With Scousers? And locals? This is surely a vision of hell on Earth . . . How did you cope?

I found myself in the middle of the pool among bobbing bodies and machine-generated waves and my strength, energy and swimming capabilities were being tested to the limit. What started out as fun rapidly turned to fear. I was now under the surface, unable to resurface. Frantically I tried to swim through all the thrashing legs of people treading water but ended up being kicked further and further below.

My swimming kicks and strokes now turned into desperate thrashing. It was at this point that my desperate need for air grew ever greater. Try as I may I just couldn't hold my breath any longer. I had to inhale. But I knew that if I did, then that would be it. Rhyl Sun Centre would be the place that I would die, aged 11. And that's when everything turned black. I stopped kicking. I stopped thrashing and I felt almost calm.

I don't know how long I was out for, only a second or two I imagine. But then that's when he came and saved me. Jesus Christ reached out his hands and raised me up. I recall breaking the surface of the water and suddenly being conscious again. I coughed and spluttered then felt my feet touch the bottom of the shallow end. I was alive! And there, stood right in front of me was the man that saved my life. Imagine Robert Powell in Jesus of Nazareth with piercing blue eyes and a crucifix tattoo between his eyebrows.

I said 'thank you' and I honestly can't recall seeing him leave. I can't recall seeing him afterwards or anywhere else in the water park but he was as real, as real as it's possible for anyone to be.

Fuck me. I am speechless. Also, thanks, Gary, for attaching the picture of yourself. The beard really suits you. And the picture of the old Rhyl Sun Centre – which, you're right, does look like a complete shit hole. And the picture of Jesus Christ, just in case I wasn't sure who he was. I'm not entirely sure whether the man that Gary saw was in fact human, but sporting a really shit tattoo, or whether it was Jesus who he spotted at the Rhyl Sun Centre.

Other people who have had near-death experiences don't see anything like that. Instead, they report a life review as they start to pass over, where the saying 'My life flashed before my eyes' comes from.

I wonder whether it's pure cringe, though. Like replaying all the times you were rude to the assistant at the supermarket checkout and now regret not thanking them when he or she pointed out the bruise on the banana.

Or what about the time you went to the wedding where there were those disposable cameras on every table. And you were so poor at the time that you pinched all of the cameras off all of the tables hoping to sell them on eBay. But that was before you got them home and realised they'd all been used. And then, when you logged on to Facebook the next week you saw that the bride had posted an appeal out to every guest.

Sorry guys, just putting a shout out. Did anyone mistakenly pick up the disposable cameras that were on every table last Saturday? Dave and I cannot find them anywhere, and the hotel staff say no one handed them in. We couldn't afford an official photographer for our big day, so these are the only happy memories we will have.

If Keeley is reading this, whose wedding I went to with my ex-boyfriend some years ago, I am truly fucking sorry.

Luckily (for me anyway), reports have said that even your life review appears calm and without judgement. It's as if you're absolved of all the responsibility of being seen as good or bad, like the weight of expectation in the mortal world has been lifted from you. All the things that you should or should not have done or could have done better, don't matter any more. Sounds fucking bliss, if you ask me. And maybe you did do some really shitty things in life because you had to, but when you look back you understand all your life's highs and lows and see things from a different perspective? A far more serene angle. I still do think Hitler was a complete cunt, though. And there are some behaviours that can never be excused.

Then there's the question of what near-deathers understand about the mortal world when they are forced back into it. Many say that they are now convinced that the body and soul do separate – that the body dies but the soul lives on. Is this the paranormal explanation? Many medics would say not and that it's all in the mind, but no one has drawn any firm conclusions yet. And no one knows why people can feel this so strongly.

Whatever does happen it can have a profound effect on those people when they live again. Many who have had a positive near-death experience, bathed in beauty, say that now, when they're faced with adversity, they don't run or hide from it but accept it and let it wash over them. Others say it's made them kinder people. They're not that arsed about material things. They have less desire to earn or keep money. (Shit . . . did I have an near-death experience without even knowing it?)

But some near-death experiences are not pleasurable at all. Some are bad. *Really* bad. Like flaming pit of inferno bad. Pitchforks, demons, the whole shebang. Pure white-knuckle terror. One of the worst negative experiences that has been commonly noted has been a lonely void where people believe they are going to be stuck for ever – think IKEA on a Saturday afternoon. If Tripadvisor did reviews it would go something like this:

> Went at the end of the school holidays. All the reports had been about the white lights and glowing orbs so I had high expectations. What a letdown. Hottest day of the year and not one place selling ice cream. And when I got shown to the photo booth with the magic selfie mirror, that was it. The door banged shut behind me and no one let me out for a fucking age, despite banging relentlessly on the door. All I could see was my own body and face for ever. Needless to say I defo won't be coming back. Fuck, actually, I will be . . .

Even if the experience is bad, many of those people report the body and soul separating too. And it can take a lot of therapy to put them back together when they are delivered back to Earth. Either way, debate rages whether any of these experiences prove there is an afterlife. But can these reports, good or bad, just be dismissed as a brain that's gone haywire and thinks it's dying? Or is there far more to it? Is God hanging out somewhere in whatever form? Is this a window into the supernatural? Proof of another realm that we pass into when we die? After all, what these people experienced is *very* real. Until we know for sure, I'm prepared to believe that when we exit this mortal world, it is definitely not the end.

✫

23

THE RANDOM UNEXPLAINED

This is an online post I stumbled across a few years ago on a forum for paranormal and unexplained sightings:

> I live on the Isle of Wight, and I was a respected member of my community. I am now a laughing stock. I have been thrown out by my wife, demoted in the local bowls club and I now live in a caravan. What for? I simply saw a dinosaur. It's unlike anything I'd ever seen before. It looked a bit like a velociraptor but I couldn't be sure. It didn't try to approach me, or talk to me. It just casually walked in front of me. I'm now desperate and reaching out. Has anyone in the local area seen it?

My heart sank like a bowling ball to the pit of my stomach. This post felt so genuine and so profound that Charlie and I couldn't stop taking about it. We even considered writing a musical about this poor man's life – how he'd seen this apparition and how events had spiralled.

We imagined how, that evening, he'd excitedly turned up at the pub and told everyone about dino-ghost but they'd shunned him, saying he'd made the whole story up; how he'd then been ostracised from his village; how his marriage had fallen apart; and how he'd lost his home. All the while he'd become more obsessed that what appeared before his eyes had been real. He needed to prove it.

But what if it turned out that the creature he'd seen *had* been real? What if it was the ghost of some prehistoric brute roaming around the countryside? Or something completely alien that he'd mistaken for a dinosaur but that held the key to another universe? Actually, that was going to be our finale. A resounding 'fuck you' to the doubters. At curtain-down the audience would have dried their tears. They'd be on their feet, fist-bumping the air, cheering for this guy. *All right, Dais, don't get carried away. You couldn't even be arsed writing it.*

Of course some clever dick had written underneath this man's post:

You say you saur it, but d'ya think hesaurus? Pure Dino-mite mate!

Wanker.

The point is that there are sightings of unexplained phenomena every single day, all across the country. Here's some of my favourites that I've been sent over email in the last few months.

- Sam reported seeing phantom rectangles emerge from the ground and disappear in the village of Pluckley, Kent.
- Liam reported once seeing what looked like a flaming fish in the sky near his North London home.

- Jean wrote with a description of something she'd seen many years ago near Worthing in Sussex – a silver mushroom hovering on the horizon.

- Paul wrote with a sighting of a caravan-like object on moorland in Wales that suddenly appeared as he was driving, before it faded out.

- Michelle saw what looked like a banana suspended in the air over a bridge on the A34 to Oxford that she swears wasn't a giant inflatable fruit.

★

Of course, there could be rational explanations for all of these. Once, I thought I saw an extraterrestrial riding a full-sized Thomas the Tank Engine. I couldn't believe it. My eyes popped from my head like fucking rockets. But I had been at a car boot near Cheltenham. When I finally composed myself and walked over to the stall, there it was, in the middle of a field at 10am on a Sunday morning in full resplendent glory: a giant plastic train with doe eyes and a wide smile with a full-sized *Dr Who* Cyberman dummy sat with its hands on the wheel.

'Want it, my love?' I remember the seller calling over.

'How much?'

'£150 the lot.'

'Thanks. How much is the train on its own?'

'Sorry, my darling, comes as an ensemble.'

'Right . . . I'll leave it thanks.'

'Righto. Just let me know if you change your mind.'

'I won't, but thanks.'

The guy was clearly insane.

But when it comes to the unexplained, I think every report should be taken seriously until proved otherwise. And I'm sure many scientists will agree. And maybe – just maybe – we are all looking for the wrong kind of evidence. We need to be alert to everything.

Take extraterrestrial life, for example. It often takes on a human-like form – a head that looks like a silver helium party balloon, bug eyes bulging and dolphin-like skin. These familiar images were conjured up in books like H. G. Wells's *The War of the Worlds* (written in the late 1890s) and *The Unknown Danger* (1933), written by Swedish author Gustav Sandgren.

The alien life form that was apparently found at Roswell in the New Mexico desert in 1947 in the now infamous Roswell Incident also took on a similar form. On that occasion, the US Army reported that they'd recovered a flying disc near a ranch in the town of Roswell. Cover-ups and conflicting theories about what it was swirled around for years. At first the tin foil, rubber strips and sticks recovered from the site were claimed to be part of a weather balloon. Decades later, authorities admitted it was wreckage from a spy device. At the time, eyewitnesses claimed alien bodies had also been discovered at Roswell. Photographs produced looked just like the grey aliens I mentioned. Now, they are known to be crash-test dummies that had been part of the test flight.

Yet again, people imagined something in a human form. But what if extraterrestrial life looks nothing like this? Or UFOs aren't flying saucers in the sky or bright flashing lights or a gargantuan doughnut descending from the heavens? It is absolutely extraordinary to think it would only need one discovery, one piece of incontrovertible proof, for the whole of humanity to change, like when Issac Newton discovered gravity. And that beardy German bloke came up with the printing press. And like when researchers with, quite frankly, fuck-all else to do with their time discovered that Viagra helps hamsters recover from jet lag (don't laugh, that is actually true).

But when you think about it – *really* think about it – that's mind-blowing. That's eight billion people on this planet whose lives would change for ever. Of course everyone would see it as a massive breakthrough. They'd all be whooping and high-fiving each other at mission control like nobody's business. News channels would be awash with commentators suddenly claiming it was never a question of if, but when.

Yet, hang on a minute. I have one question that keeps me awake at night. Has anyone actually thought this through? Yes, it would change life as we know it. But it could also be an absolute fucking disaster. Would there be enough room on the planet? How could we house a new life form? What would it mean for NHS waiting lists? Schools? Would Tesco have to order in extra sandwiches in hot weather? And a whole new aisle of self-service tills in their Express stores? Would it kick-start the collapse of civilisation as we know it? Or is that just too unbelievably bleak? Maybe we'd all get on brilliantly. Maybe they'd teach us their language, if they have one. Maybe they'd love the Greggs sausage and omelette breakfast baguette and want to take the recipe back to their planet. Maybe they'd never want to go back and would just work for Greggs and climb the ladder to be the first non-human area manager.

My mouth was agape recently when I stumbled across the

ongoing work in one of the most esteemed universities in the country – Oxford. There, astrobiologists – trust me, I didn't know they existed either – have tried to imagine alien life forms as emerging the same way they believe humans did on Earth – through Darwin's theory of natural selection. My eyes were immediately drawn to this because Darwinism is the only lesson I remember from school biology, mostly because up until that point I'd swallowed wholesale the fact that the world had been created in seven days. (And as you know I do still believe in a creator of sorts but seven days is pushing it by anyone's standards. And no one ever mentions the unpaid overtime.)

Anyway these boffins reckon that, like humans, alien life form – wherever it is – will have adapted to whatever environment they are in. Any intelligent life form at the top of life's pyramid in far-away universes will be creatures that have morphed and developed and lasted the distance – like a weird cross between Chris Packham's *Animal Einsteins* and *Gladiators*, with David Attenborough winning the race to be presenter of everything for all time. If a planet is filled with a swirl of different gasses then that life form will have learned how to live in it. If it's a planet with very little gravity then it may have fashioned itself to exist in that atmosphere too.

And while these scientists say that there's a possibility that these life forms could look just a little bit human – maybe with some legs, arms and eyes – others reckon we might be in for an almighty shock. I read about one space scientist who not only thinks extraterrestrial life is likely on Saturn's largest moon, Titan, but that it might look more like . . . wait for it . . . a jellyfish the size of a football field. *Fucking insane!* It could have arms or legs or a mouth or genitals dangling from it like giant onions, plus an orange underbelly (that does seem bizarrely specific!). And its body could be generated from silicon rather than the boring-as-shit carbon that all life form emerged from here on little old Earth. Strangely it probably wouldn't live off food but off light absorbed through its skin and chemicals sucked in through its mouth.

I have three things to say about this. Number one: this gigantic fucker is probably not going to be landing on our planet via a spaceship or a Tardis or a flying saucer. Even Ryanair couldn't charge extra to transport this. I don't even know if a parachute would do it. And two: fuck me, I thought I existed in a world of utter make-believe, but this prediction is from the mouth of an actual scientist who advises actual governments on actual things outside of this world. Somehow, I think I might be in the wrong job. And three: what an amazing opportunity for a tanning salon and cocktail bar combo. I can see it on a high street in Swindon already.

Yet despite this complete head-fuck, I do maintain my theory that one day other life forms from somewhere in our vast cosmos will emerge but that we may not see them at first simply because we're looking for something else. They could be here already – not in the form of lizards with a human skin suit but something far more mundane. Who's to say that Sam's rectangles or Liam's flaming fish aren't something far more life altering than they first seem?

In the past it's been easy to dismiss this stuff as hallucinations or delusions or utter fucking stupidity, but there's one psychologist in the UK who has been taking this stuff deadly seriously. A psychologist called Daniel Stubbings has even set up an organisation where people can openly discuss what they've seen. And he's interviewed lots of people who aren't certifiably mad but really quite sane and from all walks of life and backgrounds.

And, it seems when it comes to UAPs – that's unidentified anomalous phenomena to you and me – even NASA are waking up to the possibility that there's a shit-ton going on in this universe that's unexplained. They say that they are now concerned that people are afraid to talk about this stuff for fear of ending up exactly like that poor man who saw the dino-ghost who I began this chapter with.

In fact, NASA had its first public meeting about this shizzle in 2023. Obviously I'm paraphrasing, but it said that after decades of dismissing reports of UAPs as batshit crazy, it now didn't want to stand in the way of scientific discovery and wished to remove the stigma around people coming forward with sightings. And while it said that many sightings that had been recorded can be explained – like the supposed UFO that sent radio-wave signals off the scale but turned out to be just a pilot pinging his lunch in the plane's on-board microwave. And the potentially groundbreaking sighting from one plane that turned out to be, well, just a massive Bart Simpson party balloon – other sightings remain a complete mystery.

I, for one, hope that this ushers in a whole new era. And I may even ring Chaz with a reminder.

'Hey, mate, how's it going?'

'Good thanks.'

'Listen, remember Dino-Ghost, the Musical?'

'Fuck me, that goes back a bit. Remember it? How could I forget it? Sometimes I still think about that poor man stuck in his caravan...'

'Brilliant. Let's write it.'

★

24

THE FINAL FRONTIER

As I've reached the end of this book, I want to draw some conclusions. I feel that's what a real investigator would do, even when there may be no conclusions to be drawn. It feels proper, right?

But before I get to that, I wanted to imagine what the paranormal of the future might look like. As I've said many times throughout this weighty tome, I think ghosts, for one, are way ahead of the game. Like many of my favourite ghost stories, the following story comes from a self-published collection of experiences gathered from the length and breadth of this country.

It happened in an old croft cottage in the Scottish Highlands. It had been left to a woman by her great-step-grandmother which by my calculations is someone of Miss Havisham from *Great Expectations* era old. When this woman and her mother went to visit the cottage, her mother said she'd heard footsteps in the night. She felt someone lean over her bed. It didn't worry her. She sensed it was her great-step-grandmother checking in to see if she was okay. A while later the woman went to the cottage with some friends.

'I've arrived,' she texted her mother to let her know.

She received a reply: 'Have a wonderful weekend. Lots of Love, Mum xxx And Granny too x.'

When she got home, she questioned her mother about why she sent wishes from Granny. Granny was no longer with them.

'I didn't,' her mother replied.

It goes back to something I said way back at the beginning of this book: the idea that in 50, even 100 years' time, we're still going to be sitting around holding seances, looking in mirrors and dabbling in the art of Ouija may be for the birds. The paranormal of the future could look very different. And if Miss Havisham has mastered the technological age, then we need to be ever alert to new signs, new sightings, new everything.

It all goes back to energy. While I've drawn no firm conclusions about the haunting of my home in South Cerney, remember that truth? *Energy can neither be created nor destroyed only converted from one form to another.* I come back to it time and again in my mind. And, in this technological new dawn, electrical energy will only increase. There's gadgets galore. Looking around my home, there's phones, laptops, desktops, there's an Alexa who never fucking understands a thing I ask it. There's PlayStations and consoles, smart TVs. We've come a long way since Thomas Edison – who, by the way, was a massive believer in the paranormal – invented the humble light bulb. I've come a long way since the MiniDisc Walkman I begged for turned out to be the worst present ever. The discs were far too expensive so I could only ever listen to Macy Gray's *On How Life Is* album on repeat. Anyway, my point is: the variety of ways the paranormal can connect is growing day by day.

And when you think about it, we spend so much of our time online that it could be classed as a second home, like an Airbnb of the mind. The exact places that spirits love to haunt. Why wouldn't ghosts upsize from an old Victorian mansion confined by walls to the limitless space of the Internet if they could? A place where they could stumble freely over absolutely anything from gaming forums to porn, the online Argos catalogue to the pages and pages of ASOS with 20 per cent off selected dresses.

But let's not get carried away. If you think *I* can blur the lines between the real and unreal, well, the World Wide Web is one gargantuan seething hotbed of misinformation, fake news, deepfake images, deepfake videos, fakes of deepfakes, deep-shit fakes, fakes in even deeper shit . . . fuck . . . where am I going with this? But, you get the point. The Internet is one supercharged beast of a Chinese whisper. It makes my fondly remembered childhood sleepovers with torches and white sheets and spooky ghost stories seem like the Teletubbies in la-la land. Now, some poor fucker only has to fart online and it morphs from a faint stench and an outright denial to there being a phantom farter in the room, to this shapeshifting into some kind of paranormal presence to it then undoubtedly being the ghost of Grandad who always had appalling flatulence and never, ever owned up to the fart in the first place. Like all Chinese whispers, proceed with caution.

In the online space this kind of phenomenon actually has a name.

It's called creepypasta. Of course, yours truly stupidly assumed that was the stuff I boil up for my kids every Halloween in the shape of bats, pumpkins and ghosts. Or that we use to paint pretty pictures with. But no, I've been well and truly educated. It's the stories and images and videos that move around so fast online that everyone forgets where they come from, and this makes proving or disproving anything really fucking hard.

It's the same with the numerous stories I've read of ghosts stuck online playing *Adventures of Sonic the Hedgehog* with all their ghost mates when, 30 years later, everyone else has moved on to *Sonic Prime*. Are these true or not? And what about the bots in your Instagram feed? During lockdown I had an online tryst with a sea captain who randomly DM'd me. He thought I had a lovely picture and wanted to meet me – never mind that we were in a global pandemic and my profile shot was of Kerry Mucklowe. The more we chatted, the more he revealed about himself. He was a US officer stationed in Syria on an undercover mission. Actually, he did sound like an international man of mystery. His picture looked like he'd ripped it from a website, though. For all I know he was real, but he could easily have been a bot or a malevolent spirit trolling me online. I decided to remain sceptical and told him I was the heiress of a successful dog-cloning company. You can never be too sure. But he didn't even question it, which was odd.

And how do we know that all those truly awful status updates that appear online aren't being posted up by spirits? The online space is brilliant for passive-aggressive ghosts. The type of ghost that would write: *'Why do I bother about people when no one cares about me?'*

And everyone rallies around even though they haven't a clue who's behind the post. *'So sorry you feel that way. If you want to reach out, DM me hun.'*

But if ghosts or spirits are present on the Web or the dark Web, the fact that most of the time we can't actually see anyone online adds even more bonkers complexity to a question of already bonkers complexity. I guess, as with all of the paranormal, it pays to be open-minded and painstakingly sort the fact from the fiction – not unlike the mission I set myself in this book.

But what have I achieved? Well, you might think absolutely fuck-all. I mean, did I solve the mystery of my haunted home? Nope. But I *did* uncover a lot of theories that may, or may not, lead me to the answer one day. Did I sort the wheat from the chaff when it comes to ghost-hunting methods and what to look out for? I believe I have made a valuable contribution to that ongoing debate. Did I document with care and unbiased scrutiny the ghosts in our lives? Absolutely fucking not. But it was tremendous fun thinking about them. Plus I went above and beyond for some chapters. I mean, not many people can put 'Tried to fuck a ghost and failed' on their CV and own that failure with sheer heart-swelling pride. Did I get to the bottom of unidentified objects? Nope, but I hope I've been part of the revolution in encouraging more people to come forward with what they have seen.

But you know what the most remarkable thing of all about writing this book was? By thinking about the dead and the afterlife and past lives and ghost stories and all of this shit, I learned a heck of a lot about what it is to be human. I mean, *really* human – to be scared of stuff, to wonder about death, to love people, to miss people, to want

to be a better person. Best of all I got to read and listen to all the
stories sent into me by followers who wanted to connect in exactly
the same way.

Anyway, bollocks to all of that slushy crap. What's on TV tonight?
Oh, fucking brilliant . . . *Ghostbusters* . . .

☆

ACKNOWLEDGEMENTS

This book would not have been possible without the help of some brilliant people. Thanks to Briony Gowlett at Radar who was batshit crazy enough to makes this book happen. Sybella Stephens licked it into shape, and thanks must also go to Ailie Springall and Matthew Grindon.

My literary agent Ben Dunn was instrumental in getting this book off the ground, alongside Cathy and Rachel Mason. Thank you.

Closer to home, I'd like to give a massive shout out to my family. Mum, Dad, Charlie, Anthony and, of course, my kids Pip, Jack and our newest little nutter Benji who put in a surprise appearance during this book.

Finally, thanks must go to all my followers, fans and believers in the paranormal who sent me their stories and experiences.

★